THE
STARFOLK ARCANA

Early proof copy. Please excuse any typos!

THE
STARFOLK ARCANA

Book one of the Starfolk Trilogy

Martha Dunlop

Martha Dunlop

X

TanLea

2020
TanLea Books

THE STARFOLK ARCANA
By MARTHA DUNLOP

Produced and published in 2020
by TanLea Books

Paperback: ISBN 9781913788001
eBook: ISBN 9781913788018

Cover design by Ravven, www.ravven.com
Edited by Kathryn Cottam
Copy edited by Eleanor Leese, www.eleanorleese.com
Typeset in Garamond 12pt / 14.8pt by Blot Publishing, blot.co.uk

www.marthadunlop.com

For Murray,
Who always believed in my dreams.

CHAPTER ONE

The Hertfordshire News

'EVIL DEMON AFTER MY SOUL' CLAIMS FAUSTUS

MODEL AND IT girl Amelia Faustus has claimed an evil entity entered the home of her recently deceased mother, late last night.

The alleged attack took place hours after the death of the star's mother, Eleanor Faustus. She had been suffering from cancer for two years.

There are no witnesses to corroborate the attack story, but afterwards a source described Amelia as being pale, wide-eyed and short of breath.

Eleanor Faustus lived in the local historic city of St Albans. The house was a favourite on the popular city ghost walk, where visitors often admired the flickering street lamp outside the door, crumbling brickwork and shrouded windows.

Friends of the deceased say she was often heard talking when there was nobody else there, as well as warning people of the dangers of alien invasion. She was an admirer of well-known conspiracy theorist Robson Fall. A spokeswoman for the star said, 'Amelia is currently in a severe state of shock, after both the death of her mother and this terrifying attack. She requests that people respect her privacy at this traumatic time.'

Beth

BETH SIGHED AND slouched down in her front row seat at the TV studio. If she'd known she was going to be subjected to this drivel, she wouldn't have come. She'd been here for two hours already, and not one of the stories had been genuine. Her so-called friend and flatmate had a lot to answer for. She was pleased Laura loved her new job, and it had been obvious her friend's enthusiasm about the chat show was overblown, but this was worse than she'd expected.

She caught a movement out of the corner of her eye and turned. Laura was standing off to the side of the set, waving her clipboard at Beth. She shifted on her mile-high spikes. Her feet must have been so uncomfortable, but Laura had been determined to make an impression today. Her eyes were bright as she scanned the set, drinking in her world. This job was her triumph. Beth couldn't fault her enthusiasm, she just wished Laura had left her out of today's charade.

Seated on the dais, Katherine Haversham waited for a moment, eyebrows raised, bright red lips pursed.

'Thank you for staying with us over the break. I know this is the moment you've been waiting for. Model and It girl Amelia Faustus is here, live, on *Deep and Dark* to break her silence over the horrific out-of-body attack that took her from the media spotlight. After weeks of fear and soul-searching, she has decided to step back into the public eye. Amelia, welcome. Tell us what happened.' Katherine leaned forward. 'Start from the beginning.'

Her posture mirrored Amelia's, but their faces couldn't have been more different. Amelia was trying hard to look demure. Katherine was trying not to laugh.

Amelia couldn't have looked less traumatised if she'd arrived straight from the spa. She looked around the audience, head tilted so the glossy, black curtain of hair fell as a backdrop to the too-perfect mask of her face. Her high cheekbones had a sheen as though she had been crying, but her eyes were bright and clear. She shifted in her seat, crossing her legs and allowing the white pencil skirt to rise a little farther up her tanned thigh.

'It's been a harrowing few weeks, but my decision to speak out, to bring attention to this awful, aggressive force, has given me a new reason to get out of bed each day.'

Most people would never have noticed the tension in Amelia's eyes. Beth wouldn't have seen it herself if she hadn't felt the pressure, a coil of anger that sent a sliver of cold through Beth's chest before Amelia looped it back in.

Beth sat up, searching her body for the familiar signals that something unseen was present. She allowed her awareness to reach out. There was a buzz around her from the rapt attention of the audience. It lifted her mood, and the dread eased for a moment. She was tempted to let her guard slip, but this vanished as the thread of darkness twined its way from Amelia and out towards each member of the audience. For a moment, Beth felt it. She watched the threads in her mind's eye as they snaked out towards her. Then, before they reached her, she visualised herself in the middle of a ball of pure white light. The threads fell uselessly at her feet.

Amelia narrowed her eyes as she gazed out at the audience. She scanned the rows of people in the ultra-modern TV studio, taking in the transfixed faces, and then, Beth. For a moment her red lips tightened, but then they stretched into an attempt at a smile.

Amelia shook her head. 'I'm so sorry, Katherine, darling. I'm so easily distracted these days. It all started the night my mother died. I'm sure you can imagine how devastated I felt. To lose her was to lose a part of myself.'

Katherine nodded, her forehead drawn in sympathy.

'I slept in my mother's house that night.' Amelia's voice was soft, but the room was so silent it was easy to hear her. Beth couldn't shake the feeling that Amelia was talking directly to her, as though they were on their own, sipping wine by the fire. She peered around the room. Most people sat forwards, leaning their elbows on their laps. Amelia had them reeled in like fish on big, barbarous hooks. Beth shook her head, strengthening the ball of white light and pushing the woman's energy back. She would not be part of the catch.

'Of course, I didn't really sleep.' Amelia laughed. 'How could I? There was someone in my room. And I had not invited him to be there.'

There was a muttering in the audience. People shuffled in their seats.

Amelia waited, her head still tilted, her lips lifting in a barely perceptible smile.

'I had opened my mind,' Amelia continued, her voice even quieter now. People drew in to listen, moving forwards, straining to get as close as possible. Even the cameras moved closer. 'I wanted to see if I could feel my mother, to find out if she was still here with me in any way at all.'

'And was she?' Katherine was flushed. She leaned in too, put one hand on Amelia's arm.

'If she was, I didn't feel her. Instead I felt a man in my room. I saw him so clearly with my eyes closed. I knew in my logical mind there was no way a strange man could suddenly appear in my room with no warning, but here's the terrifying thing. For a moment I wanted him to be there, whoever he was. I wanted to connect with that ghostly intruder more than I have ever wanted anything in my life. I wanted it more than I longed for my own mother, who had only left me that day. It felt as though he was luring me in with promises of peace and love. Can you believe that?'

A woman sitting behind Beth sobbed.

Beth bit back a laugh. She was a pro at empathy, but this was ridiculous. The woman had been offered a gift and she was pretending it was a nightmare.

'Awful,' Katherine said, and Beth wondered if she was the only one who noticed the sarcasm.

Amelia nodded, and wiped the corner of her dry, unsmudged eye with a folded silk handkerchief. 'I'm so pleased you hear me, Katherine, darling. I knew you were the right person to talk to. You're so understanding, such a good listener. You do so well at letting your guests speak their truths without interruption.'

Beth coughed violently in an attempt to cover the laughter that would have attracted all the wrong kinds of attention. Katherine was notorious for being a tough interviewer and digging up the worst kind of dirt. She was never flustered, emotional or caught off-guard, but for some reason, right now, she looked furious. Her face was flushed. Her arms were crossed tightly, protectively even, over her chest.

'Cut,' a voice shouted.

The audience began to shuffle and mutter as members of the crew rushed back and forth. A pale woman with dark circles under her eyes hurried over to Amelia and started touching up her make-up. Someone with a clipboard talked to Katherine, while a camera was moved into a better position.

A man walked onto the stage, handed a glass of water to Amelia and crouched down beside Katherine.

Dressed in jeans and a fitted black top, his shoulder-length, dark-blond hair pulled into a ponytail at the nape of his neck, he looked unaccountably different. Beth massaged her neck as she watched him. She wanted to be able to say he was dressed strangely, but he wasn't. It was as though he were perfectly camouflaged to all except her. He moved seamlessly through the flow of people, a word here, a touch there, but nothing that disrupted the fast-paced movement of the crew. Beth forced herself to turn away, but she felt his presence to her left, his energy tugging at her mind.

'What made you think this ghost was there to hurt you?' Katherine's voice broke in on her thoughts. The studio had fallen silent.

'I just knew it, Katherine, darling. Haven't you ever known something deep in your heart?'

Katherine laughed, but her lips barely moved. 'It's not my heart we're here to talk about.'

Beth leaned back in her chair. She knew all about *just knowing* and she just knew something was seriously off with Amelia. Why would she feel so threatened by a spirit offering peace and love? Since when was that frightening? And why, oh why, did she feel the world needed to hear about it?

Beth felt something tugging at her mind and turned. The man from the stage was now standing at the back of the audience. He was watching her. Why did she feel she had met him before? She couldn't see him clearly from this distance and felt a weird urge to go and introduce herself, to get a clearer look. Something indefinable about his face was strikingly different to anyone she had seen before, but at the same time he was achingly familiar.

Beth blinked. For a moment his ears looked pointed, but when she looked again, they were perfectly normal.

She turned back to the set, her heart pounding, mind reeling.

Amelia was still talking and Beth did her best to suppress the annoyance that surged through her. The woman had an unreasonable ability to get to her. Beth knew she was being prickly, but something was off and she couldn't work out what.

'The spirit offered his hand.' Amelia's voice was hypnotic as she leaned forwards in her chair, looking first at Katherine and then out to the audience. She spoke softly, intimately. 'I knew if I took it, I would lose myself entirely. I would no longer be the Amelia the world recognised. My soul would be in danger.'

'In danger from what, exactly?' Beth muttered under her breath. 'Beings offering peace and love? Terrifying.'

There was a sharp intake of breath. The woman to her right pulled back, eyes wide, face pale as she shielded her daughter from Beth. The little girl watched her, leaning forwards, her face flushed, head tilted to one side.

A camera swivelled around to point at Beth. She rolled her eyes. How loudly had she spoken?

Katherine nodded to someone on her left.

Beth followed her gaze and saw the same man walking towards her. She hadn't seen his face up close, but now he held her gaze, smiling encouragement. For some reason, she felt as though he were willing her to do well. His features were fine, sculpted even. His narrow, angular face was somehow out of place in the modern and transient surroundings of the television studio. His upward-slanting eyebrows were oddly familiar.

Beth smiled back. She was determined to look serene despite the butterflies swarming in her stomach, but Amelia was watching her. The woman's almost entirely contained anger was pointed right at Beth. She strengthened her psychic protections, but the energy still seeped through, making her heart pound and her stomach feel like lead. *It's not real*, she repeated to herself over and over like a mantra.

The man crouched down and held out a microphone. 'Would you like to speak?' His voice was deep, his eyes a rich blue that seemed almost violet at the edges. His ears were profoundly normal.

'I wouldn't, but someone obviously wants to ask me a question. I may as well get it over with.'

He handed her the microphone.

She took it.

Smiling, he held her gaze for a moment too long.

'Please, introduce yourself,' Katherine said, nodding with a friendly smile.

Beth felt a moment's connection. This well-manicured and formidable woman didn't like Amelia any more than she did.

'My name's Beth.'

'And what was that you said? Could you repeat it for the benefit of the audience here and at home?'

Beth swallowed. She could see herself in one of the monitors. Her dark eyes looked huge against her pale skin. She wished she'd made more of an effort. The simple plait looked out of place in this cavernously sterile room. The indigo tunic and leggings seemed somehow from a different time. She pulled herself up, holding her shoulders straight and proud as she looked at Amelia.

'I was just wondering why you thought you were in danger? Since you didn't take the offered hand, we have no idea what would have actually happened. To suggest that it posed some kind of threat is pure speculation.'

Beth felt a rush of warmth from somewhere outside of her and caught the scent of lavender.

Sister.

The single word echoed in her mind. She shook her head. Where did that come from? She was an only child; nobody's sister.

'Excellent questions, Beth.' Katherine nodded, unable to hide her smirk.

Amelia stood up. She smoothed her shimmering white top over the waistline of her white pencil skirt. Then she reached up and scooped all of her hair over one shoulder so it hung down in a glossy dark mane to her left elbow. Despite the towering stilettos, she didn't so much walk as prowl like some kind of predator.

Beth cursed her seat in the front row. If she'd been farther back, she wouldn't have attracted so much attention, no matter how many loud comments she made.

'Beth, is it? I once knew someone who looked like you.' Amelia's voice was smooth; her smile faultless. She held out her hand.

Beth paused, and then took it. It was icy cold. She winced at the strength of Amelia's grip, but held the smile on her face.

'I'm so pleased you came, Beth.' Amelia dropped her hand and then turned to the rest of the audience. 'In fact, it's so wonderful to see all of you, to feel your love at this challenging time, and to share my story with you.'

'You don't really have a story, though, do you?' Beth felt the audience's shock as a physical wave of adrenaline. 'I'm so sorry your mother died. It was clearly hugely traumatic and I can see why your mind might turn to ghosts. But nothing happened.'

The audience muttered and shuffled in their seats. Amelia paled, pursing her lips as she glared at Beth. There was a low murmur from the woman to her right. She leaned in close to her daughter, lips moving fast as she whispered in her ear. The back of her neck was flushed where it was exposed by her scraped-back hair. She turned, pressing her lips together as she glared at Beth. Despite this, the discomfort of other people's fear was less than normal. The warmth Beth had felt a moment ago enveloped her, offering a layer of protection that allowed her to breathe.

Beth concentrated, trying to see Amelia's aura. There was nothing. She must have been shielding it, although Beth had no idea how she was doing it. Odd. She had never met anyone with that talent or inclination.

'Nothing happened because I was on alert.' Amelia narrowed her eyes at Beth. 'You would understand if you were practised in following your intuition.'

Beth gave a hard laugh. Amelia wasn't as good at reading people as she was at shielding herself from them. Not many people lived by their intuition as much as Beth. She was used to being misunderstood, but for some reason she felt oddly disappointed that Amelia wasn't more perceptive.

'Perhaps you just mistrust it?' Amelia stepped closer. The people on the front row leaned forwards, trying to get as close to her as possible. 'Do you honestly doubt my experience, Beth?' She held Beth's gaze as though attempting to entrance her.

A prickle ran down Beth's spine. She focused, calling on the lavender warmth to push Amelia back, to form a protective barrier around her mind.

'Salu,' Amelia muttered. The tip of her one exposed ear turned pink, but she held her composure.

Sorry?' Beth frowned. 'What does that mean?'

Amelia was silent for a moment, her jaw tight. For the first time she seemed disconcerted, at a loss what to say. Then she laughed. Not her normal flirtatious laugh, but a genuine chuckle. 'Oh nothing, it's an obscure expression.' Then she turned and walked up the stairs of the aisle between the rows of seats.

'Amelia,' was a whisper in the air as the audience shifted to watch her walk past, unable to take their eyes off her. A teenage girl stuck out her hand and Amelia grasped it, and then pulled her into a hug. More arms reached. Soon she was surrounded by people, touching her and hugging her as she whispered words of warning.

Beth watched her, lips pressed into a tight line. Was Amelia stark raving mad? Or was she speaking the truth? Whichever it was, her ability to enchant people was staggering.

'Ahem.' The woman to her right coughed, glaring at Beth as she nodded towards the aisle, yanking her daughter after her as Beth moved her legs out of the way. 'Don't touch her,' the woman said from between gritted teeth, pulling her daughter out into the aisle. The girl turned when she got to the steps and looked at Beth, her blue eyes wide and confused. She tilted her head and pushed a strand of hair behind her ear. She took in a breath, and then paused.

Beth raised her eyebrows, intrigued.

The woman turned, saw the silent exchange and grabbed her daughter's hand, yanking her up the steps.

Beth rolled her eyes.

A warm hand brushed against hers and she turned. The

man still stood next to her, his eyes almost purple. 'Amelia is pretty formidable. Not many people can see past her. It's a shame the audience won't remember you standing up to her.'

'They won't?'

'Look at them. She has them mesmerised. That will take up all the space in their minds.'

'You sound as if you know her well.'

'Well enough. Or, at least, I know how she works her way into people's heads. We go way back. Would you mind?' he said, slipping the microphone from between her fingers.

'Of course. Have you worked with Katherine long?'

'No. I fill in occasionally when they need more staff. It's lovely to meet you, Beth.'

'You too. Can I ask your name? I feel as though I've seen you before.'

The man smiled. 'Jonan, my name's Jonan.'

Beth's heart beat faster. 'I don't know why, but it sounds familiar.'

Jonan's smile widened. 'Maybe we'll meet again soon; then it will be even more familiar.' He winked, and then turned and walked back to the stage.

CHAPTER TWO

Beth

THE WHOLE OF St Albans seemed to have piled out of their comfortable homes onto the packed main street. The market traders looked harassed but smug as they waded through long queues of customers. Beth pushed her way past buggies, wheelchairs and dogs on leads. The overpowering stench of fresh fish made her loop away from a stall on her right towards the road. That was too much death to contend with on a Saturday afternoon, particularly after listening to Amelia's creepy stories.

The road was at a standstill. She ducked between a bus and a taxi, and made her way into the book shop. It was a relief to get out of the chaos. She walked up the stairs to the first floor and found the Mind, Body, Spirit section next to the cafe, hoping she might find inspiration. Something was off about Amelia's claims, but Beth couldn't grasp what it was. She was a veteran of paranormal weirdness, and Amelia's experience, and reaction to it, just didn't seem credible.

The whole situation jarred. Every time she thought of Amelia, Beth's heart pounded and her body flooded with adrenaline. Beth ran her finger over the spine of a book on local ghost stories. Ghosts. It was almost as though Amelia herself was a ghost. She caused the same physical sensations, the chills, the dread, the sense of being watched. But how could a living person emulate the physical impact of a ghost? Was that all her own energy, or was she dabbling in something strange?

Beth examined the books. There were titles on meditation, angels, fairies and Wicca, but there was nothing that came close to explaining Amelia's strangeness. Beth's fingers landed on a box. It was pocket-sized and resembled a small, thick book.

'*The Starfolk Tarot,*' Beth whispered. On the side of the box was a picture of a woman in white, with long, shiny dark ringlets. Her eyes were deep and intense as they gazed out at Beth. The scent of lavender drifted through the air and she was flooded with warmth.

Pulling out the box, Beth studied the pictures on the back. Faces stared out at her. They felt familiar despite their otherness. She almost heard them whispering, calling her.

Beth looked at the price. Ouch. It was more than she would usually spend. But today was her birthday and there was something about this box that made her heart race.

Beth walked *The Starfolk Tarot* over to the cashier and handed her a twenty-pound note. She bought herself a coffee and sat at one of the small, round tables. Leaning back against the iron-black banister, she ignored the drop behind. Chaotic energy streamed up from the ground floor of the shop. She closed her eyes, holding the box of cards in both hands. Unexpected excitement surged through her as she traced the cardboard, remembering the picture of the woman on the side. The shop receded until there was just Beth and the cards. At last, she felt the buzz fade into calm.

She took a breath and opened her eyes, taking the cards out of the box and laying them on the table as she sipped her coffee. She turned over a few, running her finger over the shiny pictures: Wise Woman, Mother, Strength, Temperance and Transformation. They were even more beautiful than she'd expected. The faces staring out at her seemed so real and gave her an odd sense of déjà vu.

She turned over the next card and choked on her coffee.

A man sat on a chariot, guiding two wild horses into line. His face was startlingly familiar. The same long blond hair, the same slanted eyebrows, the same smile. His violet eyes bored into hers with unnerving clarity. He was a mirror image of the man from the studio. The card was titled, Intention.

Beth jolted as something slammed into her. A woman pushed past, her bag knocking the table.

'Hey, watch what you're doing!' Beth snapped, grabbing for the cards. But she couldn't catch them all. Some cascaded to the carpet. Intention fell through the banister, floating like a leaf down to the ground floor.

'No!' Beth whispered as she watched it disappear into the crowd of shoppers below.

She turned and did a double take. The woman who had sat next to her at the studio was glaring at her, hands on her hips. Her eyes flickered repeatedly to a point behind Beth. She scowled at the images that littered the floor. 'You shouldn't be messing with that stuff. I knew you were bad news when you argued with Amelia. I never imagined you'd be into this though.'

'Why do you care?' Beth shook her head. 'We've never even met.'

'Huh!' The woman pressed her lips together. '*Tarot* attracts the wrong kind of attention,' she said, her gaze darting around Beth and never quite landing on her. 'It opens you up to evil forces.'

Beth looked behind her. Was the woman talking to someone else, or just distracted?

'There you are.' The woman snapped her fingers as her daughter ducked through the tables to stand just behind her. She gazed at Beth, her eyes large and somehow pleading. 'Come on. Quickly. Keep away from this woman. She isn't safe. *She* didn't pay proper attention to Amelia's warning.'

Beth stared after the woman, gaping, as she hurried her daughter down the stairs to the exit. Beth shook her head. How much more of this was she going to encounter today? She looked around. The people at the other tables were watching her and, despite the busy shop, there was a ring of clear space around her table.

She gathered up the cards and downed the last of her coffee, keeping her back to the room. She didn't turn to confront the people watching her. Instead, she hurried for the stairs and the fallen card.

Jumping off the bottom step she pushed her way through the crowd, peering amongst the forest of legs for Intention.

The throng cleared. For a moment she was surrounded by space and silence. There it was, lying alone on the scratchy, grey carpet tiles. Beth grabbed it, turning it over and over. She had expected shoe prints and scuffed edges, but Intention was clean and unmarked. She opened the tarot box, slid the card into the deck and then concealed the box in her coat pocket.

A blast of cold air made her shiver.

The woman from the studio was heading out the door. She turned, caught Beth's eye for a moment, and then was gone.

Beth sighed. She would be glad when this birthday was over. She was pretty sure the party Laura had organised for her tonight would be as misguided as the invitation to the TV show. But at least she had rescued Intention.

Jonan

JONAN STOOD IN the St Albans city centre pretending to listen to the brass band playing outside the white-stone town hall. Someone shoved a hat in his face and he dropped a pound coin in without a word.

Meeting Beth had shaken him. The moment she stepped into the studio, his energy had flared. His senses were heightened. He smelled her fruity perfume and the scent underneath that took him back to that other world. They had never met in the flesh. He shouldn't have known how she smelled, but it sent shivers of recognition through him.

He needed to get himself under control. Seeing Beth had triggered memories that stretched farther back than even he knew. His energy was too big, too bright for the busy and blaring Saturday afternoon street. He was usually so good at shielding his differences, blurring the brightness of his aura into a semblance of normality for those who could see it. For the rest, he was able to make his light appear to be nothing more than charisma. Right now, that kind of camouflage was impossible and even those without psychic sight would feel the discomfort of his strangeness as a tingle down their spine or a chill through their body.

He focused on creating a barrier around his aura, on making his unusual energy feel as normal as possible to those around him. People were watching him as much as the band and a gap had opened up on either side of him. Passers-by swerved a little too far away as they sped on down the pavement.

He felt a prickle over his forehead that settled into pressure on his third eye. He looked around. There was a commotion in the book shop and strange energy hovered around the entrance. He felt a brief tug to investigate but shut it down. If he looked into every energy disturbance, he'd never find any peace.

From the corner of his eye he spotted a man in a dark-blue suit, black hair slicked back, walking towards him. The man was distracted, his eyes fixed on the phone in his hand.

Jonan was just about to step out of the way when the man looked up. He started with a sharp intake of breath. The coffee he was raising to his mouth jerked, splashing all over his crisp white shirt, and all over Jonan.

'What the hell are you?' he asked, his voice squeaking as he stumbled backwards.

'What I am is covered in coffee,' Jonan snapped at the same moment the band fell silent. He spread his arms to show the dark, wet patches all over his jeans and top, not caring that everyone was staring.

The man paled. His hands were shaking. Lunging past Jonan, he looked back over his shoulder, turned the corner and disappeared.

'Give me strength,' Jonan muttered, striding down the road towards home.

He must have managed to calm his energy somewhat, because he didn't attract any more unusual attention as he wove through the crowds and down the pedestrianised walk-way to the Third Eye Spiritualist Shop.

Jonan loved the shop he ran with his aunt, Doriel. The building was old. White with black woodwork, it always looked slightly wonky. The shop, with its purple panelling and large windows, was on the ground floor. Above was a stock room on one side of the staircase and, on the other, a small room where Doriel read tarot. On the top floor, with gabled windows, was the tiny flat he shared with Doriel.

The large ground-floor windows showcased the empty shop. Only Doriel sat at the counter, tarot cards spread out in front of her, hands wrapped around a mug of tea.

The bell on the door jangled as he pushed it open. The faint smell of sage announced that he was home.

Doriel looked up, her long, hennaed plait looped over her shoulder. Little crystals and bells were woven into the waist-length braid, which stood out against her pale-purple chiffon top and ankle length skirt. 'Was she there?'

'She was.'

Doriel nodded. 'I smell coffee. Did you bring some for me?'

Jonan spread his arms wide. His shirt clung to him in great wet patches that had long since lost their warmth. 'Look at the state of me. I'm not bringing coffee, I'm wear-ing it! I scared a random guy on the street so much that he threw his coffee at me. You should have seen the look on his face. I thought I knew how to make my energy blend in whatever the circumstances, but apparently seeing Beth bull-dozes my self-control. I don't know what the man thought he saw, but it clearly wasn't good.'

Doriel tilted her head. She screwed up her face, looking thoughtful. 'I've never seen you lose control before. Do you think you can overcome it? This is going to be a lot more difficult if she triggers you that badly.'

'Don't worry, I'll figure it out. I won't be caught by surprise next time. I've overcome worse than this.'

Doriel nodded. 'Well, for now, get out of those stinky clothes and make me a proper cup of coffee.'

'Yes, your majesty!' Jonan winked. 'But what's in the cards? It has you looking serious.'

'Oh, nothing.' She swept them up off the table, scattering the spread before Jonan could get a look.

'That bad, eh?'

'Nothing for you to worry about right now. Amelia's up to something, I can feel it, but I haven't figured it out yet.'

'Up to something? You mean beyond shooting her mouth off about Salu paying her a visit?

'But why would she talk about it now? She has had star visitors since before the Triad broke up, and not just Salu. She knows they aren't ghosts, and she knows why they're there. Why would she lie?' Doriel picked up the tarot deck and started to shuffle. 'She keeps her identity as under-wraps as we do, but today she goes on national TV and lays a trail of crumbs that leads to her biggest secret. We know she's not stupid. We know she's not self-sacrificing so, I say again, why?'

Jonan shrugged. 'She knows how far she's drifting from the path we came here to walk. She knows where Salu's loyalties lie. He is Beth's brother, for goodness sake, and Beth was always born to step into Amelia's shoes if she failed. Amelia has just marked Salu, and us, as an enemy.'

'I won't believe that, Jonan. I know you're angry with her, but I know she can find her way back to the truth.'

Jonan put a hand on Doriel's back. 'We always knew she would be our biggest challenge. That's why Beth came. We just have to stay alert until we figure out which particular endgame she has in sight. I have absolutely no doubt that whatever she's up to is meticulously designed to both further her own interests and distract us so we don't get in her way.'

'No. It was never a given that Amelia would leave us. She always planned to keep the Triad together. She may not be my natural sister, Jonan, but she was always good until...'

'Until I came along and ruined things?'

'No. You were barely more than a child. She did wrong. I know that, but there should have been a way out without this happening.'

Jonan laughed. 'You keep telling yourself that. I was seventeen. I may have been a lot younger than Amelia, but I was no child. I thought I was in love. I thought I was following my path. I had seen the dreams. I was sure she was the one for me.'

Doriel sighed. 'Any of us could have told you she wasn't. You should have asked.'

'And that's all you would have said, is it? You wouldn't have warned me off her, or torn a strip off her for dating your sister's son?'

Doriel shrugged her shoulders. 'I would have also told you the girl in your dreams was not Amelia.'

Jonan closed his eyes. 'I'll always wonder if that would have changed things.'

'I'm sorry. I'm being sentimental about losing my friend. If you and Amelia had never happened the Triad might have succeeded, but Beth wouldn't have woken up. There are no easy answers.'

Jonan pulled her into a hug. Doriel had always been more than an aunt. His mother, Miranda, the third member of the Triad, was diligent but distant. Even as a small child he had turned to Doriel for comfort. When the Triad broke up and Miranda went into spiritual seclusion, Doriel had taken over parenthood seamlessly.

'I'll get you that coffee,' he said, planting a kiss on her forehead. He had a vague memory of seeing an indigo tattoo there in another lifetime, but now there was nothing, just warm, fair skin, and a few fine lines.

'You charmer, you.'

Jonan laughed, hearing the hoarseness in his voice. When his mother had found him kissing her best friend, she had walked away. It was Doriel who'd stepped up, proving to him that he still had a family, that he was worth loving. He would always adore her for that.

Jonan took the stairs two at a time and put the kettle on. He peeled off his wet, stinking top, and strode over to the bedroom. It was a small room. Everything about this flat was small, from the low ceiling to the narrow, uneven staircase. But there was enough space for a double bed, a wardrobe and a set of shelves for his books and tarot cards. Crystals were dotted around the room in every nook and cranny.

The picture on the wall caught his eye. It was a poster he'd bought years ago and had never been able to part with, despite the scuffed and torn edges. The woman in the middle was walking away, but she had turned to look at the camera. Her dark hair was bound with flowers and flowed long and wavy down her back. She wore a floaty green chiffon dress that matched the emerald of her eyes. She was the girl in his dreams. The girl that wasn't Amelia. The girl he had just met at the studio. He knew it wasn't really Beth but, somehow, that other, timeless version of Beth was looking out at him through those eyes, just as much as through Beth's own.

Beth

BETH HATED PARTIES.

She hadn't agreed to this and didn't want to be here, but Laura insisted Beth couldn't miss the opportunity to celebrate. Now, the small flat was full to bursting with Laura's friends from the TV studio, most of whom were complete strangers.

Music blared from the speakers, distorting the heavy beat and vague, computer-generated backing. People swayed as they shouted into each other's ears in an attempt at conversation.

Laura was up on the wobbly legged dining table in skin-tight black trousers and a crop-top that showed off her tiny waist and flat, toned stomach. She circled her hips to the beat, her arms up above her head, eyes hooded. Her pixie cut was damp where it was carefully styled against pink cheeks.

A man Beth didn't recognise stood at the end of the table, gaze locked with Laura's. He beckoned to her.

She shook her head, grinning, but stepped back, making space for him to join her.

He vaulted up, sending tremors through the flimsy wooden legs of the table, which was already rocking with Laura's movement.

The doorbell rang again. Beth shook her head and turned to push her way through the crowded room, leaving Laura to her seduction. The hall was no clearer than the lounge, and she had to nudge people aside in order to open the front door and squash another group into the already overcrowded space.

Beth had no idea where the ten close friends she had invited to this party had hidden themselves, and she couldn't face battling her way through to find them. The pervasive stench of beer and the stifling heat from so many bodies was making her feel nauseous. She ducked into the kitchen to grab an open bottle of wine and picked up her coat from the stand by the door. In a moment she was down the communal concrete stairs and out on the grass. Pointing her face up to the stars, she breathed in the night air and relaxed.

The wind was full of autumn and had a sharp nip to it. Beth pulled her coat tight and sat down at the base of the huge tree outside the flat. The fresh night air was a relief and she breathed in deeply. She could see this tree from the living room window. It was her touchstone. It grounded her.

She pushed her hands into her pockets to keep back the chill. Her fingers closed around the deck of tarot cards. The new, shiny box was stiff and she fumbled, trying to open it with cold fingers. Bit by bit, she slid off the lid. The deck was smooth and fitted perfectly into her small hands, so she started to shuffle. The brand-new cards caught as they slid against each other. One flew out and landed, face up on the grass. Beth leaned forwards. The light from the street lamp just illuminated the picture.

Intention. Again.

Beth reached for it, but a gust of uncharacteristically warm breeze caught it up and carried it through the air, tumbling round and round as it was swept farther away. The scent of lavender surrounded her for a moment then was gone.

Beth balanced the wine bottle on a flat bit of ground and put the cards next to it, weighing them down with a piece of flint. Then she jumped up and launched herself after the runaway card.

She hit something hard and the air was knocked from her body.

'Are you okay?' The familiar voice sent a shiver through her. She looked up, peering through the darkness. A pair of blue eyes rimmed with violet held her gaze from underneath slanted eyebrows. She stepped back. 'Where did you come from?'

The man from the studio laughed. 'The path. I think you were too busy balancing your bottle to notice. What are you doing here? Are you here for Laura's party too?'

'Laura's my flatmate. This is my birthday party.'

'Your birthday? I'm sorry. I had no idea. Happy birthday!'

Beth laughed. 'Thank you. And it's nice to see a familiar face. I can't keep up with this TV crowd, they're exhausting. Oh, sorry,' she said, picking up the wine from the ground and gulping down a mouthful. 'You're part of that crowd, aren't you?'

'Not really. I'm pretty transient. I worked at the studio today because my Aunt Doriel has connections there.' He bent down and picked something up from the ground. It was the tarot card. He turned it over and surprise flickered across his face for a moment, but when he looked up, his expression was neutral. 'She was the resident psychic on one of their daytime shows for a while. I do a day here or there when they need me, but it's not really my scene. I own the Third Eye Spiritualist Shop with my aunt. It's down by the clock tower.' He held out the card. 'Is this what you were looking for?'

'Thank you.' Beth smiled and took it from his outstretched fingers. 'Jonan, isn't it?'

'Well remembered. Are you a reader?'

Beth settled back down on the grass, leaning against the trunk. 'Well, yes. I love books. What do you like to read?'

Jonan dropped down next to her, crossing his long legs as he propped himself up on the tree next to her. 'I meant a Tarot reader.'

'Oh! No. I've never even picked up a deck before, but this one called to me. I only bought it this afternoon.'

'Interesting. *The Starfolk Tarot*,' he said, reaching for the deck. He began to shuffle.

'Is it popular?' Beth felt her face heat as she thought about the card she still held in her hand. The card with the charioteer that looked exactly like Jonan.

'It's certainly one of the most beautiful decks, in my opinion,' he said with a wink. He reached out and turned her hand over to display the picture. Then he pulled a card from the centre of the deck. 'Particularly this one.'

Beth went cold.

The card showed a side view of a woman standing at the edge of a cliff. Her long, dark hair was tied into a plait that hung over her shoulder. White and green flowers were woven into the strands, matching the long, flowing dress that billowed out behind her in the breeze. A bag clutched in her hand, she was looking up towards the few solitary beams of light that broke through the clouds. Her face was filled with expectation, a look of ecstasy. That face was familiar in its soft lines and the gentle curve of the eyebrows. A long, slender neck was encircled by a green choker to match large bright-green eyes. That face was familiar. It was her face.

She reached up to touch her own neck. She felt the familiar soft jersey of her hoody rather than the thin gauzy fabric in the picture and felt oddly disappointed.

Jonan's fingers still held her other hand. They were warm on her cold skin and tiny prickles of energy fluttered up her arm. His touch felt oddly familiar.

His lips tilted up at the edges as though he knew what she was thinking. He let her hand go.

The hoot of an owl jerked her out of her reverie. She pulled herself into the present, focusing on the sound of traffic from the main road, and the musty scent of old leaves.

'I don't understand.' She picked up the deck and started flicking through the other cards. 'Why are we both in these pictures?'

'A coincidence, nothing more. May I?' He gestured to the wine bottle.

'Of course.' Beth handed it to him and watched, head tilted to one side, as he took a swig. 'I don't believe in coincidence.'

He laughed. 'Neither do I, but do you have a better explanation?'

She watched him, trying to read the energy that should have been flickering around his body. There was nothing. She had only ever met one person who could shield their energy that effectively, and the thought sent a chill down her spine.

'Thanks for picking up my card. What does it mean, by the way?'

Jonan laughed. 'Well that's the mystery, isn't it? What do the cards mean?'

'You're not going to give me any clues?'

'Where would the fun be in that? These are your cards. I have a hunch you'll be good at reading them. And if you really want a reading from someone else, there's always the Third Eye Spiritualist Shop.'

'The shop by the clock tower, I've got it.'

Their upper arms were touching now, drawing Beth's attention to that small, warm patch of skin.

'I've never met a professional psychic before.'

'I'm surprised you're not one yourself.'

Beth narrowed her eyes. What did he know? She normally kept a safe emotional distance from people, to stop them realising how strange she was. There weren't many who could handle her talk of ghosts and unusual energies. Experience had taught her it was best to keep to herself. Only Laura had lasted any time, and she was too self-obsessed to care what Beth said.

'What do you think you've figured out about me?' she asked. She sat upright and turned to face him. 'Has Laura said something?'

'Nobody's told me anything. You seem like you have more to you. You're... interesting.'

'I'm certainly that,' Beth muttered. Putting the cards back into the box and shoving it into her coat pocket, she took another swig of wine. 'Here's to being interesting.'

'You'd be surprised how far interesting can get you with the right people.'

'And who are the right people? You?'

'I'm more interesting that you'd ever have imagined. After all' – he winked – 'they used my face on a tarot card.'

Beth laughed. 'So, what do I do with those cards? I've been looking Tarot up, and it doesn't look like a beginner sport.'

'The cards called to you. I believe you will be able to read them. But no, you can't just buy a deck and launch in. It is something you have to learn.'

'And can you teach me?'

'A little maybe, but Doriel's your woman. In her hands the Tarot has a special kind of magic.'

Beth handed Jonan the bottle. 'And there we are, back to "you should meet Doriel". What's so special about this woman, and why do you care so much about whether or not I meet her?'

Jonan leaned the bottle against the tree and stood up. 'You know, I'm not sure I can face this party. It doesn't sound like my kind of do. What do you say we get out of here?'

Go. The thought flitted through her mind. *Go with him.* 'I don't know you,' she said, 'and it's *my* birthday party.'

His eyes were huge and had deepened to indigo. 'It looks like I'm getting out of here on my own then.'

Beth held out a hand. Jonan grasped it, pulling her up from the damp grass. His skin was warm despite the chill air. For a moment she stood close, so close that she fancied she could almost sense his heart beating across the narrow distance between them.

'Thanks,' she whispered, stepping back and pushing a stray lock of dark hair behind her ear. Laura had curled it into a ringlet, but in the damp air it had stretched back into its normal light wave. Her hand felt cold now Jonan had let it go and she tucked it into her pocket, as though that would preserve the feeling of contact.

Go. The word sounded again in her mind. 'I can't go,' she said out loud and felt a wave of disappointment.

Jonan raised his eyebrows. His lips twitched into a smile, but his shoulders slumped.

'Go?' Laura skipped over the grass to them in her flip flops, her cheeks visibly flushed, even in the dark. She linked her arm through Beth's and pressed up against her with a shiver. 'You can't leave now. I have surprises planned. Plus, everyone's asking where the birthday girl is.'

Beth shook her head. 'They don't even know who I am.'

'Of course they do.' Laura laughed. 'And even if they don't, they're here to make a fuss of you. So, let them.'

Beth sighed. There were a few of her friends upstairs. It wasn't fair to disappear on them, no matter how fascinated she might be by Jonan. 'I'll be up in a minute. You go ahead.'

Jonan nodded then took a few steps backwards. 'As you said, it's your birthday party. No matter. Another time.' He turned and walked away, hands thrust into the pockets of his jeans, shoulders hunched against the chill in the air.

Beth frowned. In the glare of the streetlight, the top of Jonan's ears had elongated into points with pale blue tips. She closed her eyes tight for a moment, but when she opened them, he had gone.

She shook her head. She must have imagined it. She felt as though she had been on the brink of something, something important, something more than a brief flirtation at a party. She sighed again, grabbed the almost empty bottle of wine, and walked back down the path to the door. It would have been sweet of Laura to arrange a party if she had actually wanted one. But, as usual, her friend had only thought about herself. Beth put her key in the lock, but the door swung open before she turned it.

'Happy Birthday,' everyone chorused, as she stepped back. She felt her cheeks heat. Too many eyes were focused on her. A sea of faces waited for her to smile, to show some sign of happiness, but instead, her stomach churned and her mouth went dry. She hated being the centre of attention.

Laura stepped out into the hall, grasped her hand and pulled her inside, slamming the door loudly behind her.

'Come on,' Laura whined, dragging Beth towards the huge immaculately iced cake. 'Blow out your candles, Bethy.'

Beth blew them out in one go.

She jolted at a crash behind her. A shriek was followed by furious muttering. Beth turned around.

'Get away from me,' the man said from between gritted teeth. He was holding his hands up in front of his face, backing away from a woman with dark-blue hair.

'What's wrong, Geoff?' Laura bounded over, stroking his face and looking him up and down to find the problem.

He nodded at the woman behind Laura, who was dabbing furiously at a red wine stain that was spreading slowly over the waist of her colourful tie-dye tunic and black leggings. A pentagram swung against her chest as she dabbed at the stain, bent around it, her long blue hair obscuring her face. She looked up to find Laura glaring at her, hands on her hips. The man stood behind her, eyes narrowed and jaw tight.

'What have I done?' Her forehead furrowed and she spread her arms wide. 'You bumped into me, not the other way around. It's my drink that was spilled, over my clothes. What do you have to complain about?'

'I can see it in your eyes,' he hissed, walking around Laura and striding up to the woman. His shoulders were tight and high, his jaw jutting out. 'You remember what Amelia said?' he said, spreading his arms wide and addressing the room. 'She has been contaminated by spirits. I know it.'

'You're crazy.' The woman stepped back, her eyes wide as she looked to the left and right and realised everyone was backing away.

31

'Here.' Beth opened the front door and the woman darted through it. Then she slammed the door and leaned against it. 'Who would like cake?' she shouted.

There was a weak cheer.

'Let me after her,' the man said, crowding Beth. She could smell the stench of beer on his breath and had to work hard not to wrinkle up her face in disgust.

Beth shook her head. 'It's my birthday, and I won't have violence at my party. You are not leaving.'

'You're going to keep me here?' His voice rose in pitch, his eyebrows shooting up in surprise.

'I'm going to keep you here.' Laura sidled up to him, a large slice of cake in one hand, a new can of beer in the other. 'I'm not anywhere close to being finished with you yet. Here,' – she handed him the plate and the can – 'these are for you.'

The man leered, but he allowed himself to be led away.

Beth let out her breath in relief. What had she got herself into?

She thought of Jonan walking into the darkness, hands stuffed in his pockets. She wondered why she had let him go without her. Laura depended on her, confided in her, even leaned on her for cash. But what did that make Beth, a friend or a mother? This party had nothing to do with her, and neither did the people.

Beth had no idea how, but she would find a way to reclaim that moment with Jonan and reopen the door to opportunity. Her coat pocket banged heavily against her leg. She reached down and pulled out the Tarot deck, sliding the lid open.

Intention was the top card.

CHAPTER THREE

Jonan

THE DOOR OF the Third Eye Spiritualist Shop creaked as it opened.

Jonan looked up from the box he was unpacking and pushed to his feet, automatically ducking under the overhead beam.

'No, no.' Doriel smiled and gestured around the messy stockroom that made up the first floor of their home. 'Don't you stop. I'll get it.'

Jonan nodded and crouched back down.

He heard Doriel walk down the narrow, wonky staircase that divided the storeroom from the shop's reading and treatment room. The tiny bells stitched into the hem of her skirt tinkled as she swung her hips.

Jonan shook his head. He had no idea why she bothered with all this theatre. She was the real deal. She could have run a fabulous business in joggers and a T-shirt, but she insisted on playing to the audience. She wore flowing skirts, bells and long earrings. Her hennaed hair was braided into a loose French plait that reached her waist, sparkling with tiny crystals. She mimicked smoke and mirrors and delivered magic. She was a goddess hiding in plain sight as a walking cliché. The irony never failed to make her hoot with laughter.

The distant voice made Jonan freeze. 'I'm looking for a reading. I was told you were good.'

He dropped back from his crouch to sit on the floor, heart pounding in his chest.

She had come.

He had told her to come to Doriel, but he had never expected it to be this easy. This was the woman he had incarnated for, the one he was here to wake up. He knew his goal, but somehow it didn't feel anywhere near as important as just being in the same room as her. He had no idea how she would react to his world. She had been brought up with Earth amnesia and would probably think he was crazy. Everything he was, everything he said, was strange. Would she listen, or would she run? He had no way of knowing until he tried it.

A shiver ran down his spine.

'How kind.' Doriel's musical voice lilted, growing louder as she started up the narrow staircase.

The reading room was next to the storeroom, but separated by a hall and two old, thick walls. If he stayed where he was, she would walk right past him without ever knowing he was there.

From the excitement in Doriel's voice, he knew she had recognised Beth.

'What kind of reading are you after?'

Jonan could almost see the curious tilt of Doriel's head as she asked. Would he ever be that familiar with Beth?

'Tarot, please. Jonan said you have *the Starfolk Tarot*. I bought a deck yesterday and don't know what to do with it. I'd love to see it in action.'

'How lovely to find someone with a real interest. Did the images grab your attention, or the idea of the Tarot?'

'I have no idea. The deck was like a magnet drawing me in. I was looking for something, I just didn't know what. As soon as I found it, I felt calm again.'

Jonan shifted closer to the stairs, moving silently on the balls of his feet despite his heavy, leather boots. The door frame was covered by a curtain of ribbons with yet more bells stitched onto the bottom. He stopped. A waft of air from the stairway carried a familiar, flowery scent that made his heart beat faster. He had always felt a little at odds with this world, but Beth, that scent, they meant home.

'I love the faces on the cards,' Beth continued. 'They seem so familiar, as though they have something to say to me.'

'Then I'm sure they do. Come on through.'

Jonan pulled back the ribbons, sending the sound of tinkling bells through the room. Beth's long dark hair hung loose over her fine-boned shoulders. Her face was flushed, the pink warming her pale skin and making her eyes sparkle. High cheekbones rose in a smile that made his heart race and his energy flare. It took every ounce of control for him to calm it back down. He knew from the way her eyes widened that she had seen something. Had his eyes turned purple? Had she seen points on his ears? Or was it something else?

Beth flushed, and then her face broke into a wide smile. 'You're here! I wasn't sure whether I'd see you.'

'Jonan.' Doriel winked. 'Would you please mind the shop while I read for this young lady?'

'Beth. My name's Beth. And Jonan and I have already met.'

'Beth.' His voice was rough. He cleared his throat. 'I see the lure of *The Starfolk Tarot* was too much to resist.'

'I couldn't make any sense of it at all.' She shrugged and leaned on the door frame of the reading room. 'I tried doing one of the spreads in the book, but putting it together was something else entirely.'

The bells jingled again from downstairs.

'Jonan.' Doriel nodded at the staircase. 'Will you please go and mind the shop before someone makes off with all the crystals?'

Beth followed Doriel into the room. At the last minute she turned, watching Jonan, her head tilted to one side. Then she shook her head, smiled and closed the door.

Beth

'DO SIT DOWN, my love.' Doriel ushered Beth onto a straight-backed, wooden chair with a purple cushion that matched the cloth on the low table in front of her. There was a crystal ball in one corner and a Tarot deck in the middle. The heavily spiced air made Beth want to sneeze, but she managed to stop herself.

Doriel went over to a tall bookshelf next to a curtained window. '*The Starfolk Tarot*, let me see. I haven't used that deck in a long time, although it's always been one of my favourites.' She pulled a deep green velvet bag from a box on the top shelf and took out the familiar cards. Sitting down in front of Beth, she pulled her French plait over her shoulder and started shuffling.

'Do you have a question?'

'I need a change.' Beth sighed. 'I feel as though I'm mixing with the wrong people, doing the wrong things in the wrong places. I don't know where I should be going and I'd love some guidance. Is that specific enough?'

'That's perfect. Shuffle the cards while you think of your question, and then give them back to me when you're ready.'

Beth let her gaze wander while she shuffled. The room was small, with several huge crystals up against the walls. She recognised an enormous amethyst cathedral, but there were many others she couldn't name, pink, green, yellow, orange and black. All had round, yellow price tags stuck to them. There was a gold statue of the Buddha in one corner, and a goddess made from iron in another. Incense was burning near the door.

'Make sure you keep your mind on your question,' Doriel said with a smile. 'I don't think a reading on the merits of my decor would do you much good. Remember, the cards will respond to the thoughts that are in your mind while you shuffle.'

Beth closed her eyes, forcing herself to concentrate. She thought about Laura and how self-obsessed she was. She thought about her job, the office where she organised copycat events day after day. All the time, Jonan hovered in the back of her mind. She tried to push him out. She had no idea how psychic Doriel really was and she didn't want her to realise how much Beth was thinking about her nephew. She thought of Amelia. She had no idea why the woman was occupying so much space in her mind. She was nothing to do with her own life, but the woman's words seemed to have wormed their way uncontrollably into Beth's brain.

She opened her eyes. Doriel was watching her with an appraising look. 'I'm sorry, was my mouth hanging open, or something?'

'No, you looked perfectly serene.'

A gust of warmth surrounded her and the familiar scent of lavender.

'Salu,' Doriel whispered. She stared over Beth's shoulder, her lips raised in a smile.

'What does that mean?' Beth asked. 'Amelia said the same thing.'

'Oh, it's nothing. Have you finished?'

Beth narrowed her eyes as she handed over the deck, but Doriel looked down at the table as she started laying out the cards. Beth wondered whether she was deliberately avoiding her gaze.

'So.' Doriel looked over the cards, hovering her hand over the top. She closed her eyes for a moment. 'Right now you're on the verge of a new emotional beginning, but it's more than that. You're intuitive and this is going to become more and more central to your life.'

Beth narrowed her eyes and looked at Doriel, blurring out the solidity of the real world and focusing on the energy around the woman. She was surrounded by a vivid purple glow. Maybe Jonan was right. Maybe she was genuine.

'You're blocked by your mastery of the physical world. You have built a nice life for yourself, and you are wary of disrupting that, or showing people that you are more than the "switched-on" woman you seem to be. This ability to function at such a high level in the normal world is a blessing. Not all people of your intuitive disposition are able to do that. On the other hand, it hinders you from being who you really are because you can do so well by pretending.'

Beth shifted in her chair. Doriel was uncomfortably accurate. She wasn't sure whether to be pleased or embarrassed.

'You come from a place of sacrifice,' Doriel said. She pointed to a card of a man with pointed ears, hanging upside down from a tree. His legs looped over a branch, his long hair hanging straight towards the leafy, autumnal ground. 'You have been putting others first, believing it was for the greater good. Their needs were more important than your own, but this is a pattern for you. You are not being honest with yourself. You need to look at life in a different way.

'The underlying theme is your independence. You see yourself as the only person you can rely on.'

Beth's face heated. She was not often embarrassed. She rarely showed the world enough of herself to cause embarrassment, but Doriel was making her feel profoundly exposed.

'In your immediate future I see you starting to make things happen. You will begin to manifest that which you have longed for.'

'How do I know what to create?' Beth cut in. Her pulse raced. Doriel was hitting one button after another. The air was thick with the smell of sage and it was clogging her throat and nose, adding to the sense of overwhelm. She had no idea what she'd expected, but to have someone see her like this was alien and deeply unnerving. It was as though Doriel knew more about her than she knew herself. 'I know I'm not happy, but I don't know what I'm looking for. I'm missing something.'

'That's perceptive.' Doriel turned from the cards, leaned her elbows on the table and rested her chin on her hands. In that moment she looked much younger than Beth had first assumed. She seemed ageless, as though she were centuries old, and yet her skin was smooth, firm and flushed. Her eyes were bright with fire. The hennaed plait draped over her shoulder and brushed the cards. 'Do you have any sense at all about where you might be going?'

'Only that where I've been is wrong. I have…'

'Yes?' Doriel leaned forwards.

'Oh, nothing.'

'It's not nothing, love,' Doriel said, leaning back. 'If it were, you would have told me by now. People never hesitate with insignificant chatter. It's only the deep, dark, fascinating stuff they keep to themselves. You can say anything here. It won't leave this room and Jonan will never hear it from me.'

Beth raised her eyebrows. 'Jonan?'

Doriel laughed. The sound was oddly musical, like bells. 'No, dear, I haven't been prying into your thoughts. I don't need to.'

'Has he said something about me?' Beth leaned forwards, casting her eyes over the cards on the table, and then looking back up at Doriel.

Doriel pursed her lips, trying not to smile. 'I know you'll understand I need to respect Jonan's privacy too.'

'Of course.' Beth looked over to the door, wondering if he was still outside and whether he was listening. She knew so little about the man but, somehow, he made her feel normal. That was not something she was used to.

Doriel laughed. 'You're a strong woman, Beth. You don't need to be saved. You need to be released. You need to find your wings so you can fly on your own terms. Trust your instincts and intuitions. If you feel someone is untrustworthy, keep your guard up around them. If someone feels like home, you can trust them even if you have only just met. Your intuition is strong. It won't lead you astray.'

'And you really can't tell me about Jonan?'

'Would you be happy for me to convey your interest in him?'

'Fair point.' Beth grimaced. She got up and pulled on her coat. 'That was fascinating. Thank you.'

'One more thing.' Doriel stood and took hold of Beth's hand. Her skin was warm and slightly dry as though the autumn weather was taking its toll. She wore a perfume that was strangely familiar and tugged at Beth's heart in an unexpected way. 'Please do come to me again, love. I think you will be a friend and I would not see you isolated. Sometimes the new person in your life may play a greater role than you would have believed possible.'

'Thank you.' Beth's voice was hoarse. She coughed, looking away.

'Now, I think someone may be waiting for you downstairs.'

Beth squinted as she walked from the crooked staircase into the brightly lit shop. It was dark outside, but there were still plenty of people walking along the damp, yellow-lit street.

Jonan was serving someone at the till. He looked up at the jingle of the ribboned curtain. His lips curved into a smile. 'Do you still need me, Doriel? I thought I might walk Beth home.' He turned to Beth. 'If you'll allow me, that is?'

'Thanks, but there's no need for you to go out into the cold. I always walk alone.'

'I know, but I'd like to. May I?' Jonan smiled, head tilted to one side.

'In that case, yes, thank you.'

'Of course, you go.' Doriel nodded at Jonan, and then pulled Beth into a tight hug. 'Come back soon. I may need your help. Don't be a stranger.'

'I will,' she said, unsure what she was agreeing to. 'See you soon.'

They stepped out into the cold. A gust of wind caught her full in the face and she burrowed down into her scarf.

Jonan pulled up the collar of his jacket. 'Fancy a drink?' He inclined his head towards the pub opposite the old flint clock tower.

'I'd love to.' Beth darted across the street to the warmth of the old-fashioned black-and-white building. She had always thought it looked rather wonky, as though the foundations weren't straight. She'd never been in before but was curious. It had a strong energy to it that fizzed around the edges of her consciousness. Pulling the door open, she ducked through the low doorway. There was a gentle hum of conversation and the underlying smell of beer. A few locals were spread around the rough wooden tables, with one or two more sitting at the bar.

Jonan strode over and waved to the barman. The broad guy in his early twenties slung a tea towel over the shoulder of his fitted heavy-metal T-shirt. He took a pint glass down from the shelf. 'The usual?'

'Of course.' Jonan looked at Beth, one eyebrow raised.

'Gin and tonic please.' A chill ran down her spine. She shivered.

'Cold?' Jonan asked, taking the drinks and leading the way to a small table in the back left-hand corner of the room.

'No, there's just something about this place.'

He turned to look at her. 'You feel it then?'

'You knew?'

'Of course! I assumed you'd have gathered that much from Doriel.'

Beth slid onto the red, padded bench, behind a wooden post and leaned on the solid wood back. 'Doriel was annoyingly discreet.' She grinned and took a sip of gin and tonic. 'I was hoping she'd spill the beans on you, but she wouldn't tell me a thing. I'm not sure what I paid all that money for.'

'That is a disgrace,' Jonan said. He raised one eyebrow. 'You'd have thought the local witch would be a bit more evil than that.'

'Is that what she is then? A witch?'

'No, but some people think she is. Doriel doesn't do labels. She's herself. That's it.'

'I like her more for that,' Beth said, looking around the pub. 'What's the story with the resident ghost?'

'There was a horrible incident here a long time ago. An imprint lingers, or so the story goes. What do you feel?'

'Why are you asking me? I thought you were the expert.'

'Nobody's really an expert. We're all learning.'

'It just feels creepy to me. Sorry to disappoint.'

Jonan laughed. 'Fair enough. What did Doriel tell you? Or is it top secret?'

'She told me I needed to look at life differently, and that I was about to start making changes. Unfortunately, I have no idea what to change.'

'Did she give you any indication?'

'She said I sacrifice myself for the sake of others.'

'And do you?'

'Doesn't everyone? I don't see how that moves me forwards.'

Jonan smiled. 'What were you thinking about when you shuffled the cards?'

'Well…' Beth paused. 'Work, Laura, Amelia…'

'Amelia?' Jonan's tone was sharp. He tilted his head, eyes narrowed. 'What were you thinking about her?'

'I don't even know. I have no idea why I've let her get into my head, but she's eating away at me. I know she's just a silly celebrity trying to get attention with a ridiculous story, but I can't shake the feeling that she's somehow… dangerous? More than she seems at least.'

Jonan watched her as though he were trying to read something. She shifted in her seat, wondering what he saw. 'Amelia *is* more than she seems,' he murmured. 'Don't ever forget that, and don't doubt your instincts.'

Beth frowned and leaned forward, propping her elbows on the table, chin on her hands. 'Okay, spill. What do you know?'

Jonan folded his arms over his chest and grimaced. 'I've known Amelia for a long time. She's intense and charismatic, and she's perfectly happy to manipulate if it works to her benefit. I'm not sure what she's playing at, but we can bet it will be a lot bigger than she's making out right now.'

'But why did she pick me out of the crowd? And why can't I get her out of my head?'

Jonan smiled and raised one eyebrow. 'Do you have any ideas yourself?'

'None. There was muttering all over the audience. Why would I be pinpointed? And why have you sought me out?'

'Sought you out? You came for a reading at the shop, remember?'

Beth raised her eyebrows. 'I saw you watching me in the studio, and then you turned up at my party and insisted I needed to see Doriel. Then there's that tarot card that looks like you. And I've looked through the whole deck, you must have known I would. There's a card called The Mother, which looks like Doriel. There's one called Fear, which is the spitting image of Amelia. And, of course, there's Leap of Faith, which has me looking up at the clouds from the edge of a cliff, a floppy-eared dog at my ankles. Do you still want to tell me there's no connection?'

'No, I don't. I can tell you why Doriel, Amelia and I are in the deck. The illustrator is an old friend and she based some of the cards on us. My mother is in there too; she's the High Priestess, if you want to look her up. It's an unnerving likeness, if I'm honest, and she looks more like the card now than she did when that picture was drawn. The shocker is that you're in there too. I stared at you in the TV studio because you were familiar from the Leap of Faith. It's the first card in the whole deck. Did you know that? Anyway, hopefully you can understand now why I was staring, and why Amelia might have been interested in hearing what you had to say.'

'She's into Tarot too?'

Jonan nodded. 'Not that she'd ever admit it now, not after what happened.'

'It sounds like there's a good story in there?'

Jonan downed the last of his pint and stood up. 'Well there's certainly a story, but I'm not sure I'd call it good. It's all a bit close to the bone for me. I'll tell you one day. Shall we go?'

Beth inched her way back out from behind the wooden pillar while Jonan pulled on his leather jacket. He walked over to the door, his movements impossibly fluid as though he were an ancient hunter let loose in this timeless pub. She watched him, fascinated. The drunk and undulating crowd parted before him, not intruding into his space at all.

Grabbing her bag, she followed. She was jostled, nudged and grabbed several times before she reached the exit. He held the door open for her as she stumbled out into the street.

The lights sent welcoming beams into the chilly air. The clock tower loomed over them as they cut up towards the main street.

'You know, I'm fine to walk home from here,' Beth said, looking up at Jonan.

His angular cheeks dimpled as he suppressed a smile. 'Don't you want me here?'

'Of course I do... I mean, are you trying to catch me out?'

Jonan laughed, a deep belly laugh that lit his face. He stopped and turned, leaning against a low wall. His collar was turned up against the cold, his hands thrust deep in his pockets. 'Maybe I just wanted an excuse to spend a bit more time with you?' He tilted his head, watching her with violet-tinged eyes.

Beth's breath caught. 'Well then, I would love your company. As long as you don't think I need looking after. I've managed perfectly well on my own for a long time.'

They continued walking past the white, looming bulk of the town hall. It cast a strange shadow over Jonan, highlighting the angular cut of his cheekbones and his slanted eyebrows. He looked weirdly other and, at the same time, disarmingly familiar. 'Alone?' he asked, his voice quiet. 'Is there no family?'

'Oh, yes. They live nearby and they love me in spite of who I am. I see them regularly. I know they're there for me, but they've never seen the world the way I do. Nobody does.'

'Are you sure about that?' Jonan stopped and turned to face her. He stood squarely, legs apart, hands in the pockets of his dark blue jeans. The upturned collar of his black leather jacket only served to accentuate his long neck and narrow, sculpted face.

Beth blinked. For a moment, his ears had seemed pointed. Right now, there was only a pale pink curve. They were oddly refined, but indisputably normal.

He was still watching her. She knew he'd asked a question and was waiting for an answer, but she had no idea what he'd said. She felt like a sponge, absorbing the energy around her, as though it were life-sustaining. Something had clicked. At that moment, with this man, she felt real, normal. Her weirdness had somehow been neutralised. She knew in an indefinable way that he was just like her. That their meeting held no coincidence at all.

'Are you sure nobody sees the world like you?' He tilted his head.

'No. I'm not sure,' she said. 'I only know I have spent a lifetime looking for someone who does.'

Jonan smiled. 'Be open to the possibility that you may have found what you're looking for.'

Beth swallowed. The silence was thick. Jonan watched her, the purple of his eyes deepening. He said nothing.

'It's, erm, it's this way,' Beth said, pointing down the road towards home.

Jonan nodded and they walked on in silence.

'Here you are,' Jonan said as they arrived, too soon, at the tree in front of her flat.

'Thank you. Will you be alright walking home alone?' Beth grinned.

Jonan let out a belly laugh that washed away the tension. She giggled. He laughed again and then she couldn't stop. By the time the laughter subsided, they were both gasping for breath.

'Look, Jonan…'

'Beth, is that you? What are you doing down there?' Laura leaned out of the living room window, waving her arm at Beth. 'Who's that you're with?'

'Oh for goodness sake.' Beth sighed. 'Is there no end to her ability to ruin a moment?'

Jonan smiled, but the hilarity was gone.

Beth walked over to the communal entrance. She reached for the handle, and then turned. Jonan hadn't moved. From this distance an aura glowed around him, a shimmering purple that matched his eyes.

'Beth, are you coming?' Laura yelled again.

Jonan smiled and raised a hand.

Beth nodded, and then pulled the door open and forced herself to walk through. She jarred when the door slammed behind her, the sound like a shove against her spine. It normally took her half an hour of meditating to become this open. How had it happened so quickly when she hadn't even tried?

At the top of the communal stairs she stopped at her front door and turned the key in the lock. Inside, she stepped out of her pumps and turned on the living room light. Padding barefoot on the smooth, parquet floor, she squinted through the large, picture window into the darkness. Jonan was underneath the tree, his blond hair glinting in the moonlight. She waved.

He lifted a hand in acknowledgement.

'Beth?' Laura yelled.

She turned at the thump of footsteps.

When she looked back out the window, Jonan had gone.

'Where have you been?' Laura's voice was oddly high pitched.

'Why, what's happened?' Beth felt a familiar sinking feeling. Laura only cared where Beth was when she wanted something. It was rarely anything simple.

'I had a horrible day at the studio.' Laura sniffed and slumped down on the sofa, kicking off her flip flops and curling her legs under her. 'There was this awful woman who was ranting about Amelia's claims being made-up fluff.

She said Amelia just wanted the publicity. Can you believe that? She actually thought the poor woman used her own mother's death as a stunt?'

Beth poured herself a glass of red wine from the open bottle on the table. Several glasses were clustered round. 'Are we expecting company?'

'No, not really, just a few friends from the studio. You'll love them.'

Beth sighed. 'What makes you so sure Amelia isn't pulling a stunt? She said all the right stuff the other day, but honestly, she was far too composed to be as distraught as she claimed.'

'She's a professional.' Laura was enunciating too clearly, a sign she was angry. Her neck was stiff, her almost pointed chin tilting upwards. A vein throbbed in her jaw.

Beth sighed. 'I'm sorry, is she a friend of yours? I had no idea. I didn't mean to be insulting.'

'She's not a friend, but I know she would be if I could just meet her. We would click, instantly, and be best friends. I just need to figure out how to get an introduction. I nearly met her at the studio the other day but you distracted her.'

Beth's eyes widened. 'I didn't distract her. She interviewed me during the show and then moved on. I *really* wasn't that much of an event.'

'You were, more than you know.'

The doorbell rang. Laura jumped off the sofa and pranced out of the lounge.

Beth grabbed her wine and headed for the door. She couldn't face one of Laura's studio sit-ins tonight. She waved at the over-trendy guy with spiky hair who was leaning against the door frame, staring at Laura's chest. Then she slipped into her room and shut the door firmly behind her.

CHAPTER FOUR

Beth

A MIST HUNG over the main street as Beth walked to work the next morning. The pavements were still littered from the weekend market stalls, giving the town a used-up feel. She popped into the coffee shop below her office and bought the largest cappuccino they had, but it did nothing to clear the feeling of dread that was settling in her stomach for no apparent reason.

An engine roared and Beth looked up to see a souped-up, white car with navy striped trim and tinted windows. Loud music rattled the car and jarred Beth's sleepy body. It sped down the road, and then slammed into an emergency stop as a white van turned right towards the market. The van swerved out of the way, crashing into a pile of wooden pallets packed with cauliflowers, broccoli and potatoes. Vegetables flew around, hitting both the van and the car, smashing as they landed on the road.

The market trader yelled and leaped over the pallet, banging on the window of the van, arms waving. The guy in the car got out, pulling his baseball cap farther down over his face. He slammed the car door and strode towards the van, curling his shoulders in and clenching his fists. Then he stopped as the door of the van opened. Both the market trader and the car driver stepped back.

The guy in the van climbed out slowly, his heavily muscled arms bunching as he rolled his shoulders. He wore a muscle shirt in spite of the early chill, which showed off his intricate tattoos. 'Do we have a problem?' His voice was low, but it carried through the stillness that surrounded the growing confrontation.

The men lifted their hands in front of their faces and backed away. Beth could see their mouths moving, but their voices carried away on the wind. The car's engine revved, and then it screeched off towards the roundabout at the top of town. The market trader bent to collect what remained of his vegetables.

There was a shuffling next to Beth and she turned. The man next to her was filming. He shrugged. 'You can't be too careful. There's weird stuff going on right now.'

'Hmm.' Beth shook her head and ducked in through the door to the old building that housed the small events company she worked for. She let out a breath as the door slammed behind her and made her way up the steep, misshapen steps to the upper floor. The dim autumn morning flooded the room with shadows, so she put all the lights on full and cranked up the heating. The light flickered. She shivered as a chill shot down her spine.

'Well hello there,' she murmured to the presence in the room. 'It's nice to feel you here after all that craziness. Are you going to talk to me today? I still don't know your name.'

Beth felt a sense of laughing, but nothing more. The lights settled down to normal.

A blast of cold air shot into the room as the door swung

open. Charlie Smythe, Beth's boss, slammed the door behind him and dropped into his chair next to the radiator. He put his hands over the flat surface and shuddered. 'I do wish they'd heat this dump better.'

'You're in charge. Make it happen.'

'I wish I could.' Charlie blew on his hands, and then turned on his computer and peered at the screen. A deep line stretched between his eyebrows as he slumped forwards in his habitual position. 'I'm just a local manager. I'm having enough trouble making that budget measure up as it is. I just wish we had a nice, modern office with proper heating and double glazing. I'm not sure it's any warmer in here than it is outside. Plus, this place gives me the creeps. I don't know why.'

'Really?' Beth leaned back in her chair, propping her legs on the rung under the table. 'You don't know why? Haven't you ever met her?'

'Met who?'

'The ghost. I assumed everyone had bumped into her at some point.'

'You're having me on.' Charlie picked up the pile of paper in his in-tray and started rifling through it. The paper trembled slightly. 'There's no ghost. It's just creepy in here.'

'You believe what you like, whatever keeps you coming into work without freaking out. But did you know the old debtor's prison used to be a few doors down? If you went in there nobody was obliged to feed you. I bet there are plenty of old prisoners wandering through these ancient buildings. What's to stop them? They're free to move as they wish at last!'

'Stop it,' Charlie said. 'I get it. You think it's all a load of rubbish, that it's fun to wind up the boss. Did you see that kerfuffle outside? Any idea what was going on? I only saw the tail-end of it.'

Beth shrugged. 'Some kind of road-rage thing. Bad behaviour followed by outrage. You know the deal.'

'I do, but it's early in the morning for it. What is going on at the moment? It's like everyone's amped up. Anyway...' He shuffled his papers around, and then looked up, a smug grin on his face. 'Some big news came in on Friday after you'd left. You have a shiny new event to organise.'

'An event? At last. I thought we were done for.'

'We may be yet. I laid off the rest of the staff over the weekend. This event is the only reason you and I are still here.'

'You laid them all off?' Beth let out a slow exhale and leaned back on her chair, shaking her head. 'Why choose me to stay?' She watched Charlie through narrowed eyes, trying to pick up any clues in his energy. There was nothing. It was dull and lifeless, as though he'd given up. 'I mean, I know I'm good, but I'm pretty sure some of the others were better.'

He laughed. 'The client asked for you by name. So please, by everything that's shiny, prove them right.'

Beth took a ragged breath. 'Who's the client, and what's the event?'

'A dinner for five hundred people. Amelia as guest speaker, a band and press. There'll be VIP tables with dignitaries because the charity is using it as a key lobbying venture. Beyond those, it will be your job to sell tickets, confirm a venue, sort the press and band. If you can think of any other entertainment, so much the better. It'll be a black-tie job. They want to target the moneyed set, have an auction, raise a shed-load of cash for the charity. Oh, and did I mention? The event is two months today.'

'Two months? Are you kidding?'

'Nope. Told you it was big.'

'Urgh.' Beth dropped her head into her hands. 'What if I say no?'

Charlie shrugged. 'Then you'll lose your job. Are you sure you want to go down that road?'

Beth shook her head, squeezing her eyes tightly shut. So much for her new start. She wouldn't have time to think, let alone soul-search. Plus, she would have to work with Amelia and that woman gave her the creeps.

'They've booked Amelia already, but there's a lot of liaising to do with her office. They're handing that to you. She was the one who requested you, would you believe?' Charlie chuckled as he shook his head. 'You've hit the jackpot there. She wants you to go to one of her events so you can get a feel for the way she operates. The job does sometimes have its perks, eh!'

Beth felt as though her throat were closing. Her body filled with a panic that was completely overblown. She checked in with her heart, her stomach, her arms and legs, all were responding as though she were in a full-on panic attack, but her mind was clear and calm. Forcing herself to ignore the physical discomfort, she clasped her hands under the desk so Charlie couldn't see her shaking. 'I will of course make it work. But why did Amelia ask for me?'

'No idea. You should have told me you knew her. I would have asked for an autograph a long time ago.'

He handed over a large, yellow ring-binder. 'All the contacts and budgets are in there. Please get in touch with them today. Confirming a venue is a clear priority, but I understand Amelia has plans for that already. It should be easy to secure something with her as a draw. It'll be amazing publicity for whichever venue hosts it.'

'Is Amelia the client? I thought it was a charity event.'

'It is. Amelia's the patron.'

'But surely the charity should be choosing the venue, not the celebrity?'

'I don't think the client can believe their luck. Their instructions are to give her anything she wants as long as it's within budget.'

'Who is the client, by the way?'

'Child Refuge.'

Beth watched Charlie as he turned away and started looking through his emails. 'Charlie, how did you get this account?'

'I'd like to tell you I nursed it for months and closed the deal using my fabulous charm and witty intellect. But funnily enough it just landed on Friday evening, all by itself. Someone I'd never met called me up on my mobile and gave me the account. No build up, no questions, nothing.'

'Except they asked for me.'

'Amelia asked for you.' Charlie grinned as he nodded towards her.

'But I've barely met her. She was on that chat show I went to on Saturday morning. She put me on the spot and made an example of me on national television. That's the only contact I've ever had with her. And that was after you took the account.'

Charlie shrugged again. 'There must be a connection you don't know about. Does it matter?'

Beth let out a bark of laughter. 'Well not to you, clearly. There's something weird about it though.'

Charlie rolled his eyes. 'You're over-thinking it. It's a job and a darn good one at that. Stop complaining, get into the brief and, please, no more calling out Amelia. She's your benefactor and our only client. Be grateful. We're lucky she chose us. She'll certainly bring us some much-needed glamour.'

'Glamour? Do you really think lack of glamour is our problem? Or did you mean visibility?' Beth asked.

Charlie flushed.

'Oh no. Not you too, Charlie.' Beth sighed. 'I have no idea how she does it, but everyone loses their ability to think straight when she's involved.'

'Listen,' Charlie said, leaning forwards, 'if you're not prepared to be ingratiatingly and infuriatingly polite to her, say so now. I don't want you using this event to pick fights.'

Beth sighed. Amelia had found a clever way to control her and she had no idea how she was going to get out of it. She plastered a smile on her face. 'Of course, Charlie. You know me, I'm a pro.'

'Well make sure you are. This is our last chance to make this branch work. Unless we can do something spectacular, I'll be transferred elsewhere and you'll be out of a job.' He got up and pulled on his coat. 'I'm off. I have a pitch to get to. Will you get on to this event now?'

'As soon as you're through that door.'

He nodded. The door shut behind Charlie and Beth let out her breath in a rush. She leaned back in her chair and closed her eyes. She was used to playing a part to fit in, but this was something else altogether.

BETH WAS CERTAIN someone had set her up. Amelia's PA, Rose, insisted The Monk's Inn was the only venue option and instructed Beth to meet her there. Half an hour later, she was standing in the middle of a purely residential street. There wasn't a hotel in sight, just a row of immaculately tended houses on each side of the road and a dilapidated ruin.

She turned to leave, but a creak and a thump caught her attention. She turned back round. A wooden sign swung outside the ruin. It was filthy and hard to read, but she could just make out the damaged wording. *The Monk's Inn.*

The building was all the wrong kinds of ancient. The black timber on white walls could have been stunning, like so many of the other Tudor buildings at this end of town. Instead, the place felt dirty. The walls had aged from a bright white to a yellowing grey, which was only enhanced by the cobwebbed black beams. A rotten wooden door stood in the centre of the building, its peeling paint doing nothing to disguise the decay. The bare windows that flanked it on either side were too dirty to see through. She'd never heard of this place and now that she saw it, she wasn't surprised. How it had escaped being modernised she had no idea. This road was one of the most expensive in St Albans, there were so many wonderful venues nearby and she was stuck in this creepy old dump.

'Oh hello, darling.' A woman in her early twenties walked down the hill towards her, fighting to stay upright on the steep, slippery paving stones. 'I'm Rose. We spoke on the phone earlier. Thank you for meeting me here. I've heard a lot about you.'

'None of it good, I'm sure.' Beth grinned.

Rose flushed and gave a forced giggle. She held out her hand, limp and cold, as though offering it to be kissed.

Beth shook it, pressing her lips together to stop herself from laughing. 'I assure you, your event is in safe hands.'

'So your boss would have me believe.' Rose looked Beth up and down.

Beth raised her eyebrows. Her black trouser suit seemed dowdy compared to Rose's pencil skirt, which was so tight it impeded her ability to walk. Her sparkly ballet pumps were stunning, but her feet looked pinched and over-large where her skin bulged over the front of the narrow shoes. Beth had no doubt everything Rose wore was designer but, somehow, she had missed the mark and looked painfully uncomfortable.

'So, Rose,' Beth said, eyeing the crumbling building behind her. 'Why this place?'

'Amelia likes it.' Rose stood by the door and raised her eyebrows. When Beth didn't move, she inclined her head towards the door.

Beth took a deep breath. She wanted to tell Rose to go to Hell, but Charlie had been very clear that her job depended on her ability to deal with Amelia and her staff. So she plastered a smile onto her face, reached forwards, and tried the door handle. It didn't budge. She tried again, giving it a good shove. The heavy door creaked open.

Rose bustled through, looking down at her phone. Her long nails tapped out a rhythm on the glass as she typed, in spite of her attempts to angle the pad of her fingertip towards the screen.

The reception area was larger than Beth had expected. The black-and-white tiled floor looked original and a huge, ornate fireplace stood dirty and unused on her right-hand side. Beth kept her breathing shallow to keep the mustiness at bay. The building felt wrong on so many levels. A creeping dread turned her insides to ice. She shivered.

The reception desk was large and imposing. A balding, wrinkled old man in brown cord trousers and a brown-checked shirt stood behind it, a scowl on his face as he watched them approach.

'Are you certain I can't encourage you to look at some of the other hotels in St Albans?' Beth said to Rose, keeping her voice low so the man couldn't hear. 'This is more the territory of the local ghost walk than a prestigious event.'

'It will be beautiful,' Rose said, looking around her, nose wrinkled in distaste.

'I can imagine, but in two months? Surely that's tight by anyone's standards.'

Rose rolled her yes. 'This conversation is getting old.' She waved her hand towards the desk, turned, and started talking into her phone as she walked back towards the entrance.

Beth sighed and smiled at the man behind the counter. 'My name is Beth Meyer. I work at Page Events and we are looking for a venue. The Monk's Inn was recommended. Is there someone who can show us around?'

'There's only me.' The man coughed. His voice was thin and reedy. 'Let me lock up here and I'll take you.'

'What if someone wants to get out while we're upstairs?' Beth asked.

'There's only me,' he repeated.

'No guests at all?'

The man laughed, and then gave a hoarse cough. 'Would you sleep here?' He sat down for a moment, fighting for breath. He looked up at Beth, his eyes watery. 'The only people here are dead. They keep me company day in day out, whether I want them to or not. Chances are I'll be one of them soon, stuck in this hell-hole for all eternity. That would be just my luck.'

Beth looked back over her shoulder. Rose had only taken a step or two into the room. She was texting, apparently oblivious to her surroundings. Beth leaned her elbows on the desk and kept her voice low, hoping Rose might not hear.

'How is the hotel still open?'

'Honestly? I have no idea. The owner pays my salary once a month, so I stand on reception. So far you're the first living person fate has brought through my door.'

'Who is the owner?'

'Not a clue. I was hired through a management company.'

'And you're the only member of staff?'

'The only one. The damp and dust are destroying my lungs, but I can't leave even for a few hours. There is nobody else here.' They both glanced over to Rose, who was now running a finger along the mantelpiece, her lip curled in disgust.

The man shrugged. 'I'd love it to be clean, but it's too far gone for me to handle on my own. It needs completely gutting.'

Beth nodded. She took his thin, cold hand and squeezed it gently.

'This place is in no position to host a charity black-tie dinner and ball for five hundred people, is it?'

The man laughed again, and then broke into his hacking cough. 'Well, if it's a haunted-house theme you're running, I'd be happy to dress up as the creepy butler. But I'm afraid that's about all I can offer.'

Beth laughed and turned. She raised her voice. 'I'm sorry, Rose, I am not recommending The Monk's Inn to my clients.'

Rose sniffed. Despite being smaller than Beth, she managed to glare down her nose at her, tipping her head back and pursing her lips. 'There is no need for you to have any direct contact with Child Refuge. They have asked me to act as their intermediary. In effect, I am your client. The Monk's

Inn will be ready and staffed. It will be perfect. You will hold the event here.'

Beth swallowed. 'We only have two months. There are two beautiful hotels nearby, ready and perfect. Why this one?'

'Amelia has her reasons.' Rose sniffed, took out a compact mirror and applied lipstick.

Beth pulled out her own mobile phone and opened her contacts. Then she dialled.

Charlie answered on the first ring. 'What?'

'I'm at The Monk's Inn. It's a disaster.'

'I don't want to hear it. I'm in the middle of an important meeting.' The phone rang off.

'Give me strength,' Beth muttered, squeezing her eyes tightly shut.

'Amelia will take care of the necessary details.' Rose picked her way over to the stairs. 'Show us around please Mr...'

'Jones, but please call me Bill.' The old man coughed.

Beth stared out the front window. The sense of dread that had filled her when she walked into the hotel intensified. She heard laughing in her mind and she pushed it back, imagining a ball of bright white light around her. She stretched it out, engulfing Bill, and watched as he closed his eyes, his face relaxing.

'Well, Miss...?' Bill asked.

'Beth, please call me Beth.' She glanced at Rose, who was running a finger along the banister and examining it, eyebrows crinkled together. Beth nodded. 'Please, Bill,' she said. 'Show us around?'

'Can I hang that up for you?' Bill nodded towards the long white coat Rose had taken off. She was staring at the hooks on the wall behind her. Long cobwebs hung from one of them, and the paint was peeling off the wall.

'No thank you,' she said, her voice strangled. 'I'll hang onto it.'

Bill snorted and shook his head in disbelief. 'What kind of mad boss do you have, to send you on such a crazy mission?'

'I ask myself that every day.' Beth winked. 'So far I've not found an answer.' Since she had surrounded Bill with light, colour was coming back into his pale, sunken cheeks and his eyes were brighter. He seemed younger somehow.

'Who is this party for anyway?' Bill asked, coming out from behind the reception desk.

'Amelia Faustus. Have you heard of her?'

'Oh, I've heard of her,' Bill said, his face darkening. 'I saw her on the telly the other day. Either that woman has no idea what she's talking about, or she's telling downright lies. I'm surprised she'd want to stay in a place like this after all her scaremongering about evil spirits.'

'Shh.' Beth held her finger to her lips again and dropped her voice to a whisper. 'Don't let the ghosts hear you say that.'

Bill laughed again. He doubled over, leaning on his knees as the laughter was choked out by coughing. 'I would love to show you around, miss. It would do me good to have the likes of you here to cheer me up. I hardly ever get to leave since there's nobody to cover me.'

'You don't leave?' Beth heard her voice crack. The shivering cold was trying to edge back into her body. She pushed it back with the light. 'Ever?'

'Only to buy food. I can't remember when I last got clothes or a book.'

'Don't you have friends who could stand in while you get out for a bit?'

'Not amongst the living.' He led her into a large room.

'Oh my goodness,' Beth said, as the smell of ingrained, stale wine hit her nostrils.

'I know.' Bill shrugged. 'But the room is my favourite for all it stinks.'

The Ballroom had once, indeed, been beautiful. Now neglect hung from every delicate line. Huge, dirty latticed windows lined the far wall, beginning at the level of Beth's shoulders and arcing up to the high, ornate ceiling. Beneath the windows stretched dark wood panels that were scratched and scuffed. A huge portrait of a woman in an elaborate red dress, with a laced corset and a voluminous skirt and full ruff, hung at one end of the hall. A small spaniel sat at her ankles, gazing up at her adoringly. At the other end was a stage, with lush velvet curtains that pooled on the floor. The material was filthy but undamaged. Round, solid-wood tables and ornate dark-wood chairs were arranged around the room, their padded seats covered with frayed, red-patterned fabric.

'Bill, this place is amazing!' Beth said. 'Why doesn't the owner do something with it?' She leaned against the heavy oak bar by the doorway, peering at the shelves behind. They were well stocked with large bottles of spirits, but each one was discoloured and thick with dust.

A smile spread over Bill's face and he stood up a little taller. 'There is so much history here. Maybe one day the owner will appreciate what they have. I can only hope.'

Beth saw a shadow move out of the corner of her eye and spun around. There was nobody there. She looked at Rose, who was perched on the edge of the one of the round tables, tapping on her mobile phone.

Bill was watching her, his lips raised in a slight smile. 'You saw it?' he murmured under his breath.

Beth nodded. 'Almost. But I definitely felt it.'

Bill stepped closer. 'How do you keep it away? Will you teach me?'

'I will, of course, but not in front of her.' She tilted her head towards Rose.

'What about the bedrooms?' Beth asked, loud enough for Rose to hear. 'I'm guessing some people will want to stay overnight, especially if they're travelling to get here.'

'This way.'

Bill led them up a huge, curved staircase with an elaborately carved banister. Smaller portraits of men and women in old-fashioned draped gowns and ruffles lined the walls. Beth felt as though they were watching her, but she didn't flinch as Bill led them deeper into the hotel.

They walked past a number of wood-panelled bedroom doors before Bill stopped before a double-door. 'This is the Royal Suite. It's housed royalty, albeit a long time ago. This bedroom is in the history books, if you look for it.'

He swung the doors wide and ushered them in. Beth gasped. A huge four-poster bed with ornate oak panelling and floor-length red curtains stood in the centre of the spacious room. Matching curtains framed the windows with dirty, torn nets behind. An old, round, mahogany table stood on each side of the bed with carved legs that curved underneath the polished surface. A chandelier hung from the ceiling, its crystalline orbs covered with dust. The room was dark, shadowy, but Beth was sure the sunlight would make it stunning if the grimy windows were cleaned. She walked over to the large latticed window and glanced at the threadbare cushions on the ornate window-seat.

'Are they all like this?'

Bill shook his head. 'I wish.'

'May I?' she asked, nodding towards the four-poster bed. 'I've always wondered how comfortable these things are.'

'Be my guest.' Bill sat on an upright chair in the corner of the room.

Beth sank onto the soft bed. 'What do you think, Rose? We could give this room to Amelia? Do you think she'd enjoy playing royalty for the night?'

Rose started, and then slipped her phone into her black, patent handbag while she studied the room. She wrinkled her nose as she ran a finger over the dirty velvet of the curtains. When she took it away, a tattered cobweb hung from her long, red nail. She shrieked, waving her finger around in disgust, and then shivered and brushed frantically at the white coat that still hung over her arm. 'Amelia is used to a much more groomed environment.'

Bill laughed. 'Then I suggest you follow your friend's advice and book one of the other hotels. If you want atmosphere, we have it in spades. If you want antiques, we have original features that antique dealers drool over. This place is a treasure trove of history, but groomed it is not, and will not be unless somebody hires a cleaning crew and maintenance staff. If that's what you want, go somewhere else.'

Rose pursed her newly painted lips. They glistened, even in the dark room.

Something moved in the shadows, but this time Beth ignored it and pulled the light tighter around her and Bill. His shoulders relaxed once more.

Rose squared her shoulders. 'There will be no more talk of alternative venues. We're booking this one. I'll speak to Amelia about where she'd like to stay.'

'You do that,' Bill said, chuckling as he led them out of the suite and into the next room.

Beth did a double take. The furniture in this room was a complete mismatch to the Royal Suite. Instead of the grand, Tudor four-poster, there was a wide double bed with a curved, semi-circular headboard with arcs in alternating wood panels. Geometric, dark wood bedside tables stood on either side, and a round mirror hung above the bed, glass panels radiating out like sunbeams.

Beth shook her head. 'Is this art deco?'

'Well spotted.' Bill smiled. 'The rooms have all been done up at different times. The next one is art nouveau. For a while there was about ten years between each restoration, I'd estimate, but it's a long time since any work was done here at all. The Royal Suite is the only one that has kept its original styling.

Beth ran a hand down the scratched and dusty dark wood dresser that stood opposite the bed. 'It's tragic that this place has been allowed to fall into such disrepair. It should have been turned into a museum.'

'Are you done?' Rose poked her head around the door, her phone still stuck to her ear. 'I need to get back to work.'

'Rose,' Beth said. 'Do you like what you see? Does the Children's Refuge have the budget to renovate a hotel in two months and is it worth the investment for them? I thought they were trying to raise money.'

'Don't be ridiculous,' Rose said, pulling on her long, white coat. 'I'm sure it can be cleaned. I'll talk to Amelia about the renovations. You don't need to concern yourself with that.'

'So it won't cost the charity?' Beth asked.

'As I said, you don't need to concern yourself with that side of things.' Rose sniffed. 'Amelia likes this place, so she'll have it. Just think of the photographs of Amelia talking about the paranormal in this old-fashioned building. I don't know why I need to tell you how to do your job.'

'You don't,' Beth said.

'Then what are you whingeing about?' Rose wrinkled up her nose.

'Well, for starters, you insisted I join you to view a hotel I don't consider suitable, and then you spent the whole visit staring at your phone instead of looking at the place. Now you're telling me it's none of my concern. How am I supposed to organise an event when I don't know whether it will be in a dilapidated dump, or a renovated historic building?'

'Huh!' Rose said, sticking her nose in the air. 'I was told you were good. I can't see the appeal myself. Anyway, I have to go. I have work to do.' Rose looked as though she longed to stick her tongue out at Beth. 'You know where I am if you need me.' Turning without a word to Bill, she walked down the hall and Beth heard her footsteps on the stairs. A few minutes later a car revved, and then drove away.

'Well, she's a charmer,' Bill said, squinting as she left. 'Now that she's gone, can I offer you a drink?'

He led Beth back downstairs, walked past the reception desk and grabbed a rough walking stick with a curved handle that was propped against the wall. 'I try not to use it, but there's only so long the old back will hold up. My body's not used to so much activity.' He laughed. The hoarseness was starting to wear off now, as though his voice was warming up after a long period of disuse.

'To the ballroom?' Beth asked, but Bill shook his head. 'No, there's too much company in there. My apartment is at the back. It's cosier.'

Bill led her through a door behind reception and into a small, windowless, room. A full basket of logs sat to one side of the fire, which was glowing with red embers. Bill lowered himself down in front of the fire with a grunt. Kneeling, he piled in some kindling and blew gently. Ash floated out around him, but a small flame burst into life. He sat back on his heels, watching as the kindling took, and then put a log on top to burn.

He pulled himself up on the simple stone mantelpiece and paused, breathing heavily.

'Here, have the chair,' he said, walking over to a small, mahogany table with a crystal decanter and cut glasses. This little corner of opulence was completely at odds with the rest of the bare room.

'No, I'll be fine on the footstool,' Beth said, pulling it towards the fire. 'You sit down.' Beth perched on the edge of the stool, leaning close to the blaze and rubbing her hands to warm them up. 'I hadn't realised how cold it was.'

'It's impossible to heat this place. It's so draughty. And with nobody staying, it never seems worth the effort. I can keep my rooms warm with the fire, and I spend as much time back here as I can. What would you like to drink? Tea? Whisky?'

'A cup of tea. please. I'm still at work.'

Bill left the room. She heard him run water and then a kettle began to warm. While he was gone, she glanced around the room. There were no pictures on the bare white walls. A comfy, faded armchair was pulled in front of the fire and heaped with blankets, which were strewn around like an unmade bed. After a few minutes Bill came back with her cup of tea. He handed it to her, and then poured himself a whisky from a crystal decanter. 'Don't tell anyone,' he said with a wink. 'I'm not supposed to use anything from the hotel, but my whisky is the only luxury I have.'

'Your secret's safe with me.' Beth wrapped her hands around the steaming cup of tea. 'Have you ever met Amelia?'

'Never. I've no idea how she even knows of this dump. As I said, you're the first people who have stepped through those doors in years.'

'Interesting,' she muttered. 'So what's her agenda?' She shook her head. 'Anyway, tell me the story of this place.'

'I used to work here as a boy when it was a proper hotel, but there were always rumours of ghosts and strange things happening. That drew a few people in, but most stayed away and the place haemorrhaged money. In the end, the owner emigrated to America and left the inn to crumble. About ten years ago, someone called me up. I have no idea how he found out about me or got my number. He said he knew I had connections with the place, and asked if I would *I* look after it in return for lodging and a salary. Nobody would bother me much.' Bill chuckled. 'I hadn't realised how much I liked being bothered. It's strange being alone so much. I feel as though I've become one of the ghosts that walks these halls.'

'Would you leave if you could?' Beth's voice cracked. She cleared her throat.

'Sometimes I think I would. In a funny way, these ghosts have become my family. I have nobody else. But then I look out through the front windows and see the warm glow from the houses across the street. I imagine the lives those families live, shouting children, playful dogs, busy, busy lives. For that, I would give up everything else in a moment.'

Beth dropped her head into her hands and rubbed her forehead.

'Please, don't feel sorry for me,' Bill said with a sigh. 'I'm surrounded by fear all the time. I don't need pity too.'

'Are you very scared here?'

'Oh, it's not as bad as all that.' Bill laughed, and then started coughing.

Beth stood up and rubbed his back until the wheezing stopped.

'I'm not going to lie,' he said, his voice still raspy, 'the monks are downright creepy and they certainly set the blood racing, but they're not the only ones here. There's a girl, too. She wears a nightgown and has glossy brown ringlets and a teddy in her hand. She cries in one of the bedrooms upstairs. It breaks my heart anew every single night. I always wish I had the strength to bring her peace. That's the hardest to bear.'

'I may know someone who could help you with that.' Beth smiled. 'Let me look into it. In the meantime, I'd better get back to work. Is there a number I can reach you on?'

Bill got up and opened a drawer in the sideboard. He drew out a thick piece of paper emblazoned with an old-fashioned crest and a black fountain pen. He wrote his name and number in a careful, looping script. He shook slightly as he wrote, his pale, age-spotted skin almost tinged with blue. 'Here you are.' He held out the paper, his fingertips white where he pressed them together in an attempt to hold his hand steady. 'I hope you're real. I hope I hear from you soon.'

Beth took Bill's hands and looked him directly in the eye.

'Do I feel like a ghost? You would know better than anyone else.'

'No, you feel real.'

Beth smiled. 'I will call you, Bill, whether or not we hold the event here. Do you trust me on that?'

Bill laughed, but the sound was more brittle than before. 'Trust? I was done with that a long time ago. I haven't had cause to trust anyone in a long time.'

Beth smiled. 'Well maybe it's time we changed that.'

CHAPTER FIVE

Jonan

'AMELIA'S CLEARLY PLANNING something,' Jonan said, leaning back in his chair. 'But I can't dig in to what it is. She has herself very well shielded.'

'And the tarot cards?' Doriel asked, her hands flying as she knitted thick purple wool into a long scarf. The movement was hypnotic.

Tired as he was, Jonan couldn't take his eyes off the wooden needles as they clicked over and over. 'The Tower and the Devil.'

Doriel stopped knitting and looked up at Jonan, back straight, eyes bright. 'The Tower? So she does have something big up her sleeve. And she's using it to spread fear; we know that already.'

Jonan massaged the bridge of his nose. 'We don't know how big she will go.'

Doriel stuck her knitting needles into the ball of wool and put it down on the coffee table. 'Amelia *is* potential. There's no end to how far she can go, or how strongly she can influence people. It's so frustrating that people can't just see through the fog she puts up. She's supposed to be on *our* side, influencing people into waking up. Instead she's shutting them down through fear, taking us back to some kind of dark age.'

Jonan sighed. Doriel was right. This was the moment he and Beth had to step in. This was why they had incarnated, but surely taking a little more time over it wouldn't hurt? He'd been dreaming of Beth his whole life; he didn't want to scare her off by saying too much too soon.

'Did you hear that?' Doriel asked, tilting her head. She unfolded from the chair and walked over to the window, the bells on the hem of her long skirt tinkling. Pulling the curtains back, she opened the crooked wooden window and peered out. 'It's Beth.'

Jonan darted out of the room and took the stairs two at a time. The front door was locked and the key wasn't in its normal spot behind the counter. He scrabbled around in the drawers before finding it nestling behind a half-full cup of cold tea. He fumbled to get the key in the lock, and then shoved the door open. It swung on its hinges as he stepped out into the street. 'Beth!' he called after her retreating back.

She spun around.

Her shoulders were hunched, her hands shoved in her pockets against the cold, but when she saw him, she broke into a wide grin that set his heart racing. She stepped forwards, and then faltered. 'I thought... the shop was closed?'

'It is, but we're both upstairs and I was about to put the kettle on. Would you like to join us?'

'Are you sure? I don't want to intrude on your downtime.'

'Of course I'm sure.' He smiled.

Beth paused, her head tilted to one side.

Jonan stepped through the door, holding it wide. She seemed to take forever. His arm was frozen unnaturally in mid-air and was starting to ache, but he tried to look nonchalant. 'Don't you want to come in?'

She chuckled. Her arm brushed against his hand as she slipped through the door and moved to wait at the bottom of the stairs.

'That's right, it's the same as the reading room, just farther up.' Jonan ducked past her and up the staircase.

He heard Doriel humming in the kitchen as he stepped into the living room, and ushered Beth inside.

'What would you like to drink, Beth?' Doriel called.

'Tea please, milk no sugar.'

'Right you are.' Doriel started singing again, louder this time.

Jonan wished he'd tidied up. The room looked like an unmade bed. The sofa had creased dips in the seats where he and Doriel had been sitting. Books and newspapers were abandoned face down and half-drunk cups of tea sat on the coffee table.

Jonan wondered what Beth's home was like, and whether it was ever this messy. He watched as her eyes tracked every piece of debris from his life, absorbing clues and personal details he'd had no time to hide.

'Have a seat,' he said, gathering up papers from the sofa and putting them in a fairly neat pile on the coffee table. 'I'm sorry about the mess.'

'Oh no, it's a lovely room,' Beth said, slumping into one of the single chairs. 'Old buildings usually feel so…' She frowned. '…edgy. Your home has all the charm, but it feels peaceful.'

'Thank you.' Jonan smiled, releasing the breath he hadn't realised he was holding. 'Not many people notice that.'

He stepped past her, picking up a large log and stacking it onto the fire, watching as it caught. He had wanted Beth in his home. Now that she was here, the things they needed to talk about seemed too big, too daunting. He felt her energy tugging at him like the scent of home. In her, he felt the peace he had longed for his whole life. He knew that if he gave in to that particular pull, he'd never have the courage to tell her the truth, to take the risk that she might think he was crazy and walk away.

'Here you are.' Doriel entered the room and handed Beth a steaming mug of tea.

Jonan closed his eyes, wishing she'd go away and give him this moment with Beth. He longed for normality. He had wanted to get to know Beth properly, chatting over a glass of wine by the fire, going on a date, buying her a Christmas present. He'd have brought up her true purpose eventually, but not until she knew him. They didn't have that kind of time now, but how could she trust his outlandish stories when she barely knew him?

'Jonan, your tea,' Doriel said.

He turned around. His eyes felt tight, his jaw strained. From the flash of surprise in Beth's eyes, he knew she had seen his discomfort. 'Thank you, Doriel,' he said, hearing the strange formality in his voice.

She nodded, and then folded herself up on the sofa, her legs crossed in a lotus position.

Jonan narrowed his eyes at her, willing her to leave, but she just smiled.

'Have either of you ever heard of The Monk's Inn?' Beth asked, warming her hands on the mug.

'The Monk's Inn?' Doriel frowned. 'What is that? A book?'

'No, it's a hotel in Fishpool Street. I'd never heard of it before today and I thought I knew all the venues round here.'

'I haven't heard of it either.' Jonan picked up a tarot deck that sat on the table and shuffled. 'But it has a strong feel to it. It has the word 'Monk' in the name and St Albans is notorious for its ghostly monks. It seems like an interesting place. Why are you asking?'

'I'm arranging a charity event with Amelia as the celebrity speaker. She's insisted the evening be held at The Monk's Inn, even though it's a dump. Apparently it will be renovated, but we only have two months until the event. Why would she do that? Why not just choose an established hotel?'

'She must own it,' Jonan said, sipping his tea. 'She's certainly wealthy enough.'

'But wouldn't her representative have told me that? I asked a lot of questions.'

'They may not know,' Doriel said. She leaned back in her armchair. 'Amelia keeps a lot of secrets. She's not one for sharing details, with anyone.'

Jonan pulled out a newspaper. He opened it and laid it out on the coffee table. It was a photo from the television studio. There was a large picture of Beth, her face twisted in frustration as Amelia smiled graciously down at her.

Beth grimaced. 'When did this come out?'

'This morning,' Doriel said, her eyes narrowed as she watched Beth.

'What is it about this woman?' Beth asked. 'Two days ago I'd never given her much thought. Now she's everywhere.'

'Amelia is a particular kind of person.' Doriel picked up a large crystal ball and cradled it in her hands. 'She is more than you could possibly imagine, and has a lot less compassion than she makes out.'

'I feel that,' Beth said, pulling her feet up onto the sofa and hugging her knees to her chest. 'Her story is clearly rubbish. That experience was a gift, and she's making it into a threat. But what does she get out of it?'

'Power,' Doriel said. 'She thrives on other people's stress.'

'She is able to control energy in an unusual way,' Jonan said, sipping his coffee. 'Whenever someone around her becomes scared, she siphons off their energy. It fuels her own, makes her bigger, brighter.'

'Or darker,' Doriel added.

'Yes, or darker. Certainly stronger.'

'How do you know so much about her?' Beth asked.

'We know Amelia of old,' Doriel said, leaning over to put her mug on the coffee table. 'She has, let's say, agendas.'

'Why does she need to be stronger? What am I missing?' Beth asked.

'Amelia is planning something big,' Jonan said. 'She's spreading fear and hatred and presenting herself as the expert who can relieve the chaos. She has the potential to change everything. At the moment her power is comparatively small, but she may want to use your event to spread her influence significantly further.'

'It's only a charity ball.' Beth shook her head. I can't see anyone taking much notice of that.'

'You don't realise what she's capable of,' Jonan said, his knee jiggling up and down.

'Maybe I don't, but I can't see many people buying into her rubbish. She's just one woman scaremongering about evil spirits. Seriously, this kind of thing has been going on for hundreds of years. Most people won't buy it.'

'People have been persecuted for less for hundreds of years,' said Doriel. Her eyes shone. 'Witch burning, the inquisition, prisons, witch-hunters, religious persecution... Need I go on?'

'No, of course not. But we live in a kinder time.'

'Many people are kinder, that's true.' Jonan leaned forward. 'But I reckon there are enough people out there who are scared and looking for a scapegoat. Amelia has plenty of anger and hatred to work with.'

'I'm not convinced.' Beth shook her head, picked up the tea and cradled it in her hands. 'Amelia's argument is poisonous, but shaky. Just because we see the paranormal around every corner doesn't mean everyone else does.'

'You'd be surprised,' Doriel said with a laugh. 'I get all sorts in here. I suspect most people never tell anyone they've been for a reading.'

'Okay, but I still don't see what you're getting at. And I don't understand how you know all of this either.'

'As Doriel said, we know Amelia well.' Jonan sighed. 'And she will use your event to bring her more attention. Can you find out what she plans to say?'

'I can ask her office but, to be honest, they're running this show. I have to do everything Amelia asks or my job is on the line. Can't you find out since you know her so well?'

'We're not her favourite people right now,' Doriel said with a strained laugh.

Jonan jumped up and paced the small room. 'Can you keep us informed? Or will that get you into trouble?'

Beth leaned back against the sofa. 'I know Amelia is awful, but why are you both acting like this is the end of the world? And why do you think it's your responsibility to stop it? There are far too many layers to this that I don't understand. I'm really not sure I want to get involved. I only came over here because there is a man at the inn who is desperate to help the ghost of a little girl cross over.'

'Of course we'll help,' Doriel said, standing up and collecting the cups. She strode out to the kitchen, the bells on the bottom of her skirt jangling.

'Would anyone like another drink?' she called. 'Something stronger, maybe?' The door slammed behind her.

Beth glanced at Jonan. 'Was it something I said?'

Jonan took a deep breath. 'Beth, there's more to this than we've told you.'

'I gathered that much.'

Jonan swallowed. This was his moment. Doriel had handed it to him on a plate, but it was too soon. The personal risk was so great and it was all his. 'Why are you here, Beth?' His voice cracked, but he held her gaze.

She frowned, little lines forming between her eyebrows. Her gaze searched his face, trying to read his change of mood.

'I came to find out whether you could help the girl.'

'No.' Jonan frowned. 'I mean why are you here on Earth?'

Beth raised her eyebrows. 'Look, I'm always up for an existential chat, but weren't we in the middle of something?'

'I'm not talking theoretically. I have memories most people don't have. I remember why I chose to incarnate here on Earth, and I remember who I chose to incarnate with.'

Beth shook her head. 'And?'

Jonan closed his eyes. Growing panic pulsed around him, pushing at his defences. He got up and stepped over to Beth's chair, sitting on the arm. He reached out, and her skin was warm under his fingers when he took her hand. 'I remember the contract I made before I was born. I know what I am here to do. And I know I made that contract with you.'

Beth paled. Her jaw tightened. She turned, looking away from him into the fire. Her hand was still in his, but it was rigid, unyielding.

'We come from somewhere special, you and I,' he whispered, dropping his psychic shields, letting every raw emotion show on his face for the first time. 'That's why I look different. It's why you have had so many paranormal experiences.'

He let go of her hand, stood up and stepped back, giving her space. 'We agreed to incarnate together for a purpose.' His voice was rough. He could hear his own uncertainty, could see it reflected in Beth's eyes as she turned back to him. 'We incarnated to stop Amelia.'

He watched Beth for a reaction, but her face was a blank mask. Her hair fell down her back in a thick plait, wisps curling around her face. The light of the fire and the table lamps threw her high cheekbones into relief, making her look ethereal. He drew in a ragged breath. She was so like the girl he remembered in his dreams. He felt the energy of that connection beating at his skin, at the part of him that expanded out beyond his body. She was cracking him open, leaving him completely vulnerable.

The silence was suffocating, banging at his nerves, at his resolve. Was it too late to pretend it was all an elaborate joke?

'Look, Jonan, I'm not as green as you think. I've been around the spiritual community for a long time. I know how quick people are to decide someone is their destiny. I understand the appeal, honestly I do, but I have not seen this path for myself. I go by feel, by gut instinct and my own experiences. I don't just accept what other people tell me.'

Jonan swallowed. 'Of course not. I wouldn't expect you to. So you don't have any sense of destiny?'

Beth gave a tight smile. 'I believe I came for a reason,

but I don't know what that is. I feel my way through one day at a time.'

Jonan nodded. 'And what feels right at this moment? Destiny or no, will you help us?'

She was silent. She watched him, her head tilted to one side, her long dark plait looped over her shoulder. For a moment, he imagined there were flowers woven though the strands. He saw the flash of a tattoo in the middle of her forehead, and then it was gone. It was just Beth watching him, chewing her lip as she thought.

Tension was thrumming through Jonan's veins, working its way out through the tapping of his fingers on the arm of the chair and the racing of his heart. 'Do you think I'm crazy?'

Beth swallowed. 'I want to think you're crazy, I'm not going to lie. It would be easier, but it's not right. There's something more to it, I just don't understand what. I might help you, but I still don't understand what you want me to do.' Her eyes were huge. Jonan was in real danger of losing himself in them. Her irises shone a deep purple, and he wondered if she knew that she too had these signs of their heritage. Her energy was changing, shifting as he watched. Something was waking up in her, but would it be enough?

'Tell us things,' Doriel said.

Jonan looked up. Doriel stood in the kitchen doorway. She was dressed the same, her hennaed plait still looped over her shoulder, her long flowing skirt still skimmed with bells at the hem, but she looked completely different. Jonan didn't often see the real Doriel any more. She was so good at hiding her energy, she rarely let it out. Now, she was dazzling. She seemed taller, her eyes shone a rich purple, and her ears elongated into shimmering blue points. When she moved, she appeared to glide over the floor.

Jonan looked at Beth, her lips were parted in a gasp, her eyes locked onto Doriel's brilliance.

Jonan stood up, releasing his own energy from the hold he had become so used to keeping on it. His aura stretched, expanded and shimmered in the air as the brightness became almost palpable. His heart soared. The release allowed him to lift up and away from the Earth-plane fog, and his heart expanded with joy.

Beth's energy called to him, and he let it in, allowing her familiar light to touch his own. He saw her struggle in the creases between her eyebrows, in the white of her knuckles where she clasped her hands together. He felt her anxiety in the beating of his own heart.

'You can help us with Amelia, Beth. This is what we all came here to do.' His voice was no more than a whisper, but it vibrated, setting off the pure brilliance of an overtone that resonated through the room.

Beth's eyes widened. 'I…' Her voice cracked. She coughed. Then a barrier came down between them. She stepped back, her jaw hardening. 'Why are you doing this? You only needed to explain yourself. By trying to intimidate me, you're pushing me away.'

Jonan blanched. 'Intimidate you? Is that what you saw?' He stepped back, holding up his hands, shielding himself. 'We were being real. We can't often let our guard down, but I thought that with you…'

Beth flushed. 'Of course. Be yourselves and I will do the same. I will help you if I can, but I won't be pressured into doing things that feel wrong. And I won't believe just because you tell me to.'

Jonan let out a breath. His shoulders slumped in relief. 'Thank you. I would never ask for any more than that.'

Beth

IT WAS BARELY light when Beth jogged through town the next morning. Her breath came out in smoky gusts as she ran, the warmth inside her body a stark contrast to the biting cold on her skin.

She ran past the Third Eye Spiritualist Shop, slowing as an image of Jonan and Doriel filled her mind. Conflicting emotions warred within her, creating a knot that could have been either excitement or fear. Anticipation fizzed in her chest and a spike of irritation shot through her. Somehow they had both offended and dazzled her. Finding someone who spoke her own language was rare and thrilling, but the assumptions and condescension were maddening. What was she doing to make herself look so green?

She powered past the shop, trying to push it from her mind, to focus instead on the cold dampness of the pavement in front of her.

She increased her speed, running down Fishpool Street, and then coming to a halt in front of The Monk's Inn. She felt the familiar churning in her stomach that told her there was something there and jogged on the spot as she narrowed her eyes, using her psychic sight to scan the building window by window. When she reached the last pane on the top floor adrenaline shot through her. A tear-stained face looked out through the grimy panes of glass. Her heart slammed against her ribcage, pounding in her chest. The girl had ringlets and her face was chalk white. A light flickered behind her then went out. The face disappeared. This was the girl Bill wanted to help.

Beth reached out with her thoughts, but the energy retreated. A cloud of fear hovered around the window. Beth wondered how many people had walked down this street and looked over their shoulder in this very spot, or maybe felt someone was watching them, or worse, following.

There was a haze of energy lingering around the whole building. She wondered if that was from the ghostly monks, or the fear people felt when they unknowingly encountered a house with paranormal activity. It was a feeling she was used to and it had stopped frightening her a long time ago.

As a child, she had allowed it to scare her. The faces pressed up against dark windows made her blood pound whenever the curtains were open after sunset. The strangers she had seen sitting in a circle in her garden at night had been invisible to her down-to-earth parents, but they had left an imprint in her mind. For a long time she assumed the dread in the pit of her stomach and the shivers that filled her body were real. Now she took those physical symptoms as signals, information about what was close by, and a reminder that she needed to protect her energy. She examined the physical sensations, read them, and used them, but she never viewed them as fear.

She tuned into those feelings now. The girl's face flashed through her mind, along with the sensation of a pounding heart. Her palms felt sticky, and she rubbed them on her leggings impatiently. She pushed through the sensations, looking for light on the other side.

She hit a brick wall of energy.

It was heavy, dark, sludgy. It grew, oozing out until it spread all around her like oil. It tried to pull her in but she pushed her ball of light out around her, creating a solid wall of protection. Stepping closer to the building, she narrowed her eyes and turned her head so the hotel was in her peripheral vision. It had a muddy, grey energy around it. It pooled around the foundations of the crumbling old building and seeped its way up the brickwork, taking in more and more of the inn.

'What are you?' Beth whispered.

A shape caught her attention out of the corner of her eye. She turned her head, but there was nothing. She turned away again, looking at the hotel through her peripheral vision. A translucent monk drifted past the front door. It turned to look at her, a leer on its face. It disappeared, but she still felt it there, laughing in her mind.

CHAPTER SIX

Beth

CHARLIE JUMPED AS Beth threw the ring-binder onto her desk.

'What the hell, Beth? What are you trying to do? Give me a heart attack?'

'Maybe if I did, you could haunt The Monk's Inn too.'

'What are you talking about?'

'That hotel is haunted. Seriously haunted. Maybe we should have a creepy Halloween-style party?'

'Amelia is doing the hotel up. It will be fine.'

'Yes. And isn't that strange?' Beth sat on the edge of her desk, tapping her heel against the modesty board. 'Why would she do that? Don't you wonder at all?'

'Whatever Amelia does, I'm sure she has a good reason.' Charlie's lips turned up at the edges. His cheeks flushed.

Beth's eyes widened. 'Charlie Smythe, do you have a thing for Amelia? Of course you do. That's why you're bowing and scraping.'

'Stop it!' Charlie snapped. 'I am your boss. Don't ever speak to me like that again. I am bowing and scraping because we're going out of business and Amelia is our last chance. I'm bowing and scraping because I want to keep my job, and I'd like you to keep yours too. We've been lucky, but the world doesn't owe you, Beth, and unfortunately it doesn't owe me either.'

'I know it doesn't owe me.' Beth leaned towards Charlie. She spoke slowly, enunciating over-clearly. 'But I also know it's not acceptable to allow a charity to be conned by a duplicitous celebrity who wants to generate publicity for the opening of her new hotel.'

Charlie frowned. He pushed his chair backwards, kicked off his trainers, and propped his feet up on the desk. 'What makes you think she owns it?'

'The manager doesn't know who the owner is. He deals entirely with a middleman. They haven't had a single guest for as long as he's cared for the property, and now there's a crew coming in to renovate on Amelia's behalf in time for the event. Why pay for the work if it wasn't her hotel? And why choose a beaten-up, haunted building for a glitzy fundraiser, when there are perfectly good hotels down the road? There's something going on.'

'Okay, it's strange.' Charlie shrugged his shoulders. 'I just don't see why it matters. There's so much else to worry about right now. Just organise the event in the venue you've been given.'

'But the client...'

'The client is happy. In fact, they're beyond happy. Deal with it. It's time to let it go.' Charlie stood up and pulled out a pair of smart black shoes from under his desk. He took a black, knee-length coat from the hanger behind him, pulled it on and grabbed a couple of ring-binders from the shelves to his left. 'I'm going to see if there's any more work for us out there. Can I trust you to do the job you're paid for without aggravating anyone?'

Beth sighed. 'Of course. You know you can.'

She watched him leave, but found it almost impossible to concentrate. Her desk was piled with paperwork from caterers and staff agencies, as well as legal contracts and builder's plans, but her head was filled with what Jonan had told her.

Could there have been any truth to what he said? Had Doriel been as intimidating as she'd thought, or had the woman just let go of her mask of normality, as Jonan had suggested? Beth had always known she was different. She had spent a lifetime hiding her weirdness. What if there was a reason for that? And what if she wasn't in this alone?

The conversation had moved on so quickly she hadn't even tried to find out more, but now her mind was flooded with images. Jonan and Doriel larger than life, shimmering in the homely room. Jonan in the TV studio, his ears tapering to points. The dreams that had filled her head night after night. Dreams of floating, dreams of a brother who looked different every time she saw him, but always *felt* the same. Dreams of a woman with pale skin and long, dark ringlets, and of a man with long blond hair, a man who looked intriguingly like Jonan.

She had never felt a sense of belonging. She had never felt able to truly be herself without fear of judgment. Was this why? Was she truly alien in this strange and harsh world? The idea gave her a sense of relief, of there being a reason for her differentness that had never before been within reach.

Beth shivered. The office was getting colder by the minute. 'Are you there?'

Yes. The word floated through her mind.

'What do you want me to know?'

She wants to use the spirits.

Beth's heart pounded. Was she actually communicating with the presence, or was it all in her mind? She had imagined talking to ghosts would be like having a conversation with a physical person. This was infinitely more subtle. The words forming in her mind didn't feel like her own, but how could she really know?

'What does she want to use the spirits for?' she asked the voice.

She wants to use the spirits.

The words repeated, looping over and over in her mind before fading to nothing.

'Is that it? Is that all you can tell me?' Beth shouted into the empty space. Her hands were shaking, whether in fear or frustration she didn't know.

Tell him. The words were loud in her mind now. You are supposed to work together. Stop her.

Silence. As though a door had closed, the space she had assumed was empty now felt like a yawning void. The presence had gone, leaving her alone with the words that chilled her to her core.

Switching on the answer machine, she grabbed her coat and went into the hall, locking the office door behind her. She took the stairs two at a time and dodged through the crowds on the street, making her way to the Third Eye Spiritualist Shop. Jonan was behind the counter when she arrived. Doriel was nowhere to be seen.

'Jonan, can we talk?' she said, as he served a woman with a stack of crystal bracelets looped around her arm.

He paused for a moment, his eyes meeting hers.

The woman tutted.

'Let me clear this queue,' he said, his lips curled up

slightly at the edges, as though he was trying not to smile. 'Have a look around.'

Beth wandered around the aisles. Huge crystals sat at various points around the room, purple, yellow and white. There were shelves of tarot cards and books, stands with crystal pendants and dream catchers. In this place, Beth felt relaxed. The energy was so different to the office and a world away from the claustrophobic atmosphere of the Monk's Inn. A light pressure settled in the middle of her forehead as she tuned into the sensations the shop awakened in her.

'Is everything okay?'

Beth swung around, startled out of her daydream. Jonan stood so close that he was almost touching her. She stepped back instinctively, and then wished she hadn't. The air that had felt warm on her skin was now cold, but she didn't feel she could move back without being obvious. 'Can we talk?'

'We can, but I need to stay down in the shop. Doriel's doing readings.'

'I don't mean to sound crazy, but I just had a conversation with the ghost in my office.'

'And?' Jonan's face was serious with no hint of mockery.

'She said Amelia wants to use the spirits in the hotel. Any idea what that might mean?'

'Did she now?' Jonan leaned back against a bookshelf. His eyes glazed as he stared past her right ear. His forehead gathered slowly into a frown, and then he stood up straight. 'Of course,' he whispered. 'I don't know why I didn't think of that before.'

'Think of what?'

'Will you take me to the hotel? Doriel only has one more client, so I'll be done in an hour. Presumably you can visit the venue in work time?'

'Of course. Is something wrong?'

'I just want to test out a theory. I have an idea what your ghostly friend may have meant, but I want to visit first and see if it fits.'

The bells on the door jingled as a man in a suit walked into the shop and stood in the middle of the room looking lost.

'Do you need some help, sir?' Jonan winked at Beth, turned to the man and led him over to shelves as they talked.

Beth couldn't face going back to the office, but there was a coffee shop across the pedestrianised walkway that she'd never tried. She pushed the door open, closing her eyes and inhaling the heavenly smell of coffee and the sweet tang of sugar. The place was buzzing, but there was one small table with a single chair squeezed into a space that should probably have been left empty. She breathed in as she slid into the seat, apologising as the woman behind shot her a filthy look when their chairs touched. She rolled her eyes. What was wrong with people? Why were they were so antagonistic? The waitress took her order, and moments later presented her with a huge slice of coffee cake, laden with far too much butter icing and rows of walnuts. She scooped some up on her fork and tasted it, sighing as the sugar sparked her system.

The file in front of her was not so exciting. She opened it at the scruffy green Post-it note, her heart sinking at the rows of costs that assaulted her sense of peace. Surely there must be more to life than adding up someone else's expenses? She smiled as the woman brought her coffee, but kept her focus on the paper in front of her, determined to nail this job as quickly as possible and move on to something more interesting.

'What are you so angry about?' A voice at the table next to hers cut through her thoughts. 'You're always cross about something.'

'No I'm not,' said the woman to the right of Beth. She had long salt-and-pepper hair tied in a low bun at the nape of her neck, and a blouse with a crumpled collar that hadn't been turned down at the back. 'I'm not angry; I'm just fed up of you not taking me seriously.'

'I take you seriously,' the man said. His grey hair was badly in need of a haircut, and the skin around his neck sagged. He pursed his crinkled lips for a moment. 'It's that woman I don't trust. She's just another celebrity trying to get attention, that's all. All this nonsense about spirits, honestly!'

Beth smiled. Maybe she had been right after all. Amelia was too way-out to get proper attention in the real world.

'It's not just her,' the woman said. Her voice was strained as though her teeth were clenched. Beth glanced over and saw her knuckles turning white where she gripped the seat of her wooden chair. 'I had a dream. It was real, I know it was. One of them came for me.'

'Have you been drinking again?'

Beth watched them surreptitiously. The man's eyes were narrowed, his head turned to the side as he looked at his wife with obvious suspicion. 'You know what red wine does to you. I wish you wouldn't drink the stuff. You're paranoid.'

'No I have not been drinking.' The woman stood up. 'If you don't believe me, there's no point in us having this conversation.' She hooked her quilted jacket and navy handbag over the crook of her elbow. She caught Beth's eye as she turned her back to her companion and pursed her lips. Her cheeks reddened.

'And what do you want?' she said, leaning her free hand on Beth's table, bending down so her face was close. 'Want to see what someone looks like after they've been preyed on by a horrifying spirit?'

'Good lord, no,' Beth said, pushing her chair backwards. 'Honestly, I'm with your husband. You had a dream, nothing more. And believe me, I'm used to ghosts.'

'Huh!' the woman said, and then turned and strode out the door.

'I'm sorry. Please don't hold it against her,' the man said, picking up his newspaper, folding it and tucking it under his arm. 'That Amelia's got her terrified. She's imagining horrors around every corner. And being in this blasted town doesn't help. She's always been a bit of a ghost-hunter. Now she sees them *everywhere.*'

'Don't worry. Amelia's getting to people, I can see that.'

'It's not right that she stirs up this fear. Blasted woman. I wish they'd take her off the airwaves.'

'I hope your wife feels better soon,' Beth said, nodding at the man. As he walked past, she caught a glimpse of the headline.

VULNERABLE WOMAN ATTACKED BY AGGRESSIVE SPIRITS

Beth stared after him, and then glanced at the clock. The hour was almost up. She put her coat on the seat and wound her way to the toilet at the back of the cafe. As she went, she peered over people's shoulders, reading the headlines on their newspapers, phones and tablets. Almost everyone was reading about Amelia. The woman serving behind the counter was wearing a large crucifix over her apron. Another had a pentagram pendant. Beth's heart rate began to rise as she relaxed her protections, testing out the vibe in the cafe. There was only fear.

If Jonan was right, and Amelia was doing this deliberately, the big question was: why?

There was no queue for the loo, so she was back at the table minutes later. Stuffing the ring binder into her bag, she swung open the door to the cafe, steeling herself against the blast of cold air. The Third Eye Spiritualist Shop was quiet now. There was just one customer, and Jonan was talking to her next to the shelf of tarot cards.

Doriel stood behind the counter, a mug of steaming liquid in her hand. 'Jonan mentioned your ghost,' Doriel said, setting down the cup and coming out from behind the counter. She drew Beth into a hug. 'Does it bother you?'

Beth stiffened. She had expected Doriel to be prickly after their confrontation last night. Maybe Jonan was right. Perhaps it had only been a confrontation in her own mind. Jonan was serving the woman now, running through a box of tarot cards, and laughing as she made a joke Beth couldn't hear. Beth stifled the stab of irritation that shot through her and untangled herself from Doriel. She shrugged. 'I'm used to it. The ghost respects me and I respect her. I know Charlie hates her though, even though he doesn't realise what he hates.'

The woman with the tarot cards stuffed the crisp new box into her bag along with her purse. 'Thanks for your help, Joe; I'll enjoy these. Have a good one.' She blew Jonan a kiss and winked as she slipped through the door and out into the street.

Beth frowned, wondering at the sinking feeling in her stomach. She had no claim on Jonan. She barely knew him and was supposed to be angry with him. But whatever else had happened last night, the intimacy of it had changed something. She had seen him; seen a spark she knew he didn't show easily. She didn't want him sharing that with this woman or anyone else.

Jonan waved and gave an easy smile. Then he made his way over to Beth, grabbed his jacket from the hook and pulled it on, turning up the collar. 'Are you ready, Beth? Let's go and see this haunted inn of yours.'

Beth shivered as he opened the door to the shop. The wind was icy against her skin and she wished she'd put on a warmer coat. The smell of pasties from a nearby shop made her stomach rumble.

'Why did that woman call you Joe?'

Jonan looked at her, eyebrows raised slightly. 'Jonan is my real name, but out here, in the normal world, it can be easier to go by Joe. In the shop it's helpful to seem accessible.'

Beth nodded and fell into step beside him. They walked in silence past the expensive boutique shops that lined the narrow street. Beth was glad the road was free of traffic, because the pavement was slick from the damp weather. More than once she nearly lost her footing in her work heels. The sky hung heavy over the abbey as the road levelled out. Crows circled overhead, mingling with the occasional magpie. Their harsh calls seemed in keeping with the blustery wind that shook the trees and whistled through the old Abbey Gateway. 'It's not hard to believe it was a prison, is it?' she said, looking up at the flint archway.

'Anything feels possible here, doesn't it? There are so many stories about this place, music coming from the abbey when nobody was playing, monks drifting around, bodies disappearing from the prison. It's no wonder Amelia has fix-ated on this area. It's beautiful, but the energy is strong.'

The red-brick Georgian houses looked peaceful as they headed down the hill. It felt as though the road was sleeping, putting up a civilised front to calm the fears of modern-day visitors who didn't understand the history that overlaid each stone.

'Amelia uses fear to gain power and control. She pulls other people's emotions inside of her and burns them up like fuel.'

'You make her sound like a vampire.'

'A psychic vampire, if you like. Nothing like the blood-suckers in fantasy books. She's very real and very sinister.'

'And what are you?' Beth turned. Their faces were so close she could see his eyelashes feathering over the deep blue of his pupils. She knew she should step back, claim some head space, but she couldn't bring herself to move. 'What aren't you telling me, Jonan? What are you worried about?' Her voice was low. She felt a prickling down her whole body as she looked at him, refusing to turn away.

'I am a guy who has come here to counteract The Fear.' Jonan swallowed. His voice was rough, but he didn't look away. 'Amelia comes from a place of fear, but she is not scared. She spreads fear, increases it and builds conflict. She embodies it, feeds from it. Absorbing other people's fear makes her bigger, stronger and more able to spread anxiety. If I'm right, she wants The Monk's Inn so she can draw on the energy of the trapped spirits to increase paranoia.'

Beth gaped.

'She's one of the most highly developed psychics I know. She started off looking for truth, but somewhere along the way she became caught up in her own ego and power.'

'And you got all of this from what? That TV show?'

Jonan laughed, but there was no mirth in the sound. 'No. Amelia and I go way back. I've spent months trying to talk her out of this path, but it's made no difference. She's cut me off now, which is why I'm trying to get to her another way.'

Beth froze. Her chest tightened. She felt as though a rock was crushing her lungs. 'Through me, you mean? That's why you're getting to know me, isn't it? You need to stop Amelia, and I'm a good link.'

'Oh Beth, don't say that. I'm not being opportunistic. I've waited my whole life to meet you. I would love to delay dealing with Amelia, but she's manipulating people right now and it puts everyone who doesn't fit social norms at risk.'

'I'm sure that's not true.' Beth turned to face The Monk's Inn. It was directly opposite them now, on the other side of the road. It looked even drearier than before in the grey light, the filthy windows dull and lifeless, like unseeing eyes. She felt the pull of the building, felt it reaching out to her even though she'd only been inside once. There was a connection, if she could only figure it out. She shivered.

The air temperature had dropped.

A light flickered inside.

'Well hello,' Jonan murmured.

He pulled his hands out of his pockets and crossed the road.

Beth watched his energy shift. His aura grew brighter as he stepped closer. At the other side of the road, he turned around, tilting his head as he watched her. He raised his eyebrows, his lips quirking up at the edges. 'Are you scared?'

Beth narrowed her eyes. 'I'm not that girl.' She crossed the road overtaking him. She walked into the hotel first.

A cobweb brushed her hair as she came through the

crooked old door frame and into the dusty reception area. It smelled of damp and the fresh scent of sawdust. The reception desk was empty.

'Bill,' she called. 'Bill, where are you?'

There was silence, and then a rhythmic knocking from the ballroom. Beth looked at Jonan, frowning.

He shook his head. 'There's nothing ghostly about that.'

'How do you know?' she said. Her heart was pounding. The air was icy. A shiver ran down her spine.

'I just know.' He shrugged. 'Why don't we go and see?'

Beth walked silently across the black-and-white tiled floor. She noticed every crack and chip, avoiding anything that looked like it might creak.

Jonan followed. He seemed at ease but made no more noise than she did. She felt him behind her, felt the tingling along her skin where she imagined their energy touched and intermingled.

Her senses heightened with the contact. She felt even more aware of the energies around her, moving, undulating, trying to take back control of the space, to minimise their bodily intrusion.

Jonan stepped forwards as they approached the door, but she shook her head. She reached out her hand, steady, determined. She twisted the rusty brass knob and swung the door open.

A crash reverberated around the ballroom.

Beth stepped backwards, feeling the noise as a physical jolt. She felt Jonan's hands on her upper arms, steadying her.

'Dear God, you frightened the life out of me.' A man in a yellow hard-hat, overalls and tan steel-capped boots, put down his hammer and leaned on one of the scratched wooden tables, rubbing his chin with a dirty calloused hand.

'Who are you, anyway? I thought I was alone.'

'Isn't Bill here?' Beth asked. 'I thought he never left.'

'Is that the old guy at the desk?'

Beth nodded.

'He's at the hospital.'

'The hospital? Why?' Beth stepped into the room, ignoring the shadows hovering in her peripheral vision. 'What happened to him?'

'I honestly have no idea. He was right as rain when I arrived, went off to his little den out the back to make a cuppa, and then next thing I know there's this big bang. I went through and found him lying on the floor. No idea how he got there. I called the ambulance and they took him away.'

'You didn't go with him?' Beth said, clenching her hands into fists.

'No. I did not.' The man stepped back, his forehead drawing into a frown. 'If I skive off work, I don't get paid, and I don't want to spend any longer in this dump than I have to. Anyway, Amelia was here, you know, the celeb? She dealt with the ambulance folk. I just left her to it. My name's Henry, by the way.'

He held out his hand. Beth shook it.

'Well hopefully it won't be a dump when you're finished with it.' Jonan raised one eyebrow as he shook Henry's proffered hand.

'It'll be pretty enough.' Henry shrugged. 'But there's nothing I can do about the ghosts. You wouldn't catch me coming to a party in this place, I can tell you.'

'I don't blame you for that.' Beth said. 'Anyway, sorry to have scared you.'

'Oh, don't worry. It serves me right for being so jumpy.' He chuckled.

'One thing,' Jonan said, looking at the man, his eyes slightly glazed. 'Have you actually seen anything frightening, or does this place just give you the creeps?'

Henry looked at Jonan, his eyes narrowed. He rubbed his stubbly chin with one hand.

'Well, why would you ask that?'

'I'm a paranormal investigator,' Jonan said. He smiled, his expression open, inviting Henry to speak.

Henry stared at him for a moment, and then nodded. 'I swear someone keeps crying in one of the bedrooms upstairs. I've checked and there's no one there. I thought a child had got stuck at first. Thought I was going to have to call social services.'

'Well at least it wasn't that.' Jonan nodded. 'Thanks, Henry. Your account tallies nicely with the other reports I've been given.'

'I'm not going mad then?'

'You're not going mad. But if I were you, I'd burn a candle in here while you work. Maybe some white sage too.'

'Seriously? A candle? That's all it takes?' Henry sat on one of the chairs, propping his feet up on the battered dining table.

Jonan laughed. 'No, it's not all it takes, but it wouldn't hurt.'

'I dunno. I think there's a bit too much kindling in this place. Anyway, there's only another hour then I'm off. I'm not staying here alone in the dark. Makes you wonder how that little old guy did it, alone, all those years.'

'That little old guy was more game than you could possibly believe,' Beth said. 'Let's have a look around, Jonan. Then we can check whether Bill's okay.'

Jonan held up a hand in farewell as they walked back out into reception. 'How do you get up to the bedrooms?'

'This way,' Beth said, leading Jonan up the stairs. 'Thank you for helping me.'

Jonan shrugged. 'Helping the dead cross over is part of what I do. Plus, if Amelia does want to use the spirits to increase fear at her event, getting rid of them seems like an excellent beginning to a plan.'

Beth counted the doors as she walked along the hall, until she reached the one that ought to hide the window where she had seen the face. 'I think this is the room.'

Beth tried the handle. It turned, but the door didn't budge. She put her shoulder up against the old wooden door, turned the handle again and shoved. It swung open.

Even standing in the hall outside the room, there was a creepiness that made Beth's skin crawl and her stomach churn. When she walked in, she felt an invisible icy wave crash over her. The air temperature dropped and a churning settled in the pit of her stomach.

'I'd like to get a feel for the type of guests who have lingered here,' Jonan said, walking into the room and looking around. 'I want to see what kind of energy they have and how likely it is Amelia will be able to use them. There are spirits who are trapped and just want to move on, and then there are others that cling to the Earth plane with everything they have. They draw on fear in the environment to keep their vibration low. These are the beings I believe Amelia wants to use.'

'And you really think she's that calculating?'

'I know she's that calculating. She puts on a good act of being all sweetness and light, but her energy is very different.'

'I felt that, but I didn't realise she was this conscious.'

'Never underestimate how conscious Amelia is.'

'Well, here we go then,' Beth said, relieved that her voice came out steady.

'Here we go indeed.' Jonan rolled his shoulders. Then nodded.

Beth monitored the symptoms in her body as she looked around the empty room. The once-white walls had turned grey with age. Yellowish patches alternated with black damp. Grey and tattered net curtains hung at the window, but had been pulled down at one side. They swayed slightly as though in a breeze, but the window was firmly shut. There was a double bed in the middle of the room, naked and free of linen. Only a single pillow sat on the mattress. The bed frame was simple wrought iron and underneath was a city of dust and fluff. An old-fashioned dark-wood wardrobe stood against one wall. One door hung open, swinging on its hinges. The mirror on the inside of the door was cracked.

There were no signs of habitation. No personal effects that might have suggested someone had once loved the space.

Beth walked over to the wardrobe and ran a finger down the crack in the mirror. She opened the other door, but it was empty apart from yet more fluff. A single wire coat-hanger swung on the rail at the top.

Beth shivered. She turned to Jonan. He stood with his arms open and his eyes closed. Energy buzzed around him, bathing him in a curious brightness. He seemed larger than usual, and when she tuned into her psychic sight, the space around him was lit with a golden glow. She inched closer, hoping to pick up on some of his warmth.

'Can you feel what it is?' she whispered.

'It's a girl. She doesn't want to be here any more.'

'How do you know?'

Jonan opened his eyes and smiled at Beth. 'I asked her.'

'And she told you? Just like that?'

'Yes.' Jonan tilted his head to one side. 'Why don't you try?'

Beth closed her eyes. *Please, protect me.* She sent the thought to her guides. *And please help me to help this girl.* She felt energy building around her. There was a fizzing in the crown of her head and a tingling in her palms. She felt her heart expand, and imagined pale-pink light flooding from her, out into the room and surrounding the girl. A smiling face flashed into her mind, large eyes and shiny brown curls. The chill had dropped away. Beth felt warm. In fact, she was heating the room with her own body. She felt bigger, somehow disjointed, as though she didn't belong in her restrictive, physical form.

Beth opened her eyes. Jonan stood opposite her, hands stretched out towards hers, palms parallel to her own. His eyes were open. He smiled, slowly, as she nodded at him. She wondered if she looked as beautiful to him as he did to her. He shone, a brightness emanating from him that was similar to charisma only much, much more. At that moment she wanted nothing more than to be near Jonan. She felt a tug in her heart and found herself stepping closer. They were so close now there was barely any space between them and the fizz of his energy mingled with her own. For a moment there was no separation. They were one being, but at the same time, deliciously different and enchanting.

She forced herself to turn away from him. *Please let me see you properly, I mean you no harm.* At first she saw nothing. Then her eyes widened. The girl looked almost as solid as Jonan. Her face was streaked with tears, but light shone from her eyes. Rich brown hair fell in ringlets around her face and she smoothed down her pink-and-white pinafore with her hands.

'She's by the window,' Beth said.

Jonan nodded.

Beth stepped forwards.

She felt no fear.

When they stood face to face, Beth extended her arms until their hands faced each other, palm to palm. The tingling across her skin was so strong it felt like needles, but she welcomed the connection. There was nothing wrong here, no negativity. The energy in the room had changed and lifted. In this trance state she could see beings in her peripheral vision, knew they were flooding the room with light, lifting the energy higher and higher.

The girl was shining, a soft golden glow coming from her skin and beautiful curls. She shimmered. The air around her was flooded with gold.

Thank you. The words formed in Beth's mind. Thank you for bringing me freedom.

'Bill wanted to do it,' Beth said, feeling her eyes well up with tears.

Bill did do it, the girl said. He brought you to me. He is brave, but he is not safe because of Amelia. He knows her secrets. That is why she had him hurt. Will you find him and protect him?

'She had him hurt? What did she do?' Anger flooded through Beth. The image of the girl flickered.

Don't let Amelia scare you. Please help Bill.

Beth took a deep breath, forcing her body back into trance state. The girl's image solidified.

'When you are ready, follow the light,' Jonan said. His voice was deeper than usual, echoing in the small empty room.

I am ready, the girl said. As long as you will look after Bill.

'I will,' Beth said, feeling her energy flare as certainty filled her. 'I will make sure Amelia never hurts him again.'

Thank you, Beth. You are a true Earth angel.

The light flared to one side and Beth could just make out a woman coming forward through the beam. She shone so brightly in Beth's peripheral vision that she emitted a pure, beautiful warmth.

The girl's image flickered. She was no longer solid but translucent in the bright golden light that surrounded her.

The girl reached out and touched the woman. Then they faded into the light and were gone.

Beth closed her eyes, savouring the feeling of expansion. Joy filled her body, drumming through her like an electric current. She was hyper-aware of Jonan. Even without looking she could feel their connection, feel their energies vibrate in sync. She had never experienced this kind of bond with anyone. In this heightened state, his claims of shared destiny felt more real than she could possibly have imagined.

Beth opened her eyes, feeling the intensity recede. Jonan stood, hands shoved in the pockets of his jeans, his leather jacket pushed back. He smiled, his head tilted to one side. Beth's insides warmed so she no longer missed the light that had been there a moment ago.

'I knew you could do it,' he said, his smile widening.

Beth took an unsteady breath. 'That was amazing. Is that what you do?'

'I help spirits cross over, if that's what they want. Sometimes I help them when that's not what they want too, if they're causing trouble, but most spirits are ready to go when their vibration has been raised high enough. Really, I just stand here and ask my guides for help. They do the rest.'

'Are you ever scared?' Beth sat on the bed.

'Scared?' His forehead creased. 'There's no need. I have rock-star guides. We all do. They can take anything these Earth-bound folk can throw at them. It's the incarnated types that are really problematic.'

Beth smiled. 'Like Amelia? Speaking of whom, what are we going to do about her?'

'Amelia plans to use this venue for her games. I suggest we change the energy here so there's less negativity for her to draw on. That should reduce the power of her attempts to manipulate, for now at least.'

'Right.' Beth pushed her sleeves up. 'We've done one room; shall we move on to the next?'

Jonan smiled. 'I think we're done for today.' He opened the door and Beth rose from the bed, leading the way out into the hall.

Jonan kept pace with her as they went down the stairs. 'The girl wanted to go; she just didn't know how. The Monks are going to be a very different matter. We'll need all our strength for that battle, so I'd like to get Doriel involved. We'll be stronger with three.'

'In that case,' Beth said, wrapping her coat around her as she stepped out of the dingy hotel, 'I suggest we find out what happened to Bill.'

CHAPTER SEVEN

Beth

BETH STEPPED THROUGH the door to the hospital and immediately backtracked. A man in scrubs rushed past, narrowly avoiding crashing into her. He shouted, and then broke into a full-out run, dashing through the double doors at one end of the room.

'We'd better join the queue,' Jonan said, frowning as he looked around. 'I've never seen this place so chaotic.'

'You make it sound like you're a regular.'

'Doriel's had a few bricks tossed through the shop window. We've been here with minor stuff, but it's always been very orderly. This is like a playgroup on coffee.'

Beth pressed her lips together, trying not to laugh.

The queue shuffled forwards. The man in front of them groaned, clutching his arm closer to his chest.

'I don't know what's got in to everyone this week,' the receptionist muttered under her breath as Beth finally stepped up to the desk. 'What is the world coming to?'

'I'm looking for Bill.'

The woman raised her eyebrows but said nothing.

'He was brought in this morning from The Monk's Inn?'

'Never heard of it,' the woman snapped, pursing her lips and shoving a stray lock of hair behind her ear. 'Last name?'

Beth sighed. 'He did tell me, but I can't remember. Is there any other way to do a search?'

'You can't expect me to find a patient from a first name. We've had the world and his wife in here today.'

Jonan stepped forwards and leaned his elbows on the reception desk. He looked the receptionist in the eye. Smiling, he held her gaze until her cheeks flushed.

'I'm so sorry to bother you,' he said, his voice low. 'I can see you're incredibly busy today. Is there any way we might be able to find out where our friend is?'

She swallowed. 'Of course. Injured you say? Let me have a look.' She ran her finger down a register. 'Bill, was it?'

'That's right. It's such a pain that we don't know his surname. His closest friend asked us to look after him before she crossed over.'

The woman looked up, her pen hovering in mid-air. 'Crossed over? You mean… died?'

Jonan nodded.

'Oh no, poor man.' The woman stared into Jonan's eyes for a moment, and then shook her head as though trying to force herself to wake from a dream. 'Look, here it is.' Her finger stopped at a name on the list. 'Bill Jones.' He's in Hyacinth Ward. Go up in the lifts, it's the third turning on the right. You can't miss it.'

'Thank you so much; you're an angel helping us out like that. I hope you have a wonderful day.' Jonan smiled and the receptionist beamed. She was still smiling when she greeted the next person in the queue.

Beth snorted as they walked towards the lifts. 'Is that

how you get on in life? By charming the pants off every woman you meet?'

Jonan shrugged. 'There are worse ways.'

'But you weren't sincere.'

'Wasn't I? Bill is Amelia's first casualty. I owe him.'

They went through a set of double doors. There was a buzz as one of the doors to the lifts on their left started closing. One stride took Jonan close enough to stick his arm in between the closing doors. There was a moment's pause and they opened again.

Jonan nodded at the gap, standing aside to let Beth through.

The doctor in the lift glared at them but said nothing.

Beth leaned against the banister under the mirrored wall. The doctor's disapproval hung over them like a cloud and she looked at her feet, trying to disconnect from the energy. The door pinged open and the man dashed past them out into the hall, not looking back.

Beth scanned the hall outside the lift for a number. Nothing. She looked back at the lift controls and spotted where they were just as the door began to close. Sticking her foot in-between the doors, she felt the impact of metal, and then the door receded. 'This is it.' She ducked through and out into the hall.

Jonan followed and pressed the buzzer for Hyacinth Ward. 'We're here to see Bill,' he said into the machine.

'Bill? Oh, how lovely.' The intercom clicked off and the door buzzed open.

The woman behind the reception desk beckoned them in. 'I didn't think he was going to get any visitors. I'm so pleased you're here. Such a kind gentleman.' She beamed at Jonan, completely ignoring Beth.

She led the way down the corridor and then into a room on the right. There were four beds, one in each corner. Bill was sitting up. The other three occupants were all asleep.

'Bill!' Beth said, walking over and sitting on the edge of the bed.

Bill's eyes shone. 'You came to see me? I can't believe it!'

She drew him into a gentle hug. 'I'm so sorry we didn't come sooner.'

'I've been alright.' Bill coughed. His body seemed too frail for the violence of the spasms, which left him gasping for air as he lay back against the pillows. 'Are you sure you want to be bothered with an old man like me?'

'Of course.' Beth took his hand. 'Plus, I promised your ringlet-girl I'd look after you. She didn't want to leave without knowing you were okay.'

'She's gone?' Bill's eyes widened. 'I always wanted that, but I think I'll miss her all the same.' He looked over at Jonan.

'This is my friend Jonan,' Beth said.

'Any friend of Beth,' Bill said, holding out his frail hand for Jonan to shake.

'What happened to you, Bill?' Beth asked, leaning closer.

Bill sighed. 'Amelia.'

Beth felt a chill.

'She came to the inn, told me the hotel was hers and my time there was done. Then she did something. I can't tell you what. She made the room suffocating. I couldn't breathe. The Monks were there and she seemed to control them. They filled the room until there was no space left for me. I thought my heart was going to give out. I was... I was scared.'

A shiver ran down Beth's spine.

'Did she touch you?' Jonan's voice was steady.

'Not with as much as a finger. She stood in front of me, her eyes glowing, and then I collapsed. There's no way anyone would believe she had anything to do with me ending up in here and she knows it. Now where am I supposed to go? The inn was my home.'

'You can stay with me,' Beth said. 'I'm sure Laura won't mind…' She tailed off.

Jonan raised his eyebrows, his lips quirking up at the edges. 'With all her parties? Don't worry, you can stay with me. Our place is small, but we can make the space as long as you're okay to get up the stairs?'

'But you don't even know me.'

Jonan shrugged. 'I know enough. I can see the living as well as ghosts.'

'Thank you so much.' Bill's voice caught. 'You have no idea what you've done for me. I thought I was finished.'

He sank back onto his pillows and yawned.

The nurse stopped at the end of the bed and looked at Bill's chart. 'Come on now, time to go. He's still healing.'

'I'll see you soon?' Bill asked, his eyes glinting in the harsh, overhead light.

Beth kissed his forehead. 'You concentrate on getting better. You'll see us soon. I promise.'

CHAPTER EIGHT

Beth

'WHERE HAVE YOU been?' Doriel held out a spoonful of tomato sauce for Jonan to sample.

He went into the kitchen and kissed her on the cheek before tasting the sauce, eyes closed. 'Delicious. We were visiting Amelia's first victim.' Jonan opened the fridge, grabbed three bottles of beer and handed them to Beth and Doriel.

Doriel turned off the hob and put the spoon down. 'Who was it?'

'Bill from The Monk's Inn.' Beth picked up the bottle opener Jonan handed to her and cracked the cap from her beer. 'He's in hospital now.'

Beth followed Jonan into the lounge. He had invited Bill to stay, but where would the older man sleep? She counted five doors from the communal space. The kitchen door was open. The other four were closed. She thought they must be two bedrooms, a bathroom, and probably a cupboard. The floorplan downstairs was fairly small and the lounge was a good size, so there couldn't be much space in those rooms.

Beth sank into one of the armchairs by the fire, while Jonan sprawled across the sofa.

Doriel sat cross-legged on the other chair, picked up a ball of thick purple wool with wooden needles stuck through the middle, and a long stretch of purple knitting folded underneath. The needles began to fly, but she didn't once take her gaze from Jonan. 'What's the plan?'

'I've invited him to stay here. I know we don't really have the space, but—'

'No, it's fine. What are we going to do about Amelia?'

'We need to neutralise her,' Jonan said, with a nod at Doriel. 'Take her on at her own game, bring light where she brings darkness. We need to encourage people to stand up to her fear-mongering and see where this takes us.'

Beth took a deep breath. 'I will try to find out what she plans to say at the event. That's something she might expect me to do anyway. And maybe I can reduce the number of media who cover it.'

Jonan let out his breath in a rush. 'I'm so sorry to put you in this position, but honestly, you have no idea how much this means to me.'

Doriel smiled. 'Would you like to stay for dinner?' She unfolded herself from the chair, swinging her skirt as she headed for the kitchen.

Beth noticed that her energy flared and, for a moment, her ears looked pointed too. She watched Jonan by the warm light of the fire. 'Can I ask you a question?'

'Of course!' Jonan was smiling, finally relaxed. He lay back on the threadbare sofa, hands behind his head, legs crossed.

'If Amelia is so powerful, how are we going to stop her?'

Jonan laughed. 'We have our own kind of magic. You do too. You just need to remember how to use it.'

'Magic?' Beth rolled her eyes. 'That's storybook stuff,

wizards waving wands, turning things into toads or conjuring money out of nowhere. It's not real.'

Jonan grinned. 'Real magic is far more subtle. I'm pretty sure you use it yourself, even if you avoid the "M" word.'

'Please, Jonan, I'm trying to understand.'

He sighed and sat up, leaning his forearms on his thighs. 'I'm not making fun of you. Those memories I've told you about, they're not all about my life path. I remember what it's like not to be bound by a human body. I remember being pure energy, able to manifest at will. A body inhibits that, but we are all creators at our core. It's about knowing you can do it.'

As Beth listened, she started to feel disconnected. She was focused on Jonan's words, but she could also feel them in her energy, buzzing around her. She could see his light-body now. It was bright, brighter than she had encountered before. The pale-blue energy shimmered, narrowing into points above his ears and making him look like the figure in the tarot card.

'So.' She blinked, squeezing her eyes tightly shut for a moment and digging her nails into the palms of her hands, trying to pull herself back into normal awareness. 'You're some kind of infinite creator with great connections. Is there anything else I should know?'

Jonan laughed and leaned back on the sofa. 'We're all infinite creators, it's just that most people have forgotten how to access it. Part of my job is to help *you* remember. You are the Seed, Beth. You are potential.'

The scent of lavender spiked. Beth felt a click as she slipped into trance and her awareness expanded rapidly. She was still in her body, watching Jonan speak, but a bigger part of her separated out, expanding until she had no edges.

Sister. A voice sounded through her. She didn't need to turn; she felt him, swirling, moving past her, never quite forming. *Do you see your path? Do you feel it?*

Images flickered through her mind. Tall white pillars and a raised dais. A woman with pale skin and glossy dark ringlets. A man, hugely built, blond hair flowing down his back as he shimmered in and out of form. And Jonan, or was it Jonan? He was achingly familiar and indefinably different. His hair hung to the tips of his elbows, and was paler, just a shade darker than the porcelain skin that replaced his usual tan. His ears were clearly pointed now, flesh and blood not the shimmer of light. His violet eyes warmed as he held her gaze, building a connection between them that she knew with absolute certainty she had lost and grieved.

Her heart clenched as she saw another version of herself take his hand. Her hair was woven with flowers. An indigo dress hung from her shoulders and was gathered in around her waist, before brushing the ground with gauzy tendrils. She wanted to be that woman.

Your path, sister. Your choice. You are the Seed that can flourish or remain dormant at will.

'And if I say no?'

Then we will fade away. You will live life on your old terms, lose what you haven't quite regained. Can you bear that? When you look at this Jonan, your Jonan, can you walk away?

Beth swallowed. 'How do I know he's *my* Jonan?'

The shimmering energy solidified between the pillars, and the heavily muscled man appeared before her. He tilted his head, frowning. 'I know you have been asleep, sister, but do you *really* not know? Could you honestly forget that?'

The other Jonan turned to look at her. She gasped as the

weight of knowing hit her in the chest. It cracked her open, letting in rivers of pain and separation. Her eyes swam with tears. The man smiled, and then his face wavered. His skin darkened and a light stubble now dusted his chin. She blinked.

She was lying on the sofa, Jonan leaning over her. He placed his palm on her forehead, and then pushed her hair from her face. His gaze flickered over her, taking a tally of every movement she made. She coughed, feeling her skin flush, and heaved herself up to sitting. Her arms and legs felt like lead and her head was thick with the residue of the vision.

'What happened?' She rubbed her eyes.

Jonan straightened up and strode to the kitchen. She heard the tap running. He came back in and handed her a glass of water and a bar of chocolate. 'I was hoping you might be able to tell me that,' he said, sitting down and angling his body towards her. 'Did you faint?'

She swallowed. 'I don't think so. Let's suppose, just for a moment, that everything you've told me is real.'

Jonan froze.

Beth could hear of the pounding of blood inside her head, but she forced herself to continue. 'What is the point of it all? Where do I come in?'

He took her hand in both of his. 'What happened, Beth?' His voice was rough. His throat worked.

'I may have had... some kind vision. There was this man. He called me sister.'

'Salu,' Jonan whispered. He breathed in through his nose as the scent of lavender surrounded them. Beth saw the tension in his forehead ease a little.

Beth frowned. 'People keep saying that, but nobody will tell me what it means.'

'Where we come from, Salu is your brother. He chose not to be born this time around. He guides you from home.'

Beth's breath caught. 'My guide is my brother?'

Jonan nodded. 'Do you smell lavender?'

'Yes.' Beth shrugged. 'That happens to me a lot.'

'That's Salu, letting you know he's here.'

Beth blinked. She had always felt so alone; the idea of having a brother set her heart hammering in her chest.

You've never been alone, sweetness. The words sounded in her mind.

Jonan was silent for a few moments, his gaze directed at the window that was blacked-out by the night sky outside. He nodded as though answering a question she hadn't heard, and then turned his head, holding her gaze. 'Did you see the Triad?'

Beth frowned. 'I don't know what that is. I saw you, at least I think it was you. I saw... my brother? And a woman who looked so like me I could almost swear we were one and the same.'

'How do you feel now?'

Beth took a deep breath. 'I told you I relied on my own experience. I said I hadn't been given any evidence of the destiny you talked about. I'm going to have to revisit those assumptions now.'

Jonan let out his breath in a rush. He closed his eyes, leaning forward to duck his head between his knees. He took three deep, shuddering breaths, the muscles in his back visibly expanding and contracting. When he straightened, he was calmer. A smile spread across his face. 'That's wonderful news. Is there anything you want to know? I don't want to bombard you.'

'There's a lot I'd like to know.' She shrugged. 'I saw you

and I, and I saw my brother. But I don't understand what it's all about, or why this is happening now. That vision has left me with a horrible sense of urgency in my chest. If we could skip to the understanding part of this process, that would be great.'

Jonan seemed to slump as the tension went out of his body in a rush. He closed his eyes for a moment, took a deep breath, and then released it. He nodded, as he sat up and leaned forward. 'It all started with three women.' He pushed on his thighs with his arms, propelling himself upright and took a statue down from the mantelpiece. It was carved from dark wood and showed a woman sitting cross-legged, staring into a scrying bowl. Her hair fell past one of her cheeks and a garland of flowers rested on her head, stems trailing down her back. She was so intricately detailed that Beth gasped. 'This one is the Oracle,' Jonan said, a grin on his face. 'She is one member of the team and brings us the superpower of insight.'

He put the statue down on the table, and then ducked into his bedroom, coming out with *The Starfolk Tarot*. He flicked through the cards with a speed that could only be born of familiarity and pulled one out. The picture showed a woman, her hands cupping her heavily pregnant belly. She sat in a beam of bright sunlight surrounded by the light green of new leaves and opening buds of flowers. Her face shone. 'This card is The Mother. She is our second superhero, because she brings Nurture.' He put the card on the table, a foot away from the statue.

Beth frowned. 'Are you trying to say that I am one of those?'

'No.' Jonan grinned. 'At least, not at the moment. There is a third woman.' He took an orange from the table, picked up a knife and cut the fruit in half. Dislodging a seed with the tips of his fingers, he placed it carefully on the coffee table so that the seed, the card and the statue each stood as separate points in a triangle. 'The third woman is the Seed. She is potential incarnate. She is the greatest, and the most likely to stray. She brings the ability to change, to develop, to move forward, but she also brings the possibility of failure.'

Beth picked up the seed and put it in the palm of one hand. It was so tiny. She closed her eyes, feeling her heart beating and the swirling of nerves in her stomach. 'That's not an encouraging picture.'

'It is a hugely exciting picture.'

Beth swallowed. 'Who are the women?'

'Don't you know?' His gaze shone with violet fire as he watched her, his body tense and perfectly still.

Putting the seed back on the table, she picked up the tarot card, running a finger over the lush design. 'I thought your mother walked out on you.' She let the card fall from her fingers. It flittered through the air and landed face down on the table in front of the statue. 'Can she still stand as Mother?'

'The roles are chosen on this side of birth, as well as before. Doriel and my mother exchanged places.'

Beth raised her eyebrows. 'So that leaves you, me and Amelia. Who is this?' She picked up the seed. 'I want to claim it, but I feel I might have to fight for that honour.'

Jonan's mouth spread into a wide smile. 'Perceptive. Amelia won't give up her position lightly, but you were born to it as much as she was.'

'Are you trying to tell me I was a backup?'

Jonan laughed. He stood up, took the seed from her fingers, put it on the table and took her hands in his own.

Warmth shot through her from the simple touch. She drew in a ragged breath. The feeling of rightness that swept through her was staggering. The Jonan from her vision seemed to hover around and through him. She could feel a connection that stretched back over lifetimes.

His eyes were an even deeper purple now, specks of gold glinting in the light of the fire. His grip on her hands tightened, and then eased. 'You were never a backup to me.'

Her breath caught. She swallowed. A lifetime of feeling out of place dropped away as the unfamiliar sense of belonging engulfed her. Something she had lost began to reform. She couldn't explain what it was, but it connected her to Jonan with a sense of rightness that took her breath away.

'Dinner's ready, come and get your food,' Doriel yelled from the kitchen.

Jonan sighed and let go of her hands. 'Come on. Let's help bring the food out.'

Beth's stomach growled. She laughed. 'Gladly. I'm starving.'

The food was good and the solid, real-life texture of the pasta, tomato sauce and vegetables helped Beth feel more grounded. She heaped salad onto her plate, watching Doriel's fluid movements. She made even the simplest motion look like a dance. She caught Beth watching and smiled. 'Are you enjoying your dinner? Is there anything else I can get you?'

Pushing her chair back, she reached for a bottle of wine on the sideboard behind her and filled all three glasses.

'It feels weird, talking to an Oracle about something as ordinary as pasta.'

Doriel laughed. 'You might be surprised how fascinated I am by pasta. This world is just as absorbing as the other if you're open to the magic in it.'

'And what is the magic in you?' Beth asked, 'what do you do?'

'Oh.' Doriel waved her hand. 'You don't want to know about that. It's the magic in Jonan you want to think about.'

Jonan rolled his eyes. His dinner was almost gone already and he popped in the last mouthful of pasta before putting his knife and fork neatly together on the plate. 'Thanks for that, Doriel.'

'I'm always happy to share the limelight.' She winked, picked up his plate and walked through to the kitchen, humming as she went.

'She's right though.' Beth took a sip of red wine, and then picked up a piece of bread from the basket on the table and tore off the crust. 'You didn't tell me where you fit in to the picture.'

Jonan pushed his chair back and stretched his legs out, crossing them at the ankles. He shrugged. 'I'm a healer and a teacher. I work with energy in a more vibrant way than most people. I manifest things in my life because I see fewer restrictions. I can also impact energy around me, in another place, or even at another time. This can change the way people feel in that place.'

Beth chewed the bread slowly while Jonan talked. She frowned and put her hand over her heart. It was beating faster than normal. 'Do you control the way I feel around you?'

'No.' He smiled and stood up, walking over to the fire. 'Whatever you're feeling is all you.' Crouching down, he picked up the poker and shoved at the logs, releasing a shower of sparks. Then he reached into the wicker basket next to the fire and pulled out a gnarly, triangular piece of wood and stacked it in the grate. 'I can't control someone else; I only remove energies that are blocking them personally, or influencing them through their environment.'

Beth stood up, folded up her napkin and put it on the table next to her plate. The fire was roaring now, invitingly warm. She sat in the large, squashy armchair, leaning forwards and holding her palms so near the fire that the heat of the flames was only just bearable. 'So that's why it's always nice in here.'

Jonan turned back towards the room and smiled. 'An old building like this would normally be reeking with ancient arguments, grief and who knows what else. You know this.'

She nodded. 'My office used to be part of the debtor's prison. There's always somebody wandering around making the lights flicker.'

'Exactly.' Jonan sat down on the sofa and leaned back, stretching his long legs out towards the fire. 'I don't want to live like that so I keep my home energetically clean, but when you come in here, you also benefit. Without those external triggers it's easier to see your way forward. Helping the girl cross was a stronger example of the same thing. I lifted the energies in the room until she was able to perceive her own freedom.'

Beth watched Jonan. He was staring into the fire, a muscle working in his jaw. His dark-blond hair hung in waves around his shoulders. His presence was so strong in this place that she could see the air around him shimmer. He took a deep breath, his chest expanding, drawing her eye downwards. The top few buttons of his shirt were undone. The skin beneath was pale, almost otherworldly.

'What about now?' she whispered, her voice catching. 'Are you manipulating the energies right now?'

Jonan sat up and leaned towards her. He took her hands in his, the warm touch of his skin sending tingles up her arms.

'No, this is just us, Beth. I remember you of old, and we've always been like this. There's nothing I can do to stop it.'

'Would you, if you could?'

'I've tried, many times.'

Beth jerked her hands away, hurt searing her chest. 'Why? Why would you try to cut me out?'

Jonan's eyes darkened into a deep purple as he gazed at her. His forehead creased. She felt herself inadvertently leaning in a little closer, wanting to sink into his energy, but where before she had felt connection, now a barrier had raised.

Jonan shook his head, got up and walked to the fire. He stood with his back to her in front of the flames. 'Oh, Beth, what are you doing to me?'

Beth's eyes widened. She felt as though he had slapped her. 'What do you mean? I'm not doing anything. I thought we were sharing a moment. I thought that maybe, just maybe, you might…' She tailed off. Shaking her head, she stood up and pulled on her coat. She slid her feet into her long leather boots and zipped them up. 'I'm sorry. This was a mistake.'

'Beth, come back,' Jonan said as she strode towards the front door. 'Please, that's not what I—'

'Don't,' Beth said from between gritted teeth. 'And don't follow me through that door.'

She reached for the handle then yanked it as it stuck, pulling it with so much force she jolted backwards when it opened. She shook away Jonan's hand, and then took the stairs two at a time, only stopping when she was out on the road and back up to the properly lit main street, where he wouldn't be able to see her.

She had allowed herself to be humiliated. A lifetime of

keeping everyone at a distance, and one flash of those violet eyes had left her open and exposed. She'd seen the way Jonan charmed people at the hospital. Why had she allowed herself to believe she was different?

Beth squeezed her eyes tightly shut, rejecting the tears that threatened. She would not allow herself to be weak. She had been here before. She was an expert at dealing. She would show Jonan he wasn't the only one who knew how to distance himself.

The street was already dark, but there was a stream of people striding past, eyes fixed and glazed. Beth pulled up her collar, turning her face into the neck of her coat to avoid meeting anyone's eyes. Working in town, there was always the risk of bumping into someone she knew. That was the last thing she wanted when she felt so raw. She barely saw the pavement, slick with rain, or the bright lights behind the windows of closed shops. All she saw was Jonan's face, clear in her mind. His violet eyes transported her straight back to that place that made her ache with homesickness.

She crossed the road and walked straight into the scent of lavender. 'Salu?' she whispered.

Here, sister. The words resounded in her mind, but there was nothing more.

Beth raced up the stairs to the front door of the flat. She pushed her way through the front door, slamming it behind her. Breathing heavily, she leaned against it.

'Beth, is that you?'

Beth sighed. Bracing herself on the solid weight of the door, she pushed herself upright, wiped her eyes, painted a bright smile on her face and walked through to the living room. 'Hey, Laura, I haven't seen you in a few days. How are you doing?'

'You should have seen the day I had at work.' Laura's eyes were shining.

Beth sank into an armchair, holding her smile rigidly in place as she pushed her hands into her hair, massaging her scalp. Her forehead ached and she knew that wouldn't end anywhere good.

Laura was still talking. Beth murmured yes and no occasionally, but she had no idea what her roommate was saying. She couldn't see or hear anything except for the image of Jonan's face that burned its way through her mind taking out everything in its path.

Jonan

'DAMN IT ALL,' Jonan hissed as the sage smudging sticks he was arranging in a basket tumbled in a pile at his feet. He took a deep breath, and then crouched down to gather them up and start again.

'Maybe you should light one. You could do with a bit of serenity,' Doriel said.

'Stop reading me.'

Doriel laughed. 'Stop broadcasting then. I don't know why you sent her packing. Anyone would think she wasn't the woman you had been in love with for tens of lifetimes.'

'And look how that worked out for me.' Jonan picked up his coffee from the glass shelf of crystals on his right and took a large gulp. He spluttered as the scalding liquid hit the back of his throat, just turning in time to stop the liquid spraying the pile of sage sticks.

'I guess the hot coffee is my fault too, is it?' Doriel raised one eyebrow.

'I'm not thinking about Beth.'

'Are you kidding me? I know everything. I thought you'd figured that out by now.'

Jonan rolled his eyes. Living with an Oracle was a pain in the nether regions. She was so meek in public, but when everyone had left, she flaunted her wisdom each time he messed up. Right now, he seemed to be doing that a lot. 'Okay, so it's about Beth. But if you're such a top-notch Oracle, surely you should know why I did what I did last night.'

'True.' Doriel grinned. 'But I don't need psychic ability to work that out. You remember being left. You know the pain of seeing her walk away and the tearing grief of watching her die. You have been separated so many times, in so many ways, and you remember more of them than you want to live with. You are trying to save yourself more heartache but, and this is the kicker, it won't work. You're making it worse, and you know it. This time is supposed to be different.

Jonan took a sip of coffee. 'I don't really need to be in this conversation. Can we please move on to something more interesting?'

'Of course. Next up, why aren't you getting on with sorting things out with Beth?'

'God help me, why do I live with you?' Jonan hit his forehead with the heel of his hand. 'Will I ever get a moment's peace?'

'Are you ready for peace, Jonan? Have you got to a place where you are ready to rest? Or is there anything you still want out of life?'

'Don't be facetious.' Jonan shook his head. 'You know exactly what I want.'

'And last night it looked like you were going to get her, before you threw her out.'

'I didn't throw her out.'

Doriel laughed. 'Okay, so that was an exaggeration. You were about to get her, before you humiliated her. You blamed her for your past hurts and hit out. You really don't understand this reincarnation lark as well as I thought you did.'

'Seriously?' Jonan strode over to the desk and slammed his hand down on the wooden counter. He glared at Doriel. Her eyes were sparkling and there were lines at the edges of her lips where she had pressed them together. 'You're lecturing me on reincarnation? And now you're laughing?'

'Well you have to see the funny side, surely? You're so well prepared for this destiny it almost hurts. The world could not hope for a better hero, unless of course you choose to mess it all up on the most basic level. If you alienate Beth, you can't complete your path, the world will be left to Amelia's desires, and you will have to repeat this karma. Again.'

Jonan ground his teeth together. He knew she was right and that was what made her so annoying. He had prepared. He had worked on himself and his abilities day after day, week after week, year after year. The only thing he hadn't worked on was his relationship with Beth. He had been so convinced she would feel the connection, that it would work out so easily. Then he'd fallen into the same trap he always did. He believed in her, dreamed about her, charmed her, and lost his nerve at the last minute. He liked to think she left him, but deep down, he knew she was just more honest about what was happening between them than he was. 'You think I can't do it?'

'I think that right now you're not trying. I think you're seriously considering packing it all in because it's easier on your heart, and on your pride.

Jonan's phone rang. The inane tone cut through the atmosphere like a gong, making him jump and holding his gaze on the small, vibrating machine.

'Are you going to answer it or shall I?' Doriel tilted her head. She looked so innocent, but they both knew she had won the argument, aided and abetted by the universe and a good dose of synchronicity.

Jonan picked up the phone and slid his thumb over the screen, watching the display shift. 'Hello?' he said into the handset, pretending he didn't know who it was.

'Jonan, it's Beth.' Her voice was hard, business-like in a way he had never heard it.

'Are you alright?'

'Of course. I just wanted to let you know I'll be going to see Amelia speak tomorrow night, in London. She's given me tickets and has agreed to meet me afterwards. I'll let you know when I know more.'

'I'll…' he started, and then tailed off as she hung up. He sighed and threw the phone on the table.

'Is she as prickly as you?' Doriel raised her eyebrows.

Jonan closed his eyes for a moment and took a deep breath. 'Just, don't.' He strode past the desk and up the stairs to the flat, slamming the door to the shop behind him.

CHAPTER NINE

Beth

A SINGLE SPOTLIGHT illuminated an empty chair in the middle of the dark stage.

The booming silence gave Beth the uncomfortable feeling of being too small.

A crash from backstage echoed around the cavernous space. Someone in the audience squealed. Nervous laughter followed as people shuffled and muttered.

A chill ran down Beth's spine. She peered around her but didn't pick up anything except the undefined shapes of her fellow audience members. They had presumably chosen to be in this place. She wasn't sure whether she envied them that, or pitied their naivety.

Shaking off her unease, she checked her watch, angling it to catch the glow of the nearby spotlight. Why couldn't Rose have just told her what Amelia planned to say? Surely she didn't expect to recreate this farce in the middle of a swanky charity dinner? Or maybe she did.

Someone dropped into the seat next to her. She had been given two tickets and was only using one. That seat should have remained empty. She didn't turn around. She wanted to get out of this place as soon as she could. Making contact with her co-sufferers would only prolong the experience.

'Beth?'

The familiar voice made her heart leap. She closed her eyes, trying to calm the natural response of her body. 'What are you doing here, Jonan?'

'I wanted to be another pair of ears to hear what Amelia has to say.'

'You didn't trust me to report back?'

'That wasn't what I said.'

Beth smiled and nodded as though nothing was wrong. When she next spoke, she kept her voice low, but try as she might, she couldn't get rid of the slight tremor. 'Honestly, I know you want to keep your distance, and I'm not one to intrude where I'm not wanted. Please, feel free to head home or go and amuse yourself in London. I'll deal with this and drop you an email when I'm done.'

'Look, Beth,' Jonan started.

The spotlight went out, leaving the room in complete darkness.

When the light went on again, Amelia was sitting on the stool. She wore a cream trouser suit with a neckline that plunged to her waist, displaying a well-controlled cleavage. Her dark hair was piled on top of her head. The only splash of colour came from her perfect bright-red lips.

'Welcome, my darlings,' she said, her voice low and throaty. 'Thank you so much for coming to see me today, for sharing in what I have to tell you. Dark days are coming, darlings, and what do we have if we can't tackle them together?'

There was a shuffling throughout the audience as people moved closer to Amelia, shifting in their seats to increase the connection as her voice surrounded them in the echoey theatre.

'Oh for goodness sakes,' Beth muttered, not caring that her voice travelled across the moment of silence. This time, Amelia ignored her.

'They are everywhere.' Amelia's whisper carried like a breeze, drifting into every corner of the darkness.

Beth shivered.

Amelia stood up, walking to the edge of the stage, meeting the eyes of each person in the front row by turn. 'These spirits, they surround us every minute of every day. Some people are more susceptible than others, but you will not know who has been affected. The only way to protect yourself is to remain on your guard all the time.' She clapped her hands together once and the sound jarred through Beth's bones into the seat below her. She jolted. Her heart raced even faster than before.

'We need to wake up to what is going on around us, to jolt ourselves out of sleepy complacency. We need to take control, to push back anyone who seeks to make us powerless. Stick with me and we will do this together.'

The lights went up. Beth blinked in the sudden glare, peering around her, meeting wary eyes as people checked out their neighbours, peering furtively before looking back to Amelia.

'That's right,' she shouted, flinging her arms up above her head. 'Look around you. See who is next to you, in front and behind. Do you trust them?' Her voice rose in question.

Silence hung in the air. The tension fizzed even stronger now. Beth took deep breaths. She focused on the feel of the seat beneath her legs, on the connection between the soles of her feet and the wooden floor beneath her. She did her best to ignore the warmth that seeped towards her from Jonan and focused her awareness on the left side of her body. She felt him shift in his seat. She knew he was watching her, willing her to turn to him. She stared resolutely forwards.

'Do they look different, strange?' Amelia's voice was hushed to a whisper now, intimate, despite being blasted through the PA system.

There were mutterings as people shifted closer to their loved ones and put more space between them and the strangers next to them.

'We must protect against being infiltrated, against allowing our minds to be infected. We must protect against intrusion. We must stand strong and stand together.'

Fear swept through Beth's body. Her legs were weak and her stomach rolled. She lurched upwards to her feet.

Amelia looked at her, held her gaze. As her lips spread into a wide smile, Beth shuddered. She stumbled past Jonan into the aisle. She could feel Amelia's gaze boring into her back, but she did not turn.

She threw open the door to the foyer, letting it swing shut behind her as she leaned against the wall, fighting for air.

The usher frowned at her. 'If you leave now, you won't be allowed back in.'

'Fine by me,' she snapped, bending to lean on her thighs as she pulled air into her lungs and imagined white light surrounding her in a protective bubble.

'Someone else might have wanted that seat. Amelia is a big draw, you know. You've wasted an opportunity someone else may have valued.'

Beth straightened, feeling strength flowing back into her body. 'Whoever that person is, they've had a lucky escape from Amelia's poison.'

The man gasped.

The door creaked. Jonan slipped through and closed it quietly behind him.

'Another one?' The man glared at Jonan.

Jonan pulled himself up to his full height and rolled his shoulders. The air around him seemed to shift. Beth felt a rush of warmth and the fear lifted. The usher's face went blank for a moment, and then this forehead creased and his eyes narrowed. He looked Jonan up and down and took a step back. 'I'll... just,' he said, tailing off. Then he turned and walked away.

'Is everything okay?' Jonan took Beth's hands.

For a moment she sank into the warmth of his touch, and then the scene from the night before flickered through her mind. She pulled her hands away and squared her shoulders. 'I'm fine.' She stepped past him before he could say anything else, and strode out through the door to the weirdly empty street.

Outside, she drew the cold, crisp air into her lungs in relief. She strengthened her psychic protection, feeling Amelia's cold influence wane. Reaching into her bag, she pulled out a bar of chocolate, broke off a square and popped it in her mouth. The sugar brought her back down to Earth. As the world stopped shifting, she started breathing normally again. 'I can't sit through any more of that,' she murmured to herself.

'I'll wait with you.'

Beth jumped, and then turned to scowl at Jonan. 'For goodness sakes, you startled me. I thought you wanted to keep your distance. I can handle this conversation on my own.'

'I don't want to keep my distance.'

'You could have fooled me. Look, I'm not the clingy type. You've made yourself clear. I'll give you space, but you need to do the same for me.'

Jonan stepped back as though she'd slapped him. 'You can have all the space you want, but I need to talk to Amelia too.' His hands were clenched into fists at his side, his knuckles turning white.

'This is a work meeting, Jonan. You asked me to find out what she's going to say and I'm trying to do that, but I also have a job to do. If you want more, do it yourself. You're friends with the woman, for goodness sake. Speak to her on your own time, find out what her agenda is, but don't crash my meeting. Honestly, I need to focus on my client. I need Amelia to be open with me, not to see me linked to her... what are you to her anyway? A rival? An enemy? An ex?'

Jonan's jaw clenched. 'Why are you so angry?'

'I've been on my own for a long time. I'm not afraid to walk away. I thought we were becoming... something, but you made it clear I was wrong. Nobody gets a second chance.'

'And you think you're the only one?' Jonan snapped. 'That you've been hurt over and over without inflicting a wound on anyone else? Hurt people are more likely to hurt others. Did you know we repeat cycles throughout our present lives and on into the next and the next and the next? I remember, Beth. I remember how things went down in our last life, and the one before. I remember the whole line, back to our original agreement. I know how long it's taken us to get to this moment and I remember what it feels like when it goes wrong.'

Beth stared at Jonan. His words tumbled around her head, trying to settle into some kind of meaning that made sense. 'Past lives?'

'Past lives,' he said, sitting down on a low wall at the side of the theatre. 'Running away isn't going to help. If we keep pushing each other away, we'll just have to come back and deal with the hurt all over again.'

There was a murmur of voices as the theatre doors opened. People started flooding out.

'You're the ones that walked out.' A large man squared up to Jonan. His chin jutted forwards, his shoulders rounding as he clenched his fists and flexed his muscles. He was twice Jonan's bulk and the leer on his red face told Beth he was loving the fact. 'Amelia was putting herself on the line to save us from evil, and you got up and walked out. Has nobody taught you respect?'

'I'm sorry. I was feeling ill,' Beth said, stepping forward to deflect his focus from Jonan. 'I didn't want to disturb the show.' She closed her eyes, trying to block out the man's energy. She felt it flowing past her protections and through her system like a torrent. The fear Amelia had prodded to life mingled with this man's anger to create a frightening beast. It pushed at her as he postured in front of them.

Jonan slipped his hand into hers and squeezed it. Then he positioned himself between Beth and the man. 'You heard the lady. We're done here.'

The man stuck his chin in the air, his beer belly jutting forwards as he moved to crowd Jonan.

Jonan didn't move, but the air around him seemed to shimmer and shift.

The man paled, and then stepped back. 'What...?'

Blurring her eyes, Beth saw a golden energy emanating

from Jonan, clearing away the dark, sludgy mess that surrounded the man.

One minute he was glaring at Jonan, the next, his brow furrowed. He looked around, shaking his head in confusion. 'Sorry, mate,' he said, taking a step backwards, his shoulders slumping. 'I didn't mean to bump into you.'

Beth's eyes widened as she watched him walk away. 'What happened?'

'Amelia addled his brain or, I should probably say, his feelings. She reaches into you with her energy and expands your sadness, your anger and fear. She lifts it so it spreads out and fills your whole body, becoming the only meaning you can relate to.'

'I felt that,' Beth said, her voice small. 'But how did you make him forget?'

'The less conscious you are of what's really inside you, the less you can stay conscious when she gets a hold. In simple terms, she has the power to send people over the edge.'

'I didn't need you to protect me, you know. Did you think I'd never dealt with harassment from an idiot man before you turned up?'

'Of course not. I know you don't need looking after,' Jonan murmured. 'But I'd like to build up credit so you might feel the urge to protect me one day.'

'Urgh,' Beth huffed. She rolled her eyes. She wanted to turn her back but, even when she was angry with him, she couldn't look away. That irritated her most of all.

'Is your name Beth?' A huge man in a suit with a shaved head tipped his head back, looking down his nose at her. His hands were looped behind his back.

'Yes.' Beth stepped forwards. She was determined to

show no fear in this place. If Amelia took people's ability to behave consciously, Beth would retaliate by holding onto consciousness with as much vigour as she could.

'Amelia will see you now. Come with me,' he said.

Beth stepped forward. 'Are you sure you don't want me to come along?' Jonan asked.

Beth shook her head. 'This is my meeting. Go home, or if you want to stay, find a cafe nearby and I'll text you when I'm done.'

Jonan didn't move.

'Miss, if you want to see Amelia, you need to come now. She doesn't have much time.'

A movement to her right caught Beth's attention. She turned to see a figure in a hoody disappearing into the shadows. At the last moment, he turned and held her gaze. His face was gaunt and pale. His cheeks were sunken and his eyes burned with pain. The moment seemed to last forever, and then he was gone.

'Miss, did you hear me?' the man asked.

Beth nodded. 'I'm ready.'

She nodded at Jonan, and then turned and followed the man back into the auditorium.

Amelia still sat in the chair in the centre of the stage.

The atmosphere fizzed.

Beth paused on the stairs, feeling the energy pushing at her barriers. Now she had seen what Amelia could do, her determination to resist had doubled. She pulled the light around herself, brightening her own space.

'How interesting that we get to work together after our little… history,' Amelia said with a rigid smile.

Beth swallowed. 'I was hoping you would tell me what you plan to talk about at the charity gala.'

Amelia tipped her head to one side. 'Why are you so desperate to know?'

Beth shrugged. 'It helps me pitch the right mood for the event.'

'Well, darling, I was hoping you would stay at today's presentation long enough to get a feel for it yourself.' Amelia held her gaze, chin lifted, jaw tight.

'Oh, I got a feel for you,' Beth said. She kept her voice soft, knowing it would carry in the cavernous room. 'But what kind of impact are you looking for at the charity dinner? With such an old building we could go for a ghost theme rather than glitz, present the inn as a haunted manor?'

'That wouldn't be much of a stretch now, would it, darling?' Amelia laughed. 'Come on, Beth. I know you're trying to hold the line, to be professional. I also know you've been poking around the inn. I know you've figured out I own it. And I know you've joined forces with Jonan and Doriel. I suggest you don't believe everything you hear.'

'Why don't you tell me your side,' Beth said, feeling strength flow into her limbs. 'You're assuming I've already made my mind up about you.'

Amelia laughed. 'I think you're being paid enough to give your loyalty to me, not to your friends, darling.'

'Touché.' Beth's smile was tight. 'Why don't we get back to business. What do you plan to say?'

Amelia sighed. 'This is getting so repetitive. You will find out what I'm going to say on the night. In the meantime, take today as your guide. That's all you need to know for now.'

'Listen, Amelia.' Beth walked closer. 'I am good at what I do. I've organised a lot of events and I've never gone wrong.'

'I know you haven't, darling.' Amelia tilted her head back, looking down her nose at Beth, eyes narrowed. 'You're psychic. You use your gifts to tune into what the customer wants and what the guests will respond to on the night. It's no mystery. You may even have some skill with manipulating energy. These are the reasons I chose you. But if you think you can throw your weight around, you have no idea what you're dealing with.'

'I'm not trying to be pushy.' Beth sat on the aisle seat of one of the rows, far enough away from Amelia that she still had to project into the echoing room to be heard. 'I can only do my best if I know everything. You can trust me to keep my mouth shut.'

'Well, that's an interesting prospect.' Amelia's lips spread into a thin smile. She got up and walked down the steps from the stage towards Beth, her hips swaying. 'I wonder what it would do to you and Jonan if you refused to tell him what you found out.'

'I'm not here for him.' Beth leaned back in her chair, stretching her legs out into the aisle and crossing her ankles. 'I'm here for my client.'

Amelia looked at Beth, eyes narrowed. 'If only I believed that.'

The lights went out.

Beth swallowed. 'Hello? We're still in here. Please could you turn the lights back on.'

Silence.

'Damn,' she muttered. 'Amelia, do you know where the switches are? Maybe the lights were on some kind of timer.'

Still, silence.

'Amelia? Are you there?' Beth got up and walked to the stage. Now that her eyes were adjusting, she could see it was empty. She turned full circle. She was completely alone.

The curtains swayed. The scent of mould intensified,

and then another waft of lavender. She hauled herself up onto the stage and searched in the wings. It was dark. There was only a faint glow from the small fire exit sign. The levers and ropes threw ominous shadows that made her shudder. She felt as though something was watching her, but when she spun around, there was nobody there.

She jumped down from the stage and walked to the back of the auditorium. She could see the looming shapes of the seats. Nothing moved. The air was stifling. The lavender had faded and now the scent of mould filled the air. She reached out, closing her fingers around the cold, solid bar on the fire exit. The door wouldn't budge. She shook it. It rattled, but was wedged tight.

She walked round to the next door. It did the same. She grabbed each door in turn, shaking it over and over. None of them opened. She had been locked in.

Pulling her phone out of her pocket, she dialled Jonan. There wasn't enough signal for the phone to connect. It was nearly out of battery.

'Jonan,' she yelled at the top of her voice, hoping he might have come back for her. 'Jonan!'

She retraced her steps to the door at the back of the auditorium, rattling it with all her strength as she shouted.

Amelia's voice rang out across the dark room, bringing the sound system into life. It started with a chuckle and then built to a full-throated laugh. The sound looped over and over, eating into Beth's mind as she shook the door and yelled.

She was going hoarse. Nobody was coming. She leaned back against the door. Her hands were red and raw from pummelling the wood. She slid to the floor, feeling every groove in the surface jar her back. The room was completely silent apart from her laboured breathing. The air was too thin, too scarce. Her throat closed as her lungs fought for oxygen. There was nobody there. Everyone had left without her. Amelia was the only one who knew where she was, and from the laughter that still rang through the speakers, she clearly wanted Beth to be exactly where she was.

Jonan was her only hope.

She looked at her phone again. There was still no signal and the battery was almost done. She got up and started walking around the auditorium. Something moved on her right. She spun, searching the semi-darkness for a sign of something, anything. She turned away, looking through her peripheral vision this time. Again, there was movement.

Beth tuned into the energy. It was heavy, but desperately indistinct. She felt it again, to her right this time. Then the image of a spirit began to distinguish itself.

There was another movement, this time to her left. Another spirit began to emerge, and then one directly ahead of her.

Beth tuned into the light, setting up her protections, but her concentration was disintegrating. Every time she made progress, something caught her attention and sent her mind reeling. She lost track of how many entities emerged. It ceased to matter. All that counted was the heaviness that swirled around her, trying to suck her into the vortex of fear Amelia had created.

Beth tried to push her light out as Jonan had done, but there was obviously something she was missing, or maybe she just wasn't good enough to do it. She didn't have the strength to convert this energy. The fear inherent in the spirits was eating into her defences, pushing her buttons as she fought to hold onto optimism.

She curled into a ball, wrapping her body around her centre. She closed her eyes, pushing back the cold desolation that tried to force itself inside her, filling her with loneliness. Images flitted through her mind. Every time Laura had failed to be there for her. Every time she had faced a situation alone, or pretended to be something she wasn't. She saw herself in her mind's eye, dressed in a long sludge-coloured smock, camouflaging her quirky energy in acres of invisibility. She shivered. Cold seeped through her body, beginning at the tips of her fingers and toes. She felt the energy of the spirits stroking her now. There were no barriers. There was no protection. There was only the scent of lavender.

Jonan

BETH HAD BEEN with Amelia for four long hours. Jonan had drunk so much coffee his insides were sloshing like a reservoir. It was hard to work out where the caffeine buzz ended and intuitive warning began.

Was it possible that Beth and Amelia had been bonding for that long? Jonan's mind screamed, *No!* He knew what Amelia was like, but it seemed very early in the game for her to be playing her big cards.

He checked his phone again. There was nothing, not even a text.

A siren blared past the window. Then the scent of lavender surrounded him.

Salu. He sent out the thought.

She needs you.

'Damn,' Jonan whispered. He stood up and pulled on his leather jacket. *Where? Where is she?*

You know where. The words swirled around him and then were gone, taking the scent with them.

Jonan left a twenty-pound note on the table, strode out of the cafe and set off down the dark street at a trot.

The darkness shone as streetlights reflected in the cold, dreary puddles that littered the worn pavement. The air bit into Jonan's skin. He pulled the collar up on his jacket, put his head down and walked into the chill.

The closer he got to the theatre, the more the air cooled. His skin broke out in goose bumps and ice shot through his core. Something was wrong.

He heard Beth's voice in his head, screaming and crying by turns. He was being melodramatic, surely? His mind must be playing up his fears under the mask of intuition. The steady knowledge that grounded him most of the time was shot through with terror, fogging his psychic sight.

The road was full of people and the shop windows were brightly lit, welcoming even. The theatre was dark, shrouded with the pallor of a building too long abandoned. Jonan would never have guessed it had been full to bursting a few hours before. If he had come across it now, he would have sworn it had been unused for a decade. Where were the actors arriving for the evening performance? Where were the front of house staff preparing the foyer and the early guests milling around looking for a drink? Even a theatre on a small side street should have been teeming with life this close to Leicester Square.

He peered at the poster on the wall. It was old. The show had finished months ago.

Jonan tried the front entrance but it was shut tight. He walked around the building, wrinkling his nose at the smell of mould emanating from the brickwork. The stage door was also shut tight.

'Hello!' he shouted, banging on the door. He listened.

Nobody answered, but he was sure he heard footsteps. 'Hello!' he kept shouting and banging, hoping someone would hear him.

'Can I help you?'

Jonan spun around. The man was wrapped in a full-length black coat. His heavy, dark eyebrows were pulled tight above a slightly bent nose. Straight, receding hair in need of a cut stuck out over his ears. His lips twitched.

'I think my friend might be in there,' Jonan said, turning to look back at the door.

'I'm Oliver Colman, the caretaker. Nobody was there when I left.'

'Could you just let me in to check, please?'

'I don't let people into my theatre after hours.' Oliver turned to walk away.

Jonan tuned into the energy in the building. He reeled back as darkness flooded his mind.

'*Jonan.*' The voice in his mind was so strong it forced him backwards into the wall.

'Hey, Oliver!' he shouted, striding after the man. He grabbed his arm, spinning him around. 'I know you don't want to believe me, but she's in there. Let me in or I will break the door down.'

Oliver stepped closer, glaring up at Jonan. 'I told you, there was nobody in there when I left.'

Jonan pulled himself up to his full height, allowing his energy to expand. He was the taller, and the man cringed back.

'I know you are lying.'

Oliver flushed red and made a strangled noise in his throat. Behind him, something moved in the shadows and Jonan saw a hooded face watching him, eyes narrowed.

'How dare you speak to me like that.' Oliver's fists were clenched at his sides, but his skin had whitened, and he trembled in spite of his attempts to look resolute.

Jonan's gaze flicked back to the shadows, but the watcher had gone.

'I have no time for this,' Jonan said, his voice low. 'Let me in or I will call the police.'

'And tell them what?'

'I will report a missing person, tell them that she was last seen in your theatre, and that you refuse to let me in to check. Are you *that* sure the theatre was empty when you left?'

Oliver froze. His jaw worked. He took a deep breath, and then his shoulders slumped. 'Okay, okay, I'll open the door, but you only have five minutes.' He turned around and slipped the heavy key into the lock. It creaked as it turned. 'Where do you think your friend might be?'

Jonan stepped through the door and into the small passageway. He shivered. Paint was peeling from the walls and the place smelled musty and damp. 'She went into the auditorium.'

The man walked through the narrow corridors until he reached a low door. 'This takes us to the stage. If your friend's not in there...' He shrugged.

Jonan walked through, peering into the darkness of the wings. 'Are there lights?'

'Of course.' The room lit up, making Jonan squint, and then the lights flickered and went out.

'Damn,' Oliver muttered. 'There should be a torch around here somewhere. These lights have a mind of their own.' A moment later, he shoved a torch into Jonan's hand and another flickered into life next to him.

Jonan stepped out onto the creaky boards, moving the beam slowly around the room. At the edge of the stage he stood still, peering into the shadows.

A shape flickered through his peripheral vision, but it vanished when he turned his head. He called in his guides and felt the room fill with light, pushing the visitors back.

'Stop,' the man said from behind him. 'They belong here.'

Jonan turned. 'You can see them?'

'Did you think you were the only one?' Oliver was standing as tall as he was able, pushing his chest out. His heavy eyebrows were pulled in as he glared at Jonan. 'They're not doing anyone any harm. I will not let you send them away from their home.'

'Is that really what's best for them?' Jonan asked, spreading his hands. 'These spirits are trapped. Haunting an old, crumbling theatre is no fate for anyone.'

'They like it here. And I like having them.'

'And there we have it,' Jonan muttered, turning away. 'I'll only help those who ask.'

'Jonan?' The voice from the darkness was faint.

'Beth?' Jonan jumped off the stage, running in the direction of her voice.

He slowed as he saw her hunched against one of the exits. Her knees were pulled in to her chest, her arms hugged around her legs. She was shivering violently. Even in the dark her skin looked too pale.

Jonan crouched down in front of her. 'What happened?'

He reached a hand towards her arm.

She flinched.

'Please.' His voice cracked. 'I'd like to warm you up. You're freezing.'

Beth nodded. She allowed him to pull her to his chest, but he could feel the shudders that wracked her body. He wrapped his arms around her, holding her tight. It was like falling down a well of memories. They swarmed around in his mind as he tried to get some kind of control. He forced his arms to stay strong, to hold her without shaking as he tried to push the pain deep inside where she wouldn't sense it. How long could he stay like this before he broke open, revealing the scars he tried so hard to hide? He didn't know.

'What is it, Jonan?' she asked, her voice a little stronger. 'Has something happened?'

'Has something happened? You've been trapped in this place, alone, for hours. She left you in here with all of these...'

'They didn't do anything. Amelia is the one who poisoned this room.'

Jonan knew it. He felt it deep in his gut and the knowledge churned alongside the feeling of panic that came from her interference. Every instinct he had screamed at him to get out, but he knew the spirits would do nothing to hurt them. He had to give Beth a moment.

There was a cough from behind.

His shoulders tensed as he felt the man's gaze boring into his back.

'Are you done? I gave you five minutes.'

Jonan stood up, took his jacket off and wrapped it around Beth. He stepped towards Oliver, hands clenched into fists at his sides.

'You allowed her to be locked in here, on her own.'

'I had no idea your friend was in here.'

'It's your job to know who is in your theatre.'

Oliver paled. 'Now look here—'

'Stop!' Beth stood up and leaned heavily on the wall behind her. 'I can't bear your bickering. I'm okay. We can go now.'

'Are you sure?' Jonan wrapped his arm around her shoulders. Now that he'd touched her, he craved more contact. The memories were so strong, so physical, that they made his heart split in two.

For a moment, Beth leaned into him. He felt her warmth seeping into his side and closed his eyes, memorising the feeling. The shabby theatre receded and he surrounded them in light. Beth's energy surged.

'Come on,' he said, relieved his voice sounded steady. 'I'm taking you to the hospital.'

Beth snorted. 'What are you going to tell them? Yes, doctor, she was locked in an empty theatre and attacked by mean ghosts.' She began to shake.

Ice froze Jonan in place. His mind fogged and screams bounced around in his head. The stab of fear was so familiar, so brutally shocking, that for a moment he couldn't move.

'Oh, for goodness sake.' Oliver's voice cut through the fog. 'She's laughing, man. Calm yourself. She's not a china doll.'

Jonan closed his eyes, forcing himself to breath more slowly. 'She's laughing,' he said with a grimace. 'I'd almost forgotten laughing existed. This day is just too weird. Amelia must be getting to me too.'

'Please take me home, Jonan.'

The last thing Jonan wanted to do was bid a civilised goodbye to Oliver, but it seemed to be the only thing he could do for Beth right now, so he followed the man outside, making small talk as though nothing had happened.

Only when they had walked away from the man and left the theatre well and truly behind did he feel he could breathe.

The tube train was busy, but a woman took one look at Beth, pale and slumped, and offered her seat. Jonan knew he was over-effusive in his thanks, but he didn't care. He spent the journey on autopilot, focusing on the colour of Beth's skin, the glassiness of her eyes and the sluggish drag of her feet. When the train pulled into St Albans station, he couldn't quite remember how they had got there, and mentally sent thanks to all the souls who had helped them on their way.

His car was waiting in the car park, cold, but still comforting. Beth climbed in, hugging his jacket around her. He forced himself not to shiver, liking the sight of her in his coat.

He drove to his usual parking space and slid in neatly, his car close to the raised pavement on one side of the narrow road.

'I thought you were taking me home?'

'Not a chance. I agreed not to take you to the hospital, but I want to keep an eye on you myself. You can have my room tonight. Don't worry, I'll sleep on the sofa.'

Jonan watched her face for any signs of emotion, but it was shut tight. He wasn't surprised. He knew what it was like living as an intuitive in a world that didn't recognise your gifts. You learned to camouflage, to look normal even when you felt as though there would never be a space for you that fitted.

Jonan opened the car door. 'I'm sorry, you'll need to climb over to my side to get out.'

Beth said nothing, just scooted across the seat and climbed out into the road, adjusting her crumpled clothes.

Jonan felt the energy of the theatre on her. It made him shudder and he felt a dread settle in his chest. What exactly had Amelia done?

Jonan let them into the closed darkness of the Third Eye Spiritualist Shop. He ushered Beth up the stairs, taking comfort from her physical presence in his home.

She paused at the door.

'It's okay,' he said, stopping a breath behind her. 'I know the building is old, but we cleared it a long time ago. Everyone who had hung on here has moved on to better things. The building breathes peacefully now. Anything you feel is coming with us from the theatre. We will deal with that as soon as we get inside.'

Beth nodded, but said nothing. She pushed the door open and went in, letting the heavy door swing behind her. Jonan stood, frozen, on the stairs as the door closed in his face. She was pulling even further away and he had no idea how to get her back.

CHAPTER TEN

Beth

THE ROOM WAS warm. Beth felt it on her skin, felt the welcome burn of heat, heard the crackling of the fire. It did nothing to thaw the icy lump inside her.

She still heard the voices in her mind, felt Amelia's laughter vibrating through her body and smelled the musty mouldiness of the theatre.

Her face became rigid as Jonan came into the room, her muscles like stone. She sat as though movement would crack her.

His eyes were full of concern. He knelt in front of her, taking her hand. Tingles raced around her wrist as he traced her skin with his thumb.

She pulled away so hard that he rocked back, staring at her. His eyes were wide, lips parted. He was trying to get under her skin. She would not allow it. He wanted to make her soften, to crack her heart open. She felt what they could be together. It was so tangible she could virtually touch the image, but he had shown her a glimpse of how much he could hurt her. It would not happen again.

Their potential sparked around them, abrasive against

her raw nerves. She edged as far away from him as the small room would allow. She was at the edge of her endurance. There was so much more to this moment than she understood. She saw from his eyes that he grasped it, but he hadn't told her anything. That was not a good sign.

Beth understood the paranormal. The ghosts at the theatre hadn't frightened her, but something had got under her skin, crawling around, reaching for her heart, her mind. It was still there eating away at her, prodding relentlessly. She was in way over her head. Amelia had powers Beth hadn't ever imagined. Jonan and Doriel had knowledge that soared above her own and Jonan was reeling her in. That terrified her.

'How was the performance?' Doriel said.

Her voice sounded distant, as though Beth were listening through water.

Doriel held her gaze. She perched on the arm of Beth's chair, her head tilted. Watching Beth's movements, she allowed her eyes to flicker to the space around Beth's body.

'Stop reading me.' Beth pulled her arms tight around her chest. 'If there's something you want to know, ask.'

Doriel reached out to touch her arm.

Beth jerked it away. The woman pulled back, stood up, and then moved to the sofa. 'What happened to you, my love?'

Beth said nothing.

'Amelia happened.' Jonan's voice was rough, thick. His eyes were bloodshot, but he made no attempt to hide it. He was staring at Beth as though she might disappear.

Beth felt the fear rise. She closed her eyes for a moment, imagining her own energy pushing his back, feeling the space around her release.

He was still watching her. His lips were parted. His face

had paled. He sat on the edge of the sofa, jaw clenched, hands gripping the seat so tight his knuckles turned white.

'What did she do?' Doriel said, moving up the sofa to sit next to Jonan. She put a hand on his back.

Beth felt a stab of jealousy, but pushed it away. She wanted nothing to do with these people. They were trying to lure her in, take her autonomy. They were a threat. Her attraction to Jonan was just another of their tricks.

Jonan's shoulders relaxed a little from Doriel's touch.

Beth gritted her teeth. Her body sagged under the conflict of raging emotions. She wanted to yank Jonan away from Doriel and keep him for herself. And she wanted to run as far from him as she could. The confusion sent her mind reeling and the room drifted even further away.

Some of Jonan's words seeped through her barriers. She knew he was telling Doriel what happened at the theatre. She tried to shut his voice out, to stop it triggering the cold, shadowy memories. She put her hands over her ears, instead watching his aura as it flickered around him. The normal, smooth lines had turned jagged, fluctuating so fast she felt even more dizzy.

She closed her eyes, focusing on the feel of the chair underneath and behind her, on her hands squeezed over her ears, her eyes tight shut blocking out the room.

She was alone in her head.

Her thoughts began to drift, but a part of her mind stayed detached, noticing the ideas that flowed as though from outside.

And you thought he didn't care. The words formed in her mind. She nearly jerked fully awake, but held on to the hazy consciousness, wanting to prolong the moment. The air filled with the scent of lavender.

He told me he didn't care, she thought back and had a sense that the owner of the voice was smiling.

Does he look as though he doesn't care? Do people get that upset if they're not attached? He is as scared as you are.

That's ridiculous, she thought and sensed another smile. *Who are you, anyway?*

Salu, the voice breathed into her mind. I am your brother. You know this already.

A door slammed. She stirred, opened her eyes a crack. Doriel was gone.

'Beth?' Jonan's voice was low, close by. He was kneeling on the floor in front of her, hands reaching towards her, hesitating. His long blond hair was pushed back from his face, but a stray tendril hung over his eyes. His pale skin looked blanched, but he was still beautiful. Somehow the dark smudges under his eyes, the worry lines in his forehead, only increased his pull as he focused his attention entirely on her.

Could the voice have been right?

Her heart pounded. Her hands itched to touch his as her body swayed towards him. His eyes warmed as he registered her movement. For a moment she remembered she was supposed to be keeping her distance, but somehow that didn't seem important right now. His energy was radiating out to thaw the ice inside her. She wanted so desperately to feel normal, as though she fitted somewhere, not in camouflage, but in her full and flamboyant weirdness.

Jonan's hand came close to her face, but he stopped, unsure.

Her heart pounded. The voice echoed in her mind. *Does he look like he doesn't care?* She nodded.

He moved slowly, until his hand lay against her cheek.

Her frozen skin warmed at the touch. She leaned into him. A tingling energy came from his palm. It was mesmerising, the way it prickled over her skin like the gentlest lightning. It warmed her, thawing the ice inside her even further as it travelled through every inch of her body.

In her hyper-aware state, she felt as though she was glowing. Her energy was burning and fluctuating as the sparks triggered faster and faster over her skin, sending her deeper into a trance.

She had no idea how much time passed. She felt weightless as he lifted her up in his arms, pulling her close to his chest. She felt the beat of his heart under her cheek, the warmth of his skin and the soft fabric of his T-shirt. She breathed him in, the spice of his aftershave, and the subtle scent below that was all Jonan. Warmth flooded from his body and into hers. She sank into the sensations, her mind swimming, but somehow clearer than it had ever been.

She felt his walking as a flow that merged into the energy around her. There was no separation. They were a universe in themselves, an intrinsic part of a whole that was bigger than it was possible to imagine.

She kept her eyes closed even as he lowered her onto a bed. She sank into the soft, downy surface, felt the warm covers drawn up over her freezing body, and then nothing.

Jonan

ONE BY ONE, flames flickered to life around the room. Jonan lit a sage stick, blew out the match, and tossed it into the fire in the grate. Starting in the middle of the room, he paced out a spiral, allowing the smoke to waft out into the corners. He hummed as he walked, feeling the tension in his shoulders ease. The ritual was calming, but it was going to take more than that to still the fire that burned inside his chest.

He had never allowed Amelia to get to him before. He knew what she was like, what she could do, but this was different. This was Beth.

He felt her in the room next door. His bedroom. He felt the fear that flickered through her energy, even in sleep. He flexed his fingers, forcing them not to curl into fists. Rolling his shoulders, he took some deep breaths. His kind of fighting didn't involve throwing punches. It required that he still his mind and go deep, but his mind didn't want to quiet. He still felt the echo of Beth clutching at his neck, her frozen body pressed into his chest as he carried her.

He closed his eyes, reliving the memory. That could be all he would ever have of Beth. He had incarnated for her. She was his life path, but he might not be hers. He had come to help her wake up. After that, who knew?

'Earth Guide.' The words were bitter in his mouth as he whispered them. They were his mission, and right now he hated them more than he could have ever imagined.

'Have faith in her,' Doriel whispered.

Jonan looked up, eyebrows raised. He hadn't heard her come in. The usual jangling of bells on the bottom of her skirt was silenced. Instead she wore deep purple leggings, a tie-dyed tunic and bare feet. She moved without a sound as she walked, toe first, across the room. Picking up a stick of sage, she lit it and placed it in an abalone shell on the narrow windowsill. The smoke snaked up over the latticework of the window, which framed the inky blackness of the night sky, tinged on one side with light from the streetlamp below.

'This is part of the process, Jonan. You know how to

do this. You can reach that place of peace. Feel the knowledge deep in your bones. Absorb the knowing into your very being so it becomes as easy as breathing.'

'I know all that, but I can't just flick a switch. I can't grasp something because I want to. If I could, I would have done it by now. I know I'm stuck in a web of my own making, but it doesn't make it any easier to fight my way out.'

Doriel pulled him close. 'I know, it's hard.'

He felt warm energy flow into his back from her hands. 'Seriously? You think that will fix everything?'

'No.' Doriel's eyes glistened, but her voice was steady. 'It isn't your answer, but it might help you find it.' She held her hands out in front of her, eyebrows raised.

Jonan nodded.

She took his hands.

He felt his breathing steady as her energy flowed into him.

'You are not alone, my love. Beth has you, you have me. We all have our Earth and Spirit Guides. Your situation is rather more fraught than most, but I am doing everything in my power to help you.'

The words Jonan wanted to say stuck as his throat tightened. He nodded.

Letting go of Doriel's hands, he moved to the middle of the room and lowered himself to the floor in front of the fire. The heat from the flames flickered over his skin, trying to warm away the grief that froze his body.

Grief? Hmmm… why grief? Beth hadn't died; she hadn't even gone away. She was lying in the next room, closer than she had ever been.

He leaned into the emotion, feeling it fill his body, contracting his muscles until they hurt. He wanted to shout, to yell, to scream his anger to the heavens, but he kept his focus on the sensations in his body until he felt them release and retreat.

'Good,' Doriel said, her voice a monotone. 'Now another layer.'

Beth

BETH OPENED HER eyes and sat bolt upright. The room was unfamiliar. There were no pictures on the walls, but a golden Buddha sat in one corner, surrounded by crystals, a tarot deck, and a shell with a charred stick of white sage. There were salt lamps in each corner of the room. Navy bedding matched the simple curtains, which hung over one small latticed window to her right. A pile of books sat on the bedside table on her left. They were mainly spiritual, but there was also a dog-eared thriller that had survived some kind of spillage.

Memories of the night before flickered through her mind. They were indistinct, dreamlike. The version of her she remembered seemed strange at first, but as the fear began to trickle back in, she felt her usual equilibrium drain away.

Light was streaming in between the curtains. It was morning already. She wondered where Jonan had spent the night. He had clearly sacrificed his space for her.

She dragged herself up, relieved to find she was still fully dressed. She smoothed her shirt down over her trousers and ran her fingers through her hair, wishing there was a mirror in the room so she could see what the damage was.

Opening the door a crack, she peered through.

The room was stifling from a fire that was either still burning or had been relit. The air was thick with incense and sage. Heavy curtains were drawn over the windows and the room was dark and smoky. She reached out, feeling the wall with her hand and swore as she stubbed her toe on something hard.

'Beth?' Jonan's voice was sluggish, but he stepped lightly out of the smoke on bare feet. He was wearing soft black trousers slung low on his hips. His blond, wavy hair was tousled, and hung over muscular, bare shoulders.

Beth swallowed.

'Are you okay?'

'Hi,' Doriel called out. Her hair was splintering out of its normal plait. Her unusually comfortable clothes were creased and rumpled. 'How are you feeling today?'

Beth took a step back. 'I'm so sorry. I didn't mean to interrupt.'

Doriel laughed. 'Don't be daft, we were meditating, and it's about time we stopped.'

'It's early to meditate isn't it?'

'Or late.' Jonan yawned. 'We've been up all night.'

'All night? And you were just meditating?'

'Mainly.' Doriel stood up in one fluid motion. She stretched into a backbend, and then walked through to the kitchen, her hips swaying. 'I'm pretty sure I nodded off for a while.'

'You did. Your snoring didn't help my concentration.' Jonan rolled his eyes.

Beth wanted to laugh. She knew they were trying to lighten the mood, but she just felt confused.

As though reading her mind, Jonan grabbed a T-shirt from the sofa, pulled it over his muscled chest and drew his hair back into a neat ponytail at the nape of his neck.

Beth closed her eyes, forcing herself to ignore her

thumping heart. She wished his beautiful angular face wasn't as clear on the back of her eyelids as it was when she looked at him. 'I'm always bad-tempered in the mornings.'

There was something different about Jonan that Beth couldn't put her finger on. He seemed lighter somehow and that jarred with the darkness she felt closing in on her.

'This should help.' Doriel handed out steaming mugs of coffee.

Jonan sniffed one, closing his eyes and groaning. 'You have no idea how much I need this.'

'He says to the woman who sat up with him all night.' She rolled her eyes. This time Beth gave a tentative smile.

Jonan winked, holding her gaze.

Doriel ushered Beth to the sofa. Beth sat on the soft cushions, but held herself stiff, ready to bolt if she needed to. She wasn't sure why she felt so on edge but relaxing just didn't feel safe. She took a large gulp of coffee and the scalding liquid burned her mouth. She gulped it down, opening her mouth and pulling in the cooler air in order to calm the smarting.

'Are you okay?' Doriel put a hand on her back and Beth flinched.

She held up one hand, creating a barrier between them, and then reached over to put the coffee cup on the table. She was already pulling her hand away when she felt it wobble, and couldn't quite grasp the handle with the tips of her fingers. The cup rocked and fell over, tipping coffee everywhere.

'No!' Beth clapped her hands over her mouth, staring in horror at the mess.

'My phone,' Doriel shrieked and grabbed it up from the pool of coffee that was congealing between the piles of magazines. She shook the phone, but the screen was black. She pressed the button, nothing.

'Don't worry, I'll take it in to the shop today. It'll be fine.' Jonan took it from her hand. 'I'm sure they'll be able to fix it.'

Doriel looked about to disagree, then her gaze flickered to Beth.

'I'm sorry,' Beth whispered, trying to hold back tears. 'I didn't mean it.'

Doriel took a deep breath and closed her eyes for a moment. When she opened them again, she seemed a lot calmer. 'Of course you didn't. Look, you have coffee all over your clothes. Would you like a shower? I can lend you something dry and clean to wear home.'

Beth nodded.

Doriel opened one of the doors on to the living room. 'Here,' she said, going in first, opening a pin-neat cupboard and taking out a white fluffy towel. Doriel put a hand on Beth's arm. 'I know you don't understand everything that's happening, but we can help if you give us a chance. Tell Jonan how you're feeling. I'm not talking about a declaration of love, although feel free to do that if you choose. But he has a responsibility to help you and he can only do that if you talk to him. He won't take your feelings personally. Please, just talk to him.'

'What do you mean he has a responsibility to me?' Beth shook her head. 'And why would my feelings not be personal? Is there anything more personal than emotion?'

Doriel leaned against the door frame. 'Has he told you anything at all?

'He said he's here to wake me up, and we have to do something about Amelia. But I don't want to go anywhere near her after yesterday. She's dangerous.'

'Yes.' Doriel nodded. 'But she's only dangerous in her ability to manipulate people. She taps into the human fog that gets in the way of your cosmic hearing. We all have it. Anger, fear, disappointment, all those emotions come from human experiences, and stay around us like a thick mist, keeping us contained and blinded. In order to wake up, you have to start clearing all that gunk away. When you were shut in the theatre yesterday, Amelia plugged into your fears and lit them up like fairy lights. Now you have a choice. You can either face them in glorious detail or join the flow of people navigating Amelia's fear-based rapids. If you're ready to woman-up, we're here to help and support you. If you choose fear, you'll have plenty of company without us.' She patted Beth's arm, and then closed the door behind her.

Beth stood in the bathroom, hugging the towel to her chest. Her mind had turned into a strange and confusing place. The spirits from the theatre were gone, but a protective warmth now surrounded her. The bathroom smelled of lavender and that gave her a strange sense of safety that was at odds with the swirling pit of fear in her stomach. She wanted to lash out, to blame Jonan, Doriel, Amelia, everybody else for the turmoil. She was fighting the impulse as hard as she could, but she knew she had to either give up or reach out to Jonan. This wasn't a one-woman job.

She saw Jonan in her mind, his eyes pleading, chest bare, his body supple even after sitting still all night. She felt warm. Saw her cheeks flush in the mirror. Something stirred in her. Was it anger? Fear? She had tried to reach out to Jonan before, but he had knocked her back. It was the same pattern she'd faced her whole life.

'It has to end,' she whispered.

She stepped into the shower hoping the hot water would

pound some feeling into her deadened skin but, though she turned pink, the ice only spread, numbing her whole body.

She towelled herself off and was about to put on yesterday's crumpled clothes when she spotted a pile of clean things that hadn't been there a moment ago.

'They're for you to wear,' Doriel called through the door. 'Let me know if you need anything else.'

Beth pulled the clothes on, not caring that Doriel had come in while she was showering. The cold inside her was taking over. Nothing mattered any more.

'Breakfast?' Jonan smiled as she walked back out of the bathroom. He gestured to the small table in the corner of the living room. It was set with three plates of scrambled eggs and hot, buttered toast. 'Would you prefer coffee or tea?'

'Whatever's easiest,' Her voice was flat, but she couldn't muster the energy to do anything about it. She felt so tired. Her body had turned to lead. She could see the hope in Jonan's eyes, could see this might have been her chance with him, but it didn't matter enough any more. Following a dream was just too much effort to contemplate.

Jonan frowned and glanced at Doriel. He walked over to Beth and put his hands on her shoulders. 'Tell me what you're thinking.'

'Your hands are warm.' Beth shivered.

Jonan lifted her chin with one finger so she was looking into his eyes. They were deep and blue with flecks of gold that mesmerised her. A purple tinge around the edge of his pupils shifted as his gaze deepened.

'Stop reading my aura,' she said, pushing him away. 'Isn't a girl allowed any privacy?'

'Not when she's acting this out of character,' Jonan said,

but he stepped back. 'Please, eat. Hopefully you'll feel better after.'

'I'm fine now. Thank you.' Beth shoved the eggs around her plate for a few moments, and then pushed her knife and fork together. 'I need to get to work.'

'I can take you home to get changed.' Jonan scraped his chair back.

'I'm fine like this. You don't need to babysit me.' Beth jerked up. She grabbed her coat from the arm of the sofa and clutched it to her chest.

'Beth!' Jonan followed her as she headed for the door.

She was already out in the stairwell when he caught up with her.

'My love, you're dressed for the gym, not the office.' He stepped towards her, hands outstretched.

'Don't call me that,' Beth snapped. 'You turned me down, so quit the endearments. It's untruthful.'

Jonan's eyes widened. His jaw tensed, but he stepped out of her way.

She strode to the door of the flat, slamming it behind her.

The street was cold, but it matched the ice inside as she wove her way between the early-morning shoppers. She stopped and bought some hot coffee, hoping the caffeine would do something to perk up her dulled and lifeless senses. It made no difference.

She stopped as she caught her reflection in a shop window, blinking in surprise. Why was she wearing pyjamas? She had a vague memory of Jonan telling her she wasn't dressed for work, but his words were hazy already. What was wrong with her?

A small man with a pointy face and an overlarge hoody

was staring at her, eyes narrowed. She spun around, but he had disappeared into the crowds that surged around her. She stepped backwards and knocked into an old woman with a handful of shopping bags. The woman shouted at her, but Beth couldn't make any sense of what she was saying. She held her hands up in front of her, apologising and moving away, but there seemed to be another body to crash into with every step.

She pulled her phone out of her pocket, fumbling to get it open and unlocked with shaking fingers. She dialled Charlie's number.

'Hello?'

Beth flinched at the sharpness in his tone, and then frowned. She wasn't normally this jumpy. 'I'm sorry, Charlie. I'm going to be late. I'm not feeling well.'

'Seriously? Today? I need you, Beth.'

She sighed. 'I will come, don't panic. Just give me a chance to sort myself out first.'

'How did the performance go yesterday? Did you speak to Amelia afterwards?'

'I did.' Beth's heart raced as memories flooded her.

'Great. I'd like a full report of your plans. Arrange for me to visit the venue next week. I want to keep a close eye. Our future rests on this event.'

'Of course, Charlie.' Beth tried to make her voice sound upbeat.

There was silence on the other end of the phone. 'Is everything okay?'

'As I said, I'm ill. But don't worry. I won't let you down.'

CHAPTER ELEVEN

Beth

THE WALK, THE shower, the fresh clothes from her own wardrobe, none of it helped. If anything, they made her feel more wretched. She was running out of excuses for the weird fog that had taken over her mind and body. She felt like a prisoner, watching this strange 'other Beth' make an utter fool of her. But no matter how much she tried to rein it in, the pervasive fear pumped through her system, hauling her brain under its nauseating control.

Even alone in the office she felt it squeezing her insides to mush. Her heart rate increased as she felt the arrival of the ghost and her inner audience exasperated a little more.

Pull yourself together, she told herself. I am not that girl. I'm not the one who freaks out when a ghost pops in for tea. What the hell did Amelia do to me in that theatre? The energy was snaking around her in a way it had never done before. It chilled her, making her insides churn.

'What do you want?' she whispered.

I want your fear. The words formed in her mind.

'Why?'

It helps me stay Earth-bound. I need to stay.

'Why would you want to stay here, of all places? Is it Charlie's unique charm? Or the unpainted walls?'

I lost my baby here. I have to stay in case she returns.

'Oh, my love.' For a moment, the fear receded. Beth felt a faint glimmer of light around her, heard the gurgle of a child inside her mind. 'I can feel your baby. She's on the other side waiting for you. You won't find her here. This place just holds you in your pain.'

The energy wavered. Beth fought to remember what she had done when she helped the girl with the ringlets.

Help me help this woman. She sent out the strongest psychic call she could muster. She closed her eyes, feeling the light with every ounce of her body. It warmed her where she thought the chill would never leave, strengthened her heart and allowed life back in. The churning in her stomach eased and her chest expanded as the light warmed her from the tips of her fingers and toes towards her heart-centre. She drew in deep breaths, relishing each movement in her body, feeling life flow through her in each shift of her muscles. She could do this. She would help this woman. She would beat the cold.

She visualised the chill retreating, consumed by the fiery energy of the light that burned its way through the room.

In her mind's eye she saw figures start to form next to her. She couldn't see their faces clearly, but felt they were smiling. Great white wings rose behind them as they held their arms up in the air, beaming light from every cell of their light-bodies.

For the first time in forever, Beth did not feel alone. Years of isolation fell away, leaving her raw and healed at the same time. She felt limitless, like the ocean or the sky. Every cell in her body was a part of the infinite whole. For a moment, she saw her limits for what they were. They were barriers, nothing more.

An image of Jonan flashed into her mind. He shone like the others, but his back was bowed under an invisible weight. She felt his vulnerability as he strained his muscles, fighting to stand upright. She felt his determination not to lose contact with the one thing he longed for most of all. *But what is it? What is it that's so important to him?*

Don't you know? Doriel's voice said in her mind.

For a moment Beth saw the woman who had haunted her office for so long. Her dark hair sparkled with light. Her rags were glorious in their brightness. Beth knew she would never forget the all-consuming joy that shone from her translucent face. Her energy shifted constantly as she looked at Beth for a moment, and then was gone.

Beth blinked.

The room was back to normal but the creepiness had vanished. It was just a shabby room in need of a paint job.

Beth swayed where she stood. Exhaustion weighed her down like lead. Grabbing her bag and keys, she locked up the office and walked back down to the main street.

It was Wednesday and the market was buzzing. Huge fruit and vegetable stalls sprawled all over the pavement alongside vendors selling jewellery, scarves and pottery.

She walked down the street, steering a course between the mums with buggies and elderly people with walking sticks. There was no queue at the stall selling crusty home-made bread and sugary cakes, and the smell of strong coffee from the cafe over the road made her stomach rumble.

Half an hour later the bright sunlight warmed Beth's cold body as she ate her bread on the bench opposite The Monk's Inn, a cup of hot coffee and a thick wedge of carrot cake waiting on the wooden seat next to her. She felt a strange affinity with the place after her experience in the theatre and wondered what that meant.

There was lots of banging and clanking coming from inside the hotel where the builders worked, the usually-shut door propped wide open. Bits of wood littered the pavement outside the building and a skip sat on the narrow road, leaving barely enough room for a car to pass.

'What's going on in there, do you know?' A woman peered out of one of the houses behind Beth. 'We're used to hearing noises from that place, but these ones sound almost normal.'

Beth laughed. 'The owner's doing the place up. You may have a functioning hotel on your doorstep soon.'

The woman frowned. 'I think I'd prefer the ghosts. At least they don't get drunk and throw up in the gutter outside your house.'

Beth tried to smile. Her face just didn't seem to work the same way any more. The woman was friendly, but she seemed to be waiting for Beth to say something and that felt like too much effort.

'I have to go,' she said, packing up her bread.

'Of course, sorry.' The woman stepped back, frowning as Beth got up, crossed the road and slipped through the front door of the hotel.

She picked her way over the debris in the entrance hall, noticing Bill's reception desk was, as yet, untouched.

This time the ballroom was full of workmen, sawing, drilling and banging. The walls were now a smooth cream with cornice detailing. The stage had been rebuilt and technicians hung from above, working on complex lighting rigs. Curtains fell in lush, blue velvet waves at the front of the stage to pool on the shiny, dark-wood floor. The room lacked only the finishing touches. The floor-to-ceiling windows sparkled, but they were bare of dressings. There were no tables and the gleaming bar was unstocked.

'You're the woman who came in the other day.' A familiar man walked over, wiping his hands on his overalls before offering one, still grimy, to Beth. 'Did you find your friend?'

'I did, thank you. How is the renovation going?'

'Astoundingly. They're throwing money at it.'

'And your... visitors?'

The man put his hand on Beth's elbow and guided her into a corner, turning his back to the room so the other builders couldn't hear. 'That girl hasn't cried upstairs since you came. I can't say I'm disappointed. The monks are still here though.'

'Do they bother you?'

'Well, they haven't done anything sinister yet. Most of the men can't see them, but I don't like it when they creep up on me. I don't like being here alone, particularly after dark.'

'How's upstairs going? Have you started up there?'

'Not yet. This room's the priority, I was told. After that, reception. Then we can start working our way through the bedrooms. That way, if we don't finish they can close off part of the upstairs.'

'I guess that makes sense.'

The builder's eyes widened. He nodded at the space behind Beth.

A woman cleared her throat. 'Well, I'm pleased you approve.'

'Amelia,' Beth whispered, hearing the tightness in her own voice. She felt the cold beginning to spread again. She turned. Amelia stood, leaning against the doorframe, ruggedly perfect in her closely fitted overalls and knee-high steel-capped boots.

'I don't know how I could possibly have coped without your validation, darling.' Amelia rolled her eyes and flicked her hair over her shoulder. 'What are you doing here?'

'I'm seeing how things are progressing.'

'How nice.' Amelia inclined her head towards reception and walked out of the ballroom.

Beth considered ignoring her. She didn't want to be in a room alone with this woman ever again. Only her need to keep this job enabled her feet to move, step by step, into the reception area. She looked back over her shoulder at the building chaos. Her fingers tightened on the door handle. Open, the door gave her a link to a room full of people.

'Shut it,' Amelia whispered, her voice hypnotic.

The door slammed.

Beth looked at her hand. Had she done that?

'Did you not get the message last night?' Amelia walked towards her, eyes narrowed.

'I got the message loud and clear that you're powerful and I shouldn't mess with you. I'm just here to do my job, not to cause trouble. Was there something else you were trying to communicate?'

Amelia pursed her lips. 'You're interfering. Do I have to lock you in here too? I assure you, the monks are considerably less friendly than the inhabitants of the theatre.'

'You don't want me here at all?'

'There's no need for you to be here. I am overseeing the work. I suggest you keep to your remit. The hotel will be perfect. Work on that basis.'

Beth forced her face into a tight smile. 'Of course. Anything you say.' She kept her expression benign. She needed to be careful if she was going to continue to help Jonan. But was she? Was it really worth the risk, given Amelia's power?

'You may go. Now.' Amelia's voice rang out, bouncing on the hard edges of the room.

The ballroom fell silent. The door swung open and a sea of faces stared through the opening.

Beth nodded. Slowly, not wanting to turn her back on Amelia, she walked out of the hotel.

She sped up as she left the building, feeling the heaviness ease the farther she got from Amelia. She strode up the hill, past the rows of townhouses and up into George Street with its expensive boutique shops.

Her remit for this event was decreasing by the day. She would be a paper pusher with no influence before long. She felt her face heat as she thought about everyone watching her walk out of the hotel in disgrace. She had been all but fired. Amelia was a mistress of humiliation as well as fear.

She paused as she passed the Third Eye. She saw Jonan standing in one corner, pointing at a shelf of crystals, while he talked to a woman with long dark curls. She remembered the warmth in his eyes when he had looked at her this morning. His barriers seemed to have lifted overnight and she wondered what had come out of that meditation. She'd never even thought to ask.

Her memories of the morning were hazy as though she'd been drunk. She wondered what Amelia had done to her. She still felt so strange. She cringed, remembering how cowed she had been with Amelia this morning. She felt backed into a corner and had done what she could to survive. Now, though, that instinct seemed wildly overblown, and unrealistic.

Jonan looked up. He was smiling as he talked. His eyes widened as he met her gaze. He put his hand on the woman's shoulder, and then walked towards the door, not taking his gaze from Beth.

Beth's heart thudded. Her stomach churned. Thoughts flashed through her mind, one after the other. She saw Jonan, topless, stepping towards her in the dim, smoky room. She saw the look in his eyes, the intensity, the longing. Her heart rate increased further.

Her mind couldn't make sense of what was happening. She stepped backwards. This couldn't be right. Jonan used to make her feel good, but now he was sending her into freefall. Something was wrong.

He was near the door now.

She kept moving backwards, unable to look away.

He was shaking his head, mouthing, 'please' over and over.

She shook her own head, mirroring his movement. Then turned and ran down the street.

'Beth!'

Jonan's voice drifted to her on the breeze. She heard the longing. She knew there was something she should do differently, but her head was so cloudy. She had to get away. How could she work out what was going on when her heart raced so fast and her stomach sent so many warnings to her brain?

The town was busy now. She weaved through the shoppers, attracting a few curses as she knocked into people laden with bags.

The back of her shoulders prickled and she pulled up, looking frantically around her. A small man with pointy features and an over-large hoody stood in a shadowed doorway, watching her. As she met his eyes, he smiled.

A chill shot down her spine and she lurched backwards.

'What do you think you're doing?' an old lady shouted after her.

'Get out of my way,' she breathed, her voice shaky as she forced her frozen body to run towards work.

She took the stairs to the office two at a time, and then slumped into her chair and dropped her head between her knees as she waited for her heart to stop pounding.

'What the hell is wrong with me?' she said, gripping the side of the desk in an attempt to force her hands to stop shaking. She thought back over her behaviour that morning. Had she had some kind of panic attack? Or a breakdown? Why had she felt so afraid of Jonan of all people? And why had she given in to Amelia without even the smallest struggle? What was wrong with her?

She stood up and went into the bathroom, looking at herself in the mirror. She was pale. Her eyes were dark and wide, ringed by smudged circles. She barely recognised her trembling reflection. The features were the same, but the look in her eyes was too alien.

'Pull yourself together, Beth,' she said out loud. 'This is you.'

She fished some lipstick out of her bag, not caring that it was too dark for the pallor that had settled into her skin.

The phone rang.

Beth jumped. *It's Amelia.* The words looped over and over in her mind until she forced herself to grab the handset.

'Yes?' she snapped, hearing anger covering her panic.

'Seriously? That's how you answer the phone when I'm not there?' Charlie's voice was high-pitched.

Beth sighed. 'I'm sorry, Charlie. It's not really. I'm just... jumpy today.'

'Honestly, I don't know what's wrong with you. You do know we're on a tight deadline, don't you? I really can't afford to have you falling apart right now. Go home, sort yourself out, and come back tomorrow with your head back in the game. Can you do that?'

'It's okay. I'm fine.'

'What is wrong with you? You were on another planet this morning, and now you sound terrified. You're usually so gutsy. Are you on drugs?'

'Of course not.'

'Well thank goodness for that. Did something happen?'

Beth paused. She couldn't tell Charlie about Amelia. It wouldn't make sense. She'd never told him about her psychic experiences and this was so much more than that.

'Okay, don't tell me. But either come up with a really good story, or sort yourself out for tomorrow.

'But…'

'Go home, Beth. Go home now, or you're fired.' He slammed the phone down.

Beth gaped. Surely he couldn't do that? That couldn't be legal. Her mind whirred. If she lost her job she would have to move. Laura couldn't afford the flat on her own. Laura would hate her.

The street was still packed, but Beth didn't care. She ambled along, staring at her feet, not seeing the dirty looks she received as people swerved around her.

She pulled up short. The man with the pointy face was standing in the doorway to the coffee shop, staring at her. Stepping backwards, she looked around. When she turned back, he was gone.

'Beth.' The familiar voice tugged at her mind and she tried to focus. Jonan was sitting at a pavement table with a large frothy drink. He put his hands up. 'It's okay. I'll keep my distance. Please sit down. We really need to talk, just for a moment. Here…' He handed her some juice and a piece of cake. 'Have these.'

'Did you see him? That man in the doorway? I think he's following me.'

Jonan frowned. 'Is he still here?'

'No, he disappears every time I get a good look at him.'

Jonan stood up, pulled out the chair opposite his own, and then sat back down. 'Please, join me. He's not here now and I won't let anyone hurt you.' Beth lowered herself into the chair, shifting to be farther away from Jonan. She opened the juice and took a gulp.

Jonan watched her, saying nothing.

'Beth, I think Amelia's done something to you. Do you feel different?'

Beth nodded. 'Of course she's bloody done something to me. I've *never* been like this before. I feel as though I'm going mad.'

'This is what Amelia does.' His voice was soft. 'She controls people through their emotions, spreading a fear that paralyses them until they are completely dependent on her. Once The Fear starts, everything is affected. You stop functioning normally. Start interpreting everything differently, even your own feelings and body.'

Without dropping his gaze, he put his hand on the table, palm facing upwards. For a moment, she felt something old, familiar, a longing to touch Jonan that she thought had gone. She reached out without thinking, tracing his hand with her fingertips. The warmth of his skin started to cut through the haze. She felt a tingling coming from his palm, through her own fingers into her overwrought body. The panic shifted a little. Could he be right? 'Has she changed me forever?'

'No, my love.'

'My love?'

'Come back to the shop with me. Doriel and I can clear Amelia out of your system and get you back to your normal, sassy self. We'll do it now. There's no need for you to hang on to this.'

Beth pulled her hand away. 'You want me to go in there? Into the shop?'

'I do. I want you to come with me and I will keep you safe. Nothing will happen unless you agree to it. Nobody will hurt you. You'll be able to leave whenever you want.'

Beth looked at Jonan, and then blurred her eyes to look at his aura. His energy was filled with pure pink and green.

He wasn't lying.

He was being kind.

She stood up, slowly.

Jonan gestured for Beth to lead the way, staying close as they navigated the crowded market street. He didn't touch her. She felt his energy prickling over her skin. Her heart raced but, for a moment, that freer part of her brain wondered if maybe, just maybe, those feelings weren't fear.

CHAPTER TWELVE

Jonan

THE LOOK IN Beth's eyes sent a stab of pain through Jonan's chest. She looked so frightened. The light that usually shone from her had dwindled to almost nothing. Even her hair had lost its shine, shoved back into a tight twist at the back of her neck. She was dressed head to toe in black, well-fortified against being noticed.

Her hands shook as she clutched them together, her knuckles white from the pressure. He wondered what she had in her past that gave Amelia these emotions to work with. Amelia was able to manipulate people's feelings to an extreme extent, but even she could only work with the traumas and fears people held inside. The less negativity a person carried, the less control Amelia had over them. Beth had been hiding some heavy karma.

As she walked down the main street ahead of him, he watched her movements. Her usually confident stride had shortened into small, tentative steps. Her gaze flickered backwards and forwards as she appraised each person she passed. Since the pavement was packed, this left her with a dizzying number of opponents to measure up. At one point she lost her balance, trying to size up a man who almost escaped her notice. Jonan reached out and steadied her with his hand. She flinched and his heart split a little further. At the fish stall, her nose wrinkled and she quickened her pace as though even the stench was threatening.

There were only two customers in the Third Eye. Jonan ushered them out, murmuring apologies and pushing a bundle of sage at each of them as compensation. The man shot him a filthy look. The woman looked him up and down and then slipped a card into his trouser pocket. His smile was fixed, hard, as he locked the door behind her.

Beth stood by the till watching him deal with the customers. He saw a flicker of annoyance as the woman manhandled him and a little warmth eased the dread in the pit of his stomach.

'Are you locking me in?' she asked, her gaze darting around the shop.

'No, I'm locking them out. I want to be able to concentrate on you without being interrupted by customers, or worried about the shop being looted. I promise you can leave at any time. Look, I'll leave the key right here.' He put the key on the counter, tucked under the lip of a dish of tumbled crystals. Beth would be able to find it here, but it wasn't visible through the windows.

She nodded, her lips curling up at the corners.

Jonan's heart lurched. In her, he saw so many of the other women she had been. He had loved them all. A very loud part of his soul screamed at the knowledge that she was beyond reach and, even with Amelia so close by, he wasn't able to protect her. *She can protect herself*, a voice said in his mind.

Really? he thought back. How's that going so far, do you think?

She is learning. That is as it should be. The words settled in his mind, the truth of them grating at his heart.

Beth hadn't believed him. Now Amelia had done her thing. He hadn't been able to stop it from happening. Would he be able to put an end to it now? Surely Beth would work with him after this? He just had to fix what Amelia had broken, and hope she was willing to risk a repeat performance. Jonan sighed. What were the chances of that?

Doriel followed them up to the flat and closed the door behind them.

Jonan nodded to the sofa and Beth sat down. He saw her gaze dart to his bedroom door and wondered what she was thinking.

'Can I have a word, Jonan?' Doriel said. She was smiling, but her voice was sharp.

Jonan stepped into the kitchen.

'What the hell's going on?' Doriel whispered.

'I have no idea what Amelia did to her yesterday, but she's got into her head. What we did last night hasn't fixed it. Beth's as jumpy as a rabbit and isn't thinking straight.'

'I've never seen Amelia hit anyone this hard.' Doriel shook her head as she peered through the kitchen door. 'She's always been brutal, but look at the amount of dark energy hovering around Beth. It's no wonder she can't think properly. She's operating in a thick fog of fear.' Doriel put a hand on Jonan's arm and he jerked it back, darting a look out into the living room.

Beth was staring into the fire. She didn't seem to have noticed.

'Come on, Jonan. You're the Earth Guide. Have a bit of confidence in yourself. If you get this jumpy Amelia has a real victory on her hands. If Beth's going to lose the fear, she needs you to model the Light. Now, let's get Beth out of the cave Amelia has put her in.'

Jonan nodded. He rolled his shoulders and walked back into the room, kneeling in front of Beth, where she sat on the sofa. Her feet were planted on the seat in front of her, knees hugged in to her chest.

Beth turned her head away, looking at him from the corner of her eyes.

Jonan knew what she was doing. He had used the same technique many times when he was learning to see energy. He didn't blame her for reading him, but her wariness made his heart break. He held his hands out, palms facing up.

'May I?' he asked.

Beth nodded.

Jonan took her hands. They were so small and fine boned that they were dwarfed as he held them, trying to warm her frozen, clammy skin. He closed his eyes, allowing himself to drift into the feeling of togetherness.

The energy was ancient, built over lifetimes. Jonan closed his eyes, feeling his heart opening as he visualised light surrounding them.

Help me to help her. He sent out the thought and felt his heart expand as the room filled with light figures. They drew into a circle with Jonan and Beth at the centre. There were more guides than he had encountered before, and he wondered how many were Beth's.

'What's happening?' Beth whispered.

'What do you feel?'

'I don't know. Normally everything's so clear. Right now, I can feel something going on around me. I think there's someone here, but it's like I'm trapped in a box and I can't see through the sides.'

'That's a good metaphor. Amelia has put you in that box, and right now I'm calling in our guides to help you out of it, if that's what you want?'

'I don't know. Guides can be misleading. They might be trying to trick me.'

'My love, true guides have only your best interests at heart. It's *people* that are misleading.'

'I don't know. How am I supposed to recognise whether or not these are true guides?'

'You will be able to, but right now you're in your box and you can't see. Could you trust me to look after you until you're ready to know yourself?'

Beth's jaw clenched. Her hands balled into fists within his own. 'I don't know.'

What do I do? Jonan sent out the mental call to the beings circling them.

She must decide. You cannot force her. The answer was clear.

His heart sank. But she's not in her right mind.

Amelia does not have the power to take away her sense, only to control which emotions lead it. Beth is fighting her own demons, and she must make her own choices. As an Earth Guide, all you can do is show her the path. It must be her decision to walk down it.

Jonan pulled the light around himself, calling for more protection. Fear pulsed from Beth like the beat of a drum and it ate into his equilibrium, pushing at his boundaries with incessant determination. *Model the light,* he thought to himself. *She must choose for herself; you only need to show her the path. But I have to really show her, not just talk a good sales pitch.*

Jonan stood up, letting go of Beth's hands. He closed his eyes again and reached his arms out wide to the sides.

'Doriel,' he said, his voice resonant as he lifted into trance. 'Join me.'

She stepped out of the kitchen, drying her hands on a blue tea towel. She watched them for a moment, and then nodded, threw the tea towel over the back of an armchair and walked over to Beth.

'I'm just going to stand behind you,' she said softly. 'Are you okay with that?'

Beth nodded.

Doriel waited a moment, before mirroring Beth's nod and lifting her arms wide.

Jonan felt his energy flare as Doriel rose into trance to join him. Doriel was powerful. Her added brightness expanded him further until he had no sense of beginning or ending at all.

Beth tensed at the energies surrounding her, and then her muscles relaxed and she started to breathe more evenly.

The fire flared in the grate. Jonan caught the scent of white sage and wondered briefly whether Doriel had thrown some into the fire. He smiled at her nod and closed his eyes again.

He felt huge as he stood there, towering over Beth, expanding beyond the confines of his own human form. He saw it and felt nothing but love for the vessel that carried him in this lifetime. He had spent so many lives with this woman. They had endured so much pain and fear together and now it hovered around them, polluting the atmosphere and poisoning their own bodies against the spirits that longed to grow.

Some of that fear is mine. Jonan sent the thought into Doriel's mind.

And that you can clear, she sent back. Jonan looked at Beth in his mind's eye. She was small, contracted and surrounded with dark energy. She was shaking, vibrating at such a slow speed that he wondered how she was managing to keep going.

He saw the golden cord that bound them, stretching from his heart to hers. It was bright, but surrounded by murk and he focused on clearing away all that was his, or that did not belong to Beth. As the darkness cleared, her shaking reduced. She expanded a little and looked ever so slightly brighter.

Sensing that more beings had joined, Jonan opened his eyes. Everywhere he looked he saw a version of Beth as she had been in another lifetime. The Beths were everywhere, their cords glowing gold, or muted to a dull darkness.

Jonan allowed his heart chakra to open even wider, seeing pure, pink energy flowing out into the room to every version of Beth. *Please help me*, he called out to them with his mind and felt, rather than heard, their murmur of assent.

The beings created a circle around Jonan and Beth.

Please let me disconnect from my pain so I can help Beth, Jonan called. In response he saw a flicker of images, his own soul through lifetime after lifetime. He saw so many pictures that his heart ached. He saw his own pain reflected back at him over and over, through countless rejections. He focused on love and imagined the fear formed into a thick, grey cord. In his mind's eye, he raised a flaming sword and brought it down on the cord with such force that he shuddered and stepped backwards as it severed. Jonan imagined lighting each end of the cord and watching it burn up until it fizzled out.

You have done well, the beings thought into his mind. One of his guides stepped forwards and started drawing out the energy. Feeling the tension subside he released the breath he had been holding.

When Jonan opened his eyes, Beth was looking at him. Her eyes were bright, her lips parted as her gaze roamed his face and body. 'What happened?' she whispered.

'I released some of my fear. Would you like me to do the same for you?'

Beth

JONAN LOOKED LIKE an angel. He was glowing, his energy so bright and clear Beth had to resist the compulsion to shade her eyes. He was all she could look at in the little room. He felt like home. She felt his energy surround her, warming away the cold numbness and, for a moment, she felt almost like herself again.

'Would you like me to do this for you?' Jonan asked.

She stared at him, wondering how he could make her shine like that.

Then Jonan stepped backwards and her world darkened. Without his energy around her, she fell back into the pit Amelia had put her in, only this time it was worse. This time she saw exactly what that poisonous woman had done. The moment of relief illuminated how badly things had gone wrong.

She clutched at her throat. Her airways constricted. Her heart was ready to burst from the fear that pumped through her system.

She nodded.

Jonan stepped closer. As his energy surrounded her again she gasped, drawing in air like a drowning woman. She sank into the sensations, allowing her eyes to close. She felt

Jonan standing in front of her, his energy so familiar, so bright next to her own, which she now saw was dulled beyond recognition. She felt waves of light wash over her, and then something began to build. She opened her eyes.

Jonan and Doriel stood on either side of her, arms spread wide. Even with her normal sight, she could see their auras glowing with pure white light. She stared, transfixed, as the energy flickered around them, surging towards her, drawing out the heaviness that swamped her soul. She saw herself from the outside, reliving the events of the last few days. As she watched, the pictures floated away, each layer leaving her mind a little clearer.

Jonan and Doriel lowered their hands. Slowly, silently, they stepped out of their positions. Jonan sat next to Beth on the sofa. He leaned back, letting his head sink into the soft cushions, closing his eyes. His body was so close, but it didn't touch her own at all. With the fog lifted, she longed to shift a little closer, but he surely wouldn't want that after the things she had said.

Beth focused on her body, looking for differences, but everything felt normal, just as it should be. Her heart rate was calm. Her mind was clear. She felt none of the panic that had driven her over the past few days. All she felt was embarrassment.

'What the hell was that?' Beth said.

'We cleared away Amelia's interference,' Jonan said. He sat up, pushing his hair out of his eyes. Turning his body towards her, he reached out, brushing her fingers with his own, sending tingles along her skin.

Beth froze.

Jonan moved backwards, giving her the space, she no longer wanted.

She swallowed. 'I really appreciate what you did. I meant, what did Amelia do to me? I don't even recognise the woman I became. She had me shivering and shaking at the idea of upsetting her, being near anybody, even coming in here, for goodness sakes.'

'Amelia doesn't like us.' Doriel sat in the armchair opposite and pulled her legs up, crossing them on the seat. 'We work in opposite directions. She doesn't want you anywhere near us, so she focused your fears to keep you away.'

'She was manipulating me.'

'She was.' Jonan leaned back. Now the glow had subsided she saw the dark circles under his eyes. 'But she can only manipulate the energy you already have. The best way to protect yourself is to get rid of the baggage you're hiding.'

'What do you mean?' Beth drew back. Jumping up, she started pacing as the fizzing began again in her stomach.

'Sit down,' Doriel said, nodding towards the sofa. 'You're getting drawn back in. We've cleared Amelia's energy, but she's triggered your own patterns and now they've come out to play. We need to deal with them, or you'll spiral back down.'

'You make that sound so easy,' Beth said, forcing herself to sit back down.

'That's what I'm here for,' Jonan said, his voice smooth and hypnotic. His eyes were purple in the dim light of the living room and the blue points on the tips of his ears burned more brightly than ever.

'I promised to help you. I have been waiting for this moment my whole life, but I need you to stop pushing me away.'

'I think that's my cue to leave.' Doriel winked as she uncurled from the chair. 'I'll be in the shop if you need me.

You never know, the customers we kicked out might even come back if I'm really lucky.'

There was silence when the door shut behind Doriel.

Jonan sat back in the chair, looking at Beth. There was tension in his jaw and his arms were crossed over his chest.

Beth sighed. 'I can see I'm hurting you, but I have no idea what I'm doing wrong. I'm used to being able to read people, but the rules are different with you. Everything's different and I can't find my balance. I know I was horrible to you over the last few days and I really didn't mean anything I said. Please, will you forgive me?'

'There's nothing to forgive. You're not doing anything wrong, but until we face the anger you felt towards me when you were under Amelia's influence, we're never going to be able to move forwards. What were the emotions that drove you? What made you push me away? What images came into your head when you looked at me?'

Beth thought back through the hazy memories. Already they felt years old, as though they'd happened to her in another life. 'Every time I saw you my heart raced. My skin felt strange. You sent my body into panic and I had no idea why. That scared me.'

'How do I make you feel now?'

'Now?' Beth flushed, but said nothing.

'I'm not trying to trick or embarrass you, but I need to know whether you still experience any of that. I would never hurt you and I don't want to frighten you.'

'You don't frighten me now, but...'

'But?'

'You still make my heart race.'

Beth had never seen Jonan so still. His eyes were dark, his lips parted. He took in a long, ragged breath, and then leaned forwards and took hold of her hand. Without saying a word, he placed it on his chest. The fabric of his top was soft against her skin and she felt the hard, lean muscles underneath. His chest rose and fell with each breath, which grew faster as she held her hand there.

'My heart is racing too.'

'You wanted to keep your distance.' She swallowed, trying to focus on the feel of the sofa at her back, on the floor beneath her feet as an anchor. 'I've been honouring your request.'

'We all make mistakes. We are all capable of being led by fear. Don't let anyone tell you any different. I had my own demons to face. At that moment, I was losing, but I've moved on. You can't possibly imagine how sorry I am that I pushed you away.'

'What happened in those lives you keep talking about?'

Jonan sighed and let her hand drop as he leaned back into the sofa. 'There are so many. We've lived whirlwinds of variables and I haven't seen them all.'

'You're not going to tell me, are you?'

'That's not my place. You'll find out what you need to know in your own time without me planting images in your head.'

'But how do I find out? You told me I needed to clear fear, but I don't know how to do that.'

'You've done enough for tonight. Give yourself a chance to heal from what Amelia did to you. We'll deal with what comes as and when it surfaces.'

Beth sighed. Jonan had moved away and the moment of magic seemed to have passed. She thought back over the conversation, wondering whether she'd done something wrong. She'd been so sure he was about to kiss her.

Her phone rang. She groaned and picked it up.

'Hey, Charlie,' she said using her best professional voice. 'I'm sorry about today. I shouldn't have come into work.'

'No,' Charlie sighed. 'You shouldn't, and you shouldn't have gone to the hotel either. I need you at work for eight o'clock tomorrow. Amelia is coming in and she's not happy.'

Beth sighed. 'I'll be there.' She hung up the phone. 'Did you catch that?'

Jonan nodded. 'I could come with you?'

'I've told you before, I don't need a babysitter. Amelia may have got to me once, but she won't do it again.'

'Will you at least come here afterwards so I can see what state you're in?'

'I'll come as soon as I can reasonably get away. Charlie's in a filthy mood. I think he has a thing for Amelia, so he's not going to like the friction. Apparently, we're going out of business unless we secure her patronage, which doesn't sit well.'

Jonan shook his head. 'There's more to this than I've realised.'

'What about Bill? Where does he fit in to it all?'

'I'm not sure, but I'm bringing him home tomorrow.'

Beth looked around the room and shook her head. 'Where are you going to put him?'

'He can have my room. I'll sleep on the sofa.'

'You offered him a permanent home.'

Jonan shrugged. 'Don't worry about me.' He smiled. 'We've got bigger things to worry about than where I'm going to sleep.'

'Oh no you don't. Stewing over where you and Bill are going to sleep will be like a holiday compared to the prison my mind has been over the past couple of days. And thinking about tomorrow's meeting won't be much better.'

Jonan sighed. 'Of course. This is Amelia you're dealing with. Don't worry, worst case scenario you lose your job and you can always work here. You'd be a natural.'

Beth frowned. Her career had been everything to her but, right now, it felt so unexciting.

There was something surprisingly appealing about the idea of working at the Third Eye. In this space anything seemed possible.

She frowned at Jonan, wondering what he saw. Had that been a throwaway comment, or did he know something she didn't? She had always felt restricted, had always felt she didn't fit in. But in this moment, as her old life started to crumble, the possibilities seemed infinite. She felt the bubbling of a new awareness, a new reality, a new understanding of what she herself might be capable of.

WORKING AT THE Third Eye seemed increasingly appealing as Beth walked to her meeting the next morning.

The day was so full of potential pitfalls and Beth wished she could turn around and go back to bed. She would have to convince Amelia she was still in The Fear. At the same time, she was going to have to placate Charlie, who saw her as putting his only account at risk.

'Where the hell have you been? Amelia is due any moment.' Charlie glared at her as she walked into the office, coffee in hand. He was pale, his eyes bloodshot, his lips too rosy, as though he had been biting them. 'Have I not got through to you how important this meeting is?'

Beth sighed. 'You have, Charlie. That's why I've turned up here at eight when I'm exhausted after being ill. I promised I would be here. I've never gone back on my word. You have no reason to mistrust me.'

'After yesterday I have no idea what to expect from you.'

'Leave it, Charlie,' Beth snapped as she sat down. 'I have apologised enough.'

Charlie stared, eyes wide, mouth hanging open. 'What has got into you?'

'That's exactly what I was wondering.' Amelia's voice sent chills through Beth, and then fire surged through her. She would not bow down to this woman.

She looked her in the eye without flinching. 'Amelia, how nice to see you. I'm afraid I was a bit off-colour when I saw you yesterday, but I'm better now. I'm so sorry if I said anything inappropriate while I was unwell.' Beth held her gaze. *I know what you are*, she thought, trying to project the words to Amelia.

Well, let the games begin. The words formed in her mind. Beth shuddered.

'I'm so pleased you're feeling better,' Amelia said, eyes narrowed, 'but really, I feel your state of mind is inappropriate. You're off the project.'

Beth swallowed. A wave of dizziness encompassed her, but she pushed the woman's energy back, seeing herself grow in stature as she called up a solid wall of light between her and Amelia.

'But…' Charlie's voice was weak. 'You can't, I mean, please don't, I mean, I need her.'

'Of course you don't.' Amelia's voice was quiet, but hypnotic. 'You are the boss. The big guy. You are far more appropriate to head up such a prestigious event. When I asked for Beth I thought she was the best. I was wrong. You are all I need.'

Beth's mind clouded as she listened, but she pushed the murk back. A strange ringing sounded in her ears, and then drifted away when Amelia stopped talking. Beth shook her head and felt clarity return.

Charlie's eyes were glazed and dull. His gaze ranged over Amelia's tight-fitting pencil skirt and asymmetric top. It must have been made from something expensive, because it hung and clung with perfection.

Beth rolled her eyes.

Amelia's lips turned up and she walked over to Charlie, swaying her hips in the figure-hugging fabric. She perched on his desk and leaned in close.

Charlie's eyes glazed as he looked down her cleavage. 'Of course, Amelia. I will do whatever you want.'

'Of course you will.' Amelia stood up and pulled on her long, belted coat. 'I expect you to manage the handover internally. That's where your involvement will end, Beth. I only work with people who are responsive to my... needs.'

'Your needs?' Beth stood up and walked around the desk until she was eye to eye with Amelia. 'Was it your need that I be locked in that theatre after dark? Was it your need that I be turned into an emotional wreak? I'm struggling to see how all of that benefits you.'

'I see your friends haven't enlightened you as much as I thought they would.'

'My friends have plenty to say about you, but I'd like to hear your side.'

Amelia laughed.

The sound woke Charlie from his daze.

'Are we sorted, Amelia? Beth can fill me in on the details, and if there's anything specific you'd like, please do call me. I'll pick up the phone at any time for you, day or night.'

'Well I might take you up on that offer,' Amelia purred.

Charlie swallowed.

Amelia smirked and rolled her eyes. 'Anyway, I'm done. I'll be seeing you, Beth. You can be sure of that.'

The door swung shut behind her.

Charlie and Beth sat in silence, staring at the door as it settled back into position.

'Well,' Charlie said, a little breathless, his face flushed. 'That was certainly an interesting meeting.'

Beth waited for the fury. He had been clear Amelia was the only reason she had a job. Could she really work at the Third Eye?

Charlie's eyes darted around the room as though he were looking for something, checking out the space for risks. 'Show me how far you've got with your guest list. I want to vet it and see if there's anyone who shouldn't be allowed entry. You can't be too careful about who you associate with, you know.'

'But I thought you wanted to raise as much money as possible?'

'I do, but if we bring in people with the wrong ideas, contagion could spread.' He leaned forward, resting his elbows on the desk. His eyes shone with an unnerving light she hadn't seen before. 'Haven't you been listening to Amelia? She said the spirits surround us every minute of every day. She said we won't know who has been contaminated. The only way to protect ourselves is to remain on guard all the time. We need to be wary of anyone different or strange. That's the only way to make sure we're not infiltrated. We have to be strong.'

Beth swallowed. Memories of the theatre shivered through her body with physical force. Even repackaged and spoken in Charlie's voice, Amelia's words had the power to freeze her heart and set her mind reeling. She took a deep breath to centre herself. 'Charlie, where did you hear those words? You were not in the theatre when Amelia spoke them.'

'That performance was televised. Didn't you know? *Everyone* has seen it. I've watched it over and over. I pretty much know it by heart.'

'Why?' Beth shook her head. 'Why would you watch it once, let alone over and over?'

'Amelia is protecting us.' Charlie's gaze darted around the room.

'What are you looking at?' Beth frowned, squinting into the corner, trying to see what he was focusing on.

'I'm just checking for spirits. I don't know what I'm looking for so I have to stay alert. I've never seen a spirit. I didn't believe in them a few days ago. Now I have to be vigilant enough to spot them and protect myself. Do you have any idea how terrifying that is?'

Beth sighed. 'You're fine, Charlie. I have seen and felt spirits my entire life and there are none here today. Please don't put too much store in what Amelia says, she's—'

'What?' Charlie cut across her, his voice shrill. 'You see spirits? I knew you were weird. You've been infiltrated. That's why you have it in for Amelia.'

Beth held her hands up. 'I do not have it in for Amelia and I haven't been infiltrated by anyone or anything. In fact, I am better placed to avoid being messed with, because I know what I'm dealing with. You can trust me, Charlie.'

'Trust? Trust? What is trust?' Charlie muttered, but he turned his face down towards the paperwork on his desk, muttering to himself as he drew his finger down the list of names.

Beth sat back in her chair. Charlie was mirroring her own earlier behaviour, and that knowledge sent chills through her. She remembered that feeling of fear, of suspicion. She felt echoes of it in the energy that wafted from Charlie like poisonous gas.

She gulped at her coffee but it was cold and that just added to the sinking feeling in the pit of her stomach. 'I have to get out of here,' she said, pulling her coat on and heading for the door.

'Hey.' Charlie followed and stood in front of it, his hands braced on either side of the door frame. 'You can't go. I can't do this without you.'

Beth gaped. 'Amelia just fired me and you want me to stay?'

Charlie shook his head backwards and forwards, backwards and forwards. The movement didn't stop, but he barely seemed aware of it. He just kept going, compulsively, talking through the shake. 'I won't fire you. I won't. I need you. Can't do this alone. She doesn't have to see you. Doesn't have to know you're here. You're not hers, you're mine.' He looked up at her, his gaze meeting hers in steely desperation. 'I need you.'

Beth frowned. She scooted her chair closer to Charlie and took his hand in both of hers. It was icy cold and shaking. 'She's right, Charlie. You're the best. You don't need me. I know you're not used to doing the grunt work any more, but remember how you got to where you are now. You've got this. She's your only client and she'll ditch you too if I stay.'

'I'm a salesman. I sell your expertise. I've never organised an event in my life.'

'But I thought…'

He shrugged. 'Yes, well. I may have exaggerated my experience slightly. But I knew I could do *this job*. I'm not supposed to do yours as well.'

Beth took a deep breath. His fear was pounding at her

temples and she was finding it hard to hold her focus. 'So you haven't worked on events at all?'

'I have, but I supported the people planning the events. I didn't run them myself.'

'You supported them by…?'

'Admin mainly.' Charlie looked down at the desk, not meeting her eye.

'And central management don't know this?'

'As I said, I'm a good salesman.' Charlie smirked.

Beth groaned. 'Don't look so pleased with yourself. You're in it deep now. You haven't got a clue, you've fired everyone apart from me, and Amelia hates me.'

'That pretty much sums it up.' The smirk was gone. Charlie's forehead creased as he chewed his lip. His hands were clasped together on the desk. He did nothing to hide their shaking. 'Can you fix it for me?'

'I'm off the project. I need to find a new job.' An image of the Third Eye flickered through her mind. She hoped Jonan had been serious when he suggested she could work there. It wasn't the way she'd imagined her career panning out but, in this moment, it felt like a safe haven.

'You can't be off the project.' His voice was high pitched. 'You have to help me. I'm finished without you.'

'Amelia will know.'

Charlie's chin wobbled.

Beth sighed. The image of the Third Eye flickered, and then was gone. 'Okay, I'll do it, but you have to help me. I'll coach you on how to manage this. I'm not doing all the work and giving you the credit.'

'Anything,' Charlie said.

'And no vetting the guest list. I won't make those kinds of concessions to that woman.'

Charlie paled. He let out a long, controlled breath, and then nodded. 'Whatever you need. And thank you.'

'Here's the file.' Beth dumped it on Charlie's desk. 'Read it. Come up with your own ideas and we can go through them later. I have to go out.'

'But...' Charlie stood up; his eyes glistened. 'You can't leave me.'

'Yes. Yes, I can and I will. Learn the file. I'll be back later.'

She grabbed her bag and bolted through the door. She heard Charlie calling, but didn't look back.

CHAPTER THIRTEEN

Beth

'WELCOME TO *The News at Eight.*' The presenter stood on a blustery street. She pushed a strand of blonde hair out of her face, tucking it behind her ear away from the reach of the wind. 'Three weeks ago, Spirits were confined to spooky Halloween stories, but in record time the threat posed by our unseen visitors has become accepted reality. Today we are in Central London, outside the theatre where renowned super-model, It girl and thought-leader Amelia Faustus explained the measures we should all be taking to protect ourselves.'

She turned at an angle from the camera and thrust the microphone into a woman's face. The woman jolted back-wards, her eyes widening, and then flushed at the over-re-action. She looked into the camera, her gaze darting around, looking for threats, and cleared her throat.

The presenter gave a tight smile. 'You were in the audi-torium when Amelia made her latest announcement. Have you changed your behaviour in light of what she said?'

'Oh yes.' The woman cleared her throat again. 'I am far more careful who I speak to now, and I keep my children away from anyone who seems odd.'

The presenter tilted her head to one side. 'What do you mean by odd?'

'I mean unfamiliar, strange. Anyone who does not look and act like us.'

The presenter took a small step back. 'It has been claimed by some that Amelia's announcement has led to a rise in hate crimes against minorities. Do you have any thoughts on this?'

'I'm not prejudiced; I never have been. But we have to face facts. There is something out there and it targets certain people. We can only keep ourselves safe by remaining vigilant and staying away from anyone who is different or strange.'

The presenter nodded, frowning. 'I'm so pleased you mentioned facts, because I am struggling to find any. If you could share your sources with us, I know we would all be far better placed to protect ourselves.'

The woman stepped back, her eyes wide. 'Amelia is my source. What else do I need?'

The journalist held up a hand. *'Of course, thank you.'*

The picture panned out to show a greying man with red-rimmed eyes standing on the other side of the presenter.

'Sir, can you tell me how Amelia's announcement has impacted you?'

'Have to stay safe,' he muttered, looking into the camera and then away. 'But how? How do we keep away from a threat we can't see? Anyone could be infected. Anyone could be a risk.' He looked the presenter up and down, and then inched backwards, before turning and scuttling off down the street.

She stared after him, her face impassive. 'And there's the rub. How does anyone know how to keep themselves safe?'

'I can tell you.' A girl walked up, long skirts flowing to her ankles, her hair hanging loose to her waist. 'This woman, this Amelia, has poisoned people with her fear. They are punishing those they have lived with happily for decades. Those of us who don't fit the mould are suddenly viewed with suspicion. I had a brick thrown through my window last night. It narrowly missed my eighty-year-old grandmother. How can that be excused in any way? Amelia is poison. She has to be stopped.'

'You have to be stopped,' a voice yelled from the other side of the street. 'Weirdos like you need to be put in your place so you stop infecting society. You need to sort yourselves out or get out.'

The girl pursed her lips. 'You see? This is what it's like, but this is the very least of it. Please don't just follow this woman. Please, hold on to your sense of what is right and wrong.'

The picture cut out.

The newsreader in the studio was still shuffling papers. His eyes widened, but he put the pile down and cleared his throat.

'How have you changed your own behaviour in the wake of the recent revelations? We would love to hear from you. Please do send us your stories and pictures. Now for today's other news…'

'Wow, the woman with the big skirt has lost the plot,' Laura said, stuffing crisps into her mouth. She shuffled round, propping her legs up on the sofa and sliding down to lean her head on the armrest. 'I'd kill to spend time with Amelia. You're so lucky to have met her.'

'Laura, you have no idea what you're talking about. Amelia is not what she seems.'

'Nobody ever is, but she's got more about her than any-one I've come into contact with. Plus, there aren't many celebrities who'd put their names on the line like she's doing. I should know. I work with them every day at the studio. And she is getting loads of flak.'

Beth laughed. 'She's not doing this out of generosity.'

'And you would know this how?' Laura sat up and slammed her bottle down on the coffee table. 'Your psychic powers have told you she's got terrible intentions, that she's out to take over the world and rule it for her own dreadful purposes? Is that it?'

'You'd be surprised,' Beth said, trying for humour, but knowing from the look on Laura's face she'd fallen short. 'Look. I'm not trying to turn you against anyone, or make you agree with me. I'm just asking you to hang on to your own sense of reason and remember not to give up on basic human kindness. As long as you do that, you can't go wrong.'

'You can if you hook up with people who want to steal your soul.' Laura sat up hunching over her knees. 'None of us know who these people are.'

Beth clenched her teeth, forcing herself not to speak. She knew what it was like to be under Amelia's influence. She wouldn't lose a friendship over it. Her heart pounded as she felt that familiar energy ooze from Laura and wash over her. 'I'm off to bed; I'll see you tomorrow.'

'Bethy, don't go, we need to talk about this. I've seen you going into that Third Eye shop and it scares me. You don't know those people.'

'Actually, Laura, I do.' Beth's heart was racing. She clenched her hands into fists in an attempt to stop them shaking. She felt the force of Amelia's energy pushing at her through Laura, but fury bubbled up inside her and she couldn't make herself walk away.

'I know what I brought home when I spent time with Amelia. I know what she did to me, and that I'm still suffering from her interference. I also know who it was that healed me. Amelia is a lot cleverer than you. Make your own decisions, but back off and let me make mine.'

Beth strode out of the room, Laura's open-mouthed shock burned into her memory. Her hands shook on the door handle, but she managed to get it open and race down the stairs. The warren-like building, full of small flats, was stifling. There was no movement, no love in this place. People had either settled here to die or were passing through on their way to somewhere better. She felt the dissatisfaction like a rope around her throat.

The air was cold and crisp and went some way to calming her physical symptoms of panic. She walked over and stood against her tree, her back pressing into the rough bark as she imagined herself growing roots into the grass, grounding herself in the open air, under the stars. She heard a television turned up painfully loud, the sound pulsing through the ground and into her feet. Amelia's voice blared through the wall and chilled her, sending images of the theatre through her mind. She took deep breaths, pushing the pictures back.

The shrill ringing of her phone made her jump, but it brought her into the present. Once again, she became aware of the tree at her back. The wind stung her cheeks, which inexplicably, were wet. She fumbled the phone out of her pocket, nearly dropping it in her attempt to unlock it with cold fingers. It was work, the out-of-hours press line.

'This is *The Daily*. I need a press pass to Amelia Faustus' charity function. Can you courier me one as soon as possible?'

'I'm sorry, what did you say your name was?'

'Oh for goodness sakes. Who I am talking to?'

'This is Beth Meyer, PR for the event. I'll need your name, job title and publication to consider you for a pass.'

There was a furious silence. The man was breathing heavily into the phone. I'm from *The Daily*, for goodness sake.'

'Send me your details. I'll get back to you as soon as I can.'

The man hung up.

The phone rang again. This time it was a woman from the local news, but the exchange didn't go any better.

Beth started walking. She couldn't go home and face Laura right now. She didn't want to be anywhere near the office either. There was only one place left to go.

'ARE YOU COMING in, or are you just going to stand on the street and talk on your phone all night?' Jonan had been watching Beth pace outside his front door for the past ten minutes.

'It's the press. All of a sudden they all want to come to the event. I've tried to keep it quiet, but Amelia must have put out an announcement herself.'

The phone rang again. Beth groaned, and then switched it to voicemail. 'I'm starving. Shall we get some dinner?'

'Love to.' Jonan grabbed his jacket from the hooks behind the desk, stepped outside and shut the door behind him. He locked it, slipping the key into his pocket. 'I didn't want to believe it, but I guess a media storm was inevitable. Amelia has always lapped up media attention, and they love her glamour and drama. Whether they stand with or against her, and I'm sure there will be those on both sides, she's a great story.'

'That's a lot to stand up to.' The pelican crossing started beeping and Beth ducked over. 'Let's go here,' she said, heading into a large French restaurant.

A suited waiter led them to a table in the middle of the room, handed them menus and poured water. 'Can I get you some drinks?'

'Thank you, but we'll look at the menu first,' Beth said, her voice ringing, shockingly loud, across the suddenly silent room.

She laughed as the chat resumed. 'I hate it when that happens.'

'Beth, Beth is that you?'

Beth froze. The voice was so small and hesitant, but oddly familiar. She turned. 'Charlie? What are you doing here? How did you find me?'

Charlie was standing behind her, hands gripped tightly together so that his fingers whitened. His face was pale, his eyes bloodshot, clothes rumpled.

'Charlie, has something happened?'

'It's the spirits. They're coming after me.'

The air around Beth felt heavy, and then suddenly light. An itch danced across the top of her head and she felt an expansion in her chest.

Charlie looked back over his shoulder every few seconds, forehead furrowed. His foot was tapping.

Beth saw his distress, but it wasn't reaching her any more. She looked at Jonan. He was staring at Charlie, but his eyes were glazed. He nodded without looking at her.

'Have you spoken to Amelia about this?' Beth asked.

'I can't.' Charlie shuddered. 'I don't want to bother her.'

'You don't want to bother her?' Beth said, pushing her chair back. 'I thought she was on a mission to protect people in your situation.'

'No.' Charlie's voice cracked. 'She's on a mission to protect people *from* people in my situation, and I'm scared. I've seen what happens to the infected.' Charlie pulled out a chair and slumped into it, his elbows on the table, head hanging.

'You're right.' Jonan's voice was low. 'Amelia uses people until they pass their sell-by date. If you've crossed that line, it may be time to walk away.'

'Don't say that.' Charlie slammed his hand down on the table. He glared at Jonan, his red-rimmed eyes wide, jaw set. 'You have to help me.' He turned to Beth. 'You told me you understand spirits. Make them go away so I can carry on as normal.'

Beth looked over at Jonan.

Jonan sighed. 'Charlie, there are no spirits attached to you. Amelia has manipulated you. She's made your own fears feel foreign, and that makes you fear anything different. We can help you, but you need to understand: Amelia is not telling you the truth.

'She's not lying. She's protecting us.' Charlie's jaw was tight now. His face was flushed and his hands clawed around the edge of the table in a death grip. 'Who is this man, Beth? Why are you with him?'

'He is my friend and you should listen to him. He knows what he's talking about. You don't have to do this event. Walk away. No job is worth this, Charlie.'

'If I do that, we'll both be out of a job.'

Beth shrugged. 'So be it. I'm out of a job anyway. Your only client refused to have me on her account. You'd find something new without any problem. It's the best thing for you, and you know it. You could go to a company that isn't fighting for its life. Go somewhere with big budgets and huge clients. This company is done.'

'This,' Charlie said through gritted teeth, 'is going to be the most important charity event ever held in St Albans. It may be the most important event held ever. But you know it will fold without someone organising it. Why are you trying to sabotage it? What do you have against Amelia? Are you in league with the spirits?' Charlie's gaze was flickering around the room, his breathing fast. Even Jonan's protections weren't enough to stop Beth feeling this amount of fear and her heart was starting to pound. This was not going to work. Amelia had him too firmly in her grip.

Beth sighed. 'No, Charlie, I'm not. And I'm sure you're right. Ignore me.'

Charlie slumped. He nodded, his head hanging heavy as though he wanted to fall asleep where he sat. 'Well, good.' He looked up at Jonan. His eyes narrowed. 'I still don't know who you are.'

'I'm someone who can help you feel normal again, if you want me to.' Jonan was so still he didn't appear to be breathing. He radiated a magnetism that outshone his chiselled features. He was otherworldly.

Beth's breath caught.

Charlie jumped up, tensed now in spite of his earlier lethargy. He backed away, wringing his hands in front of him.

'If you change your mind, Beth knows where to find me.' Jonan spoke quietly, but his voice carried across the restaurant like a wisp of smoke.

Charlie swallowed, nodded, and backed all the way to the door. Then he was gone.

Beth sighed. 'She's got to Charlie now. She's hemming me in, throwing me off the project, but not leaving me a free exit. I can't do right, can I?'

Jonan shook his head. 'Not by Amelia, but you can do right by everyone else.'

'By Charlie?'

'I'm not sure about Charlie. He has so much fear circulating through his system that everything you say will feel like a threat unless you agree with him. The best thing we can do for Charlie is to deal with Amelia.'

There was a crash from the doorway. Beth frowned and scooted her chair backwards. 'That's the man who's been watching me,' she whispered. 'The one in the doorway with the pointy face and the hood. Do you see?'

He was arguing with a large, waiter, gesticulating wildly. He pointed at Beth, but the waiter shook his head. Suddenly he made a dash for Beth. His hood fell back from his face, exposing greasy hair shoved back from his pale, stubble-lined face. He shoved a phone in Beth's face.

'Tell me, what's Amelia's secret?' he demanded, looking back over his shoulder at the waiter closing in on him. 'Tell me, Beth. I know you know something. What happened in that theatre when you were alone with her? Why were you there for hours after she'd left? Are you in league with her? What are you planning?'

'You've been following me,' Beth said, her voice steady despite the adrenaline pumping through her system.

'I'm sorry, ma'am.' Another waiter, even larger than the first, strode up to the table. 'He won't bother you again.' The two men hooked their hands under the man's armpits and hauled him out.

'You know something!' he yelled as they dragged him towards the door. 'That woman is evil and if you don't speak up, you're no better than she is.'

'We have to go after him,' Beth whispered to Jonan. It felt as though the whole restaurant was watching her.

The waiter came over, pad in hand, and raised his eyebrows. 'Can I get you anything to drink?'

'I'm sorry, I need to speak to that man. Thank you so much for your help. No need to keep the table for us.' She stood up and pulled her coat on.

'Are you sure?' Jonan said, standing up. 'That man was under Amelia's influence too. I could see it. He is probably coming more from fear than knowledge.'

'I'm sure, but he's been following me and I want to know why.'

Jonan nodded to the waiter. 'Another time.'

Beth wanted to duck her head as she walked out the door, to avoid the inquiring looks of other diners, but Jonan held his head high, smiling at everyone who met his gaze. A kind of glow surrounded him. It was invisible to most, but people watched him anyway, drawn irresistibly to him.

Outside, the sky was clear and black, the stars undimmed by the street lamps nearby. The black-and-white Tudor buildings looked wonky at the best of times, but now the shadows made them look weirdly malformed. Jonan's hand found hers, the warmth grounding her as she stepped into the silvery shadows of the full moon.

Beth squinted down the road in both directions. 'We have to find him,' she murmured to herself.

'You mean the man we just threw out?' One of the waiters came up behind her.

Beth nodded.

'He's over there in the doorway to that shop. He's been waiting for you, I guess. We've called the police so he won't be there long. I suggest you stay inside. Eat something. Drink. We'll let you know when it's all done out here.'

'Thanks, but no.' Beth started out into the street.

A horn blared. Brakes screeched as a car spun out of nowhere, just stopping before it hit her.

Beth barely registered Jonan's hoarse shout, or the yelling of the driver. She had seen the man. He was in the doorway of an old Tudor shop, hands shoved in his pockets as he watched her. His face was blank.

His thin lips spread into a tight smile as she approached. His hair was once again hidden under the hoody that shadowed his features, but the expression on his face as he yelled at her in the restaurant was branded into her memory. His clothes all seemed too big, as though they were hand-me-downs from an older and larger brother.

'What do you know?' Beth asked, stopping in front of him.

'I know you were at the theatre,' he snarled. 'I was there, waiting at the door. I saw you go inside, but you didn't come out. At all. Amelia left by a side door, a scarf wrapped around her head, huge sunglasses covering her face as though she were some 1950's film star. She signed a few autographs, posed for selfies with the girls who had been waiting by the stage door, and then disappeared. I have no idea how, but one minute she was there, and then she was gone.' He glared at her, hands clenched into tight fists at his sides.

Beth stepped back at his anger. 'Are you press?' she said, narrowing her eyes.

The man laughed. 'Do I look like a journalist?'

Beth studied him for a moment. 'No, you don't.'

He advanced on her, pulling himself up straight, pushing his shoulders back and owning his full height. 'Why are you protecting her?'

Beth laughed, but it was hollow. 'Protecting her? I'm not protecting her. Why are you watching her?'

'That nasty, fear-mongering parasite? Let's just say I have

my own reasons to hate Amelia. Are you saying you're not working with her?'

'Absolutely not!' Beth said. 'I'm trying to stop her.' She turned to glance at Jonan. He was standing behind her, his whole focus on the man. Switching to psychic sight, she saw him reaching out his energy, trying to calm his aura.

'Stop it!' The man retreated into the shadows of the doorway. 'I know what you're doing. You manipulating people's energies to get your own way. You are like her.'

'No,' Jonan said, putting his hands up and stepping backwards. 'I'm not like her at all. I can help protect you from Amelia. I can help you clear her interference.'

'And then I'll be stuck with your interference. I'll do this on my own, thank you very much. Keep away from me. I just want to speak to Beth.'

'It's okay, Jonan. He won't hurt me.' Beth took Jonan's hand for a moment. He looked at her, surprised as her fingers closed over his. She squeezed, nodding in what she hoped was reassurance. 'I've got this.'

Jonan stepped back several paces.

'What do you want from me?' Beth spread her hands wide.

'I want to know Amelia's secrets. I want everything. Every bit of dirt on her spotless white suits. I want to know every bad thing she's done, and every bit of damage she's inflicted. Then I'm going to make her suffer. She's going to pay for what she did to me.'

'What did she do to you?'

'She took my Molly.'

'Molly?'

'My wife. Molly was always happy and sociable. She was the one people turned to when they were down and needed picking up. She worked at the Children's Refuge helping kids who had nothing. That was what she lived for, helping those kids, and having a family of our own one day.' He looked at the ground and swallowed. 'Things had been particularly tough for a while. Times were hard and there were a lot of kids in need. The charities had to work overtime to try and make any difference at all.' His voice was quieter now, hoarse with emotion. When he looked up at Beth, his eyes were red. 'When Amelia joined the charity as an Ambassador and offered support to the workers, it felt like a dream come true. Molly wasn't interested in celebrities, but she was enamoured by Amelia. She talked about her all the time. That was fine, at first, until the stories got weirder and weirder. This was a long time before Amelia did that damn interview, but she was talking about spirits even then.' He paused, eyes closed as he took a few deep breaths. 'She had Molly terrified to go out, scared of meeting people through work. My social butterfly turned into a hermit. She cried night after night. Amelia visited often, but Molly was always worse after she left.'

He leaned back against the wall, his throat working as he tried to keep his breathing controlled. When he started speaking again, Beth moved closer, leaning in to hear his cracked whisper. Then one day she was gone. She'd left a note saying she'd she didn't trust me anymore. She thought I had been taken over by spirits. I have no idea where she went. I relive that moment, over and over again. It haunts me every moment, waking and sleeping. She was everything, all I had. Our family was yet to come. Amelia stole her soul, poisoned her imagination and left her unable to think herself out of her mental prison. She obliterated the lives we were supposed to live.

Beth knocked a tear from her cheek and cleared her throat, but it was still hoarse. 'I'm so sorry. I knew she was poison, but this...' She shuddered.

The man shrugged his shoulders. 'Amelia's clever enough to cover her tracks every step of the way. Her fingerprints aren't anywhere because she doesn't touch with her physical hands. Her impact is far more sinister. My life is ruined. And I want to ruin her.'

'What's your name?' Beth asked, stepping closer.

'None of your business.'

'Listen, I agree with you about Amelia, but I don't have anything to tell you. I am doing what I can to stop her, but I want a positive solution from this, not mass hysteria. Giving you dirt to bash her with won't solve anything.'

The man glared at her, and then his shoulders slumped. 'If that's all you have to say, you'd best stay out of my way.'

He strode towards her and would have walked straight into her if she hadn't stepped to the side at the last moment. She watched him walk away, shoulders hunched, head down into the wind.

Beth shivered and wrapped her arms around her middle. 'The game has changed,' she said, not moving.

Jonan stepped forwards and put his arm around her waist, pulling her into his warmth. 'We can't fix this tonight. Tomorrow we'll bring Bill home. Come back to mine. I'll cook. Doriel's out. It's a rare chance for some peace and quiet.'

'Do you want me to leave you to it? To your peace?'

Jonan reached up and stroked a strand of hair away from her face. 'I'd rather you didn't, but if you want to go home, I'll walk you.'

Beth's heart was pounding. She shook her head. She'd

been to his house so many times. She'd even slept in his bed, but they'd never really been alone. The cramped quarters upstairs were difficult with three, would be impossible with four once Bill arrived. 'No, I'll come with you.'

CHAPTER FOURTEEN

Beth

THE FLAT WAS dark and quiet, quieter than Beth had ever felt it. Doriel wasn't noisy but her presence had a definite buzz that electrified the room.

With her gone, Jonan's energy felt so much stronger. It enveloped Beth, wrapping her in a sense of safety she hadn't felt before.

Her heart beat fast, but without Amelia's interference, she knew it wasn't fear. She fell into the feeling, allowing herself to recognise the joy and anticipation that had been hidden underneath gnawing anxiety.

She felt her energetic connection to Jonan. Whenever he moved, she sensed him as though he were an intrinsic part of herself. They shifted around each other. Every mundane movement became beautiful as their link intensified.

Jonan lit the fire, and then moved through to the kitchen and started taking a rainbow of vegetables out of the fridge, green, red, yellow and deep purple. He found a small knife in a drawer and started chopping. 'There's wine on the rack in the lounge. Why don't you open a bottle.'

'I don't know anything about wine.'

'It's okay, pick anything. It's all there to be enjoyed.'

Beth went back into the sitting room and looked around. She had never noticed a wine rack but, sure enough, there it was tucked in the corner next to Jonan's bedroom door. She pulled a bottle from one of the slots, and then went back into the kitchen and opened it with the corkscrew that lay on the worksurface. Delicious smells were starting to waft around the kitchen as the pan sizzled.

She poured the wine and handed Jonan a glass. He sipped it. 'Hmm, good choice.'

'How long have you lived here with Doriel?'

'Oh, for an age.' Jonan shrugged. 'I moved here shortly after I started the job. There's a certain freedom in sharing a space with another intuitive.'

'Wow, I can imagine. That would be a dream.' Beth sighed. 'I've been friends with Laura for a long time, but she's a drain. She only talks about herself and I always feel tired when I'm with her.'

'People like us attract people like Laura.' Jonan threw a handful of asparagus into the wok. 'But you don't have to live with them.' He winked.

Beth laughed. 'True, although the deed is done now.'

Jonan leaned back against the kitchen counter. He gazed at Beth, head tilted to one side. 'Life can be better. Your life could be magical.'

Beth swallowed.

The silence was so complete she felt frozen to the spot. The air was thick with energy. Her heart pounded. She took a deep breath as Jonan stepped towards her, reached out one hand, touching her fingers lightly with his own. She felt a jolt of electricity at the contact and released herself a little more into the current that fizzed between them.

There was a crash.

Jonan started. He frowned at the tinkling of broken glass. 'It's coming from the shop. Stay here.'

In a few steps he was out of the kitchen, across the small living room and onto the stairs, grabbing a long, sharp umbrella from a stand as he went.

For a moment Beth just stared, and then she grabbed the knife Jonan had been using to cut vegetables and weighed it in her hands. It was small and flimsy, nothing like the knives people armed themselves with in films. This one felt as though it would barely be equal to cutting a carrot.

She gripped the flimsy knife in her right hand and ran down the stairs on the balls of her feet. She stopped at the bottom and heard raised voices. Shielded by the staircase wall, she peered around the door.

A large man, twice the size of Jonan, with short dark hair, wearing black joggers and a hoody stood facing her. His muscled legs were planted firmly apart, his knees slightly bent as though he were preparing to fight. He clutched a large black fabric sack in one hand, and held a two-foot-high wizard carved from amethyst in the other. The glass cabinet to his left was smashed and a metal shelf stack lay diagonally across the floor in front of him, smaller crystals scattered everywhere. Jaw set and protruding, he glared at Jonan, but his shoulders were high round his ears and his skin was pale and glistening.

Jonan stood with his back to Beth, relaxed in socks and jeans. He leaned on the umbrella, a smile on his face, showing no signs of stress.

The man's gaze flickered up towards Beth. Jonan turned. His eyes widened as he spotted her. He paled and shook his head as a frown creased his forehead.

Instead of retreating, Beth stepped out into the shop. 'Looking for a Christmas present for someone, are we?'

The man sank into his knees, swaying slightly from foot to foot. 'Who are you?'

'I think you've got that wrong,' she said, leaning against the wall. 'I'm supposed to be here. Who are you?'

The man's gaze flickered down to the sack and the carved crystal. 'No need to go in to that. I'm done here.'

Jonan stepped closer, resting one hand on a bookshelf. 'You've got what you wanted, have you? Ready to make a packet with your loot? There's one thing you haven't considered though. With Amelia casting aspersions on everyone outside the mainstream, crystals aren't exactly doing a roaring trade right now. You're more likely to be branded a threat than paid handsomely for your efforts. Unless, of course, someone sent you here with instructions?'

Jonan looked relaxed; his body wasn't braced for any kind of struggle. His eyes were unfocused. He leaned up against the shelf of books now, as though he were simply chatting about the weather. Tuning into her psychic sight, Beth looked deeper. His energy was huge, radiating out to fill the room and beyond. It shone a bright white and gold as he filled the space around him. His space.

The other man's energy was as contracted as his body was huge. A dull, muddy colour, it swirled visibly around his tense muscles, stirring up the fear that so obviously held them rigid. She saw a ball of dark energy hovering around his solar plexus. A strand of it reached into his body. She sensed the echoes of it all around her, in the fear that pulsed through and out of him.

'Is this Amelia's work?' she said. She stepped closer but saw him tense even further and froze. She remembered the paralysis vividly, knew deep in her bones how volatile he was right now.

Jonan nodded.

'If you don't mind me asking, sir.' Beth kept her voice neutral. 'I'd like to know what you're afraid of?'

'Him,' the man hissed, pointing at Jonan. He stepped back. 'He's one of them, I can smell it.'

'One of whom?' Beth took another step forward.

'Get back!' the man said from between gritted teeth. 'Get away from me. Don't even think of touching me. I won't hesitate to flatten you if you try.'

Beth held her hands up and stepped back.

'You clearly came here to rob me.' Jonan's voice was low, his posture neutral, but his eyes were narrowed on the man's face and his jaw was tight. 'But that doesn't explain why you're still here.' He straightened, and then stepped forwards, slowly. 'I could have you arrested for trespass.' He paused.

The man's chest was heaving. His lower jaw protruded and a vein throbbed in his neck.

'Leave now.' Jonan's voice was quiet. 'Tell Amelia that if she has any questions she can contact me directly. She has my phone number.'

The man pressed his lips into a thin line. 'Amelia does not appreciate being threatened.'

'Nobody appreciates being threatened, me included. Now, give me my crystals back and get out.' Jonan jostled the door so it jingled.

The man shook his head. 'You're just as she described you.' He looked Beth up and down. 'Watch yourself, girlie.'

'Girlie? Are you kidding me?' Beth raised her eyebrows. 'Amelia's really done a number on you.'

He opened his hands, smirking as the crystals dropped to the floor. The wizard carving smashed with a crack that reverberated through Beth's bones. Shards of crystal flew across the floor. He strode out of the shop. Pausing outside the door, he took out his phone and looked the building up and down as he started talking into it.

Jonan

JONAN SLAMMED THE door shut and pulled the bolt across. Looking around the room, he sighed. It was only stuff. He had to remember that it was only stuff. Nobody was hurt. He did a mental tally of the damage. The shelves weren't broken but too many of the crystals were. Finances were tight enough already without this kind of loss. He squatted down and picked up the single intact piece of the wizard, weighing it in his hands.

'Was it worth a lot?' Beth put a hand on his arm.

'A few thousand pounds.'

'Ouch.'

Jonan sighed as he put the fragment on the desk, and then opened a cupboard and took out a broom.

'Shouldn't you leave the evidence for the police?'

'The police? We didn't have much luck with them when the brick was thrown through the window. I can't see why they'd be any more interested now.'

'That can't be right. Look at this place.' Beth stretched out her arms. 'They have to be interested in this.'

Jonan frowned. Something glinted on the floor, something shiny. 'What's that?'

He reached it in two strides, bent down and picked it up. It was an old-fashioned Polaroid shot. Bill stared out of the picture, eyes dark and pleading. His skin was pale and waxy. Sweat gleamed on his forehead as he tried to stagger upright. He was in a dark room. Jonan flicked on the overhead light to see better. 'It's Bill,' he whispered.

He moved the picture closer as he tried to pick up something in the man's surroundings that might help locate him, but the bare brick wall and concrete floor could be anywhere.

A hand touched his arm, and he felt Beth lean into him, peering at the photograph. 'That doesn't look like the hospital,' she said, her voice hoarse.

Icy fingers shot down Jonan's spine. 'No. It doesn't.'

Jonan put the picture down and picked up a box of matches from the payment desk. He took three cream-coloured candles in metal tins from the side of the desk and spaced them evenly across the glass. He lit them, and then put a stick of sage into one of the flames. When it caught, he breathed in deeply, and then put it in a brass cup with a bed of herbs in the bottom.

'What are you doing?' Beth asked.

'I want to see what I can pick up from the photo, but I'm pretty scattered right now. The candles and sage are to help me centre.'

'I can help.' Beth took his hand and closed her eyes.

Jonan felt the knot in his chest ease as her warm fingers closed around his. He closed his eyes, feeling the drop into trance as a welcome relief from the incessant challenges of physical life. At first there was peace and he felt a fizzing connection travelling up his arm from Beth's hand. He focused beyond that into the air around him and the stones that lay smashed across the floor. He felt the energy of the intruder, saw Amelia's imprint on him, and the fear and confusion that seemed so at odds with his size and confrontational demeanour. Jonan searched further, focusing on the photo and on Bill.

He could see Bill in his mind's eye now, could feel his agitation. He could see the bare brick wall, feel the cold, hard concrete biting into Bill's bony kneecaps. Bill looked up and seemed to recognise Jonan. His lips moved, but Jonan got no sense of what he was saying. *What is happening?* Jonan sent out the thought.

The answer didn't come from Bill, but from one of Jonan's guides and he repeated the words aloud for Beth's benefit. 'Bill is in trouble. He has been moved to a place that is less in line with his personal wellbeing. He is trying to send a message to you, but is not practised enough in the art of telepathy. Urgh,' Jonan groaned, opening his eyes and doubling over to lean on his thighs. His heart raced and stomach rolled from the fear that still poured through his connection to Bill.

Beth's eyes widened. 'What's happening? Are you okay?'

'I'm fine, but Bill's fear is potent and hard to throw off.'

'If Bill can't contact you, can you contact him?'

'I tried, but there's too much fog around him. Amelia's got to him. He won't hear anything helpful through that.'

'Maybe Amelia has him at the hotel?'

Jonan nodded. He took his leather jacket from the hooks by the door, pulled it on and shoved the polaroid into his pocket. 'There's only one way to find out. Shall we go?'

Beth let out her breath in a rush. 'Yes. At last, something we can actually do.'

It was eleven o'clock and the temperature outside was dropping. There were still plenty of people milling about outside the shop, drinking and laughing. For most people it was a normal Friday night.

Beth wished she were one of them. She couldn't help the feeling Amelia was closing in on them with a stranglehold. Everywhere they turned, they found her. She talked through the press, sent intruders into their space, and got into the hearts and minds of their friends and the people on the street. She was in the newspapers, in people's conversations. As they walked, they heard her name repeated from so many lips, Amelia, Amelia, Amelia.

'If I hear one more person say her name, I'm going to scream.' Beth hugged her arms around her middle against the cold.

Jonan took her hand.

She froze, but warmth spread from his fingers into hers, and up her arm. The world receded as her awareness focused in to that single point of contact.

She hadn't even realised she'd stopped walking until their arms stretched, and then he stepped back towards her. His approach shielded her body from the prickling cold of the night air, setting it alight with warm awareness. She looked up.

His blue eyes were dark pools that drew her in so she couldn't look away.

'You're not frightened of going to the hotel, are you?' He reached up, brushing a strand of hair away from her face.

'Ghosts don't scare me.'

'But ghosts didn't take Bill from the hospital.'

'No, they didn't.'

'It's okay to be scared. We've had a crazy night and we don't know what we'll find at the hotel. My heart is racing too.'

He took her hand and placed her palm on his chest, over his heart. She felt it beating fast through the rough weave of his shirt, felt warmth gathering between them. Their bodies blocked out the wind and her hand was sheltered by the stiff collar of his leather jacket. She felt the heat of his body through her palm and the prickling of his energy where it touched her own. His heart beat in unison with hers. She had never felt so connected to her body, or so separate from the world around her. There was only Jonan.

He moved closer. She froze as a stab of fear shot through her, but she pushed it back. She would not give Amelia the power.

Jonan winced. He closed his eyes tightly and took a deep, shuddering breath. Then he stepped back.

'No, please, I'm just nervous. It doesn't mean anything.'

Jonan opened his eyes and searched her face. 'I don't want to frighten you. I have no idea how far she pushed her fear into you.'

'I want this, Jonan.'

'Are you sure?'

She nodded, closing the space between them. Her long coat was a barrier she didn't need, didn't want. It stopped her from feeling his warmth against her, but she recognised his energy, felt the prickling against her skin under her clothes. She closed her eyes, immersing herself in the feeling of being this close to Jonan. She felt as though she had been waiting for this moment her whole life, as though something connected them across timelines she didn't even know were there. She recognised Jonan at a bone-deep level, and yet she marvelled that they had met so recently. This moment was all there was. She would never let it go.

His lips were feather light when they brushed hers, sending tingles across her skin. She leaned into him and felt him relax, pulling her close as she melted into him, losing her sense of where she ended and he began.

She felt his thumbs on her palms, marking spirals on her skin, felt his lips trace her jaw as she leaned into him.

'Get a room,' a male voice shouted and the rowdy laughter jarred her out of the trance.

Beth shook her head as the men passed, tripping over each other as they wove drunkenly across the pavement.

Jonan pulled her into his side.

'Did Amelia get to you too?' Beth whispered, leaning into his body.

His breath caught. 'Yes,' he said, his voice rough. 'In another lifetime, but it's one I remember well.'

'Was I there?'

'You were.'

Beth nodded. Something was fizzing below the surface, a pain deeper than any she had experienced in living memory.

'Don't block it,' Jonan said, pulling her in front of him. His eyes were hooded, blank, as he gazed at her. 'Let it in, through and out.'

'But I'll be vulnerable.'

'You're already vulnerable. Awareness makes us strong. She plays on people's blind spots.'

Beth nodded. She took a deep breath, leaned into Jonan, and sank into the energy.

She felt the screams. Didn't know whether they were hers or someone else's. They seemed to envelope her, permeating and surrounding her like a whirlpool that dragged her under.

As the picture cleared, she saw the woman standing in front of her, saw the flaming torch. The look in the woman's eyes was so familiar, it sent fingers of ice threading their way down her spine as the cold spread through her body, fighting the heat that seared the skin on her face.

Her throat hurt. The screams must have been her own. Her voice was hoarse now, dry, burned from the choking smoke and the ash that surrounded her as the wood burned.

Other shouts rose in volume as her own drifted away. She heard the voice of her beloved, heard the pain and anguish as his deep voice cracked, broke her open so her sadness filled the fire, fanning the flames with greater fuel.

She felt the relief as she left her body, her energy drifting to the man on his knees by the fire, held back from the flames by the guards. She surrounded him, wrapping her energy around him like a blanket as he wept and keened. She felt his shudders as he broke apart in grief, as pain wracked his body and soul, leaving scars that would hold through lifetimes.

She watched as her body screamed one more time, wishing she could tell her beloved that she felt nothing now, that her pain was over despite the death cries that shook her physical frame. She felt him convulse with the body that was no longer hers. Then, as she crumpled into the flames, he collapsed, spent and unconscious on the ground.

She felt the touch of his energy on hers. She didn't need to look: she felt him so completely as their vibrations blended in the shimmer of the heat haze from the fire.

'It is done,' she thought to him, knowing he heard her. She felt his grief, his understanding, the pain at their parting.

'I won't remember this,' he sent into her mind.

She opened her heart to his. 'No, but try to feel me. I will always be with you.'

He fought as his energy drifted back to his body, but that only made the pull greater.

'I love you. Always.' She sent the words to surround him

like a mist, as he settled back into his body, shuddering as he woke to his new, broken reality.

'It is done.' The words vibrated through her energy as she felt the pull of the light.

'Oh please, no!' Beth slumped in the cold night air, feeling the warmth of Jonan's arm around her waist, holding her upright.

'Here, there's a bench. Let's sit for a moment.'

Beth sank onto the rough, cold slats, hugging her arms around her middle. The moon was huge and round above her in the black, inky sky. She closed her eyes, still seeing the flames, feeling Jonan's grief.

'Did that really happen?'

'Yes,' he whispered and the pain was still raw in his voice. 'It happened. Did anything come into your mind as you watched? Does it connect with now in any way at all?'

Beth closed her eyes and took a deep breath, eyeing the scene from a distance this time. 'Amelia. She committed me to the flames. We've been here before.'

'We have, but this time it will end differently. The only way I will lose you this time is if you walk away.'

Her breath caught as he kissed her again, pulling her close. 'Is that a promise?' she murmured as he pulled back to look at her.

'It's an intention,' he said. 'Come on, let's go and find Bill.'

CHAPTER FIFTEEN

Beth

THE MONK'S INN was dark and Beth felt a cold dread settle in her stomach as they approached. There didn't seem to be anyone nearby, but she felt the skin prickling on the back of her neck and kept turning to look behind her. There was nobody there.

Jonan reached for the handle, but the door didn't budge. 'Is there another way in?'

Beth walked to the side of the building and tried a small, dilapidated, wooden gate. It creaked open. 'I'm not sure where this leads, but it's worth a try.'

The path on the other side of the door was narrow with a dirty, whitewashed wall on one side, and a high wooden fence on the other. There was rubbish on the floor and Beth stopped as a rat ran across the path just in front of her.

There was a door at the back. It gave way a little, and then opened as Beth pushed it, scraping along the floor as though something heavy leaned up against the opposite side.

Voices came from deep inside the building.

Beth reached out, grasping Jonan's hand. She nodded. 'Let's go.'

They walked through a narrow hall and into the main reception area. It was dark apart from a crack of yellow light around the edges of the door into Bill's living room.

'Look!' Beth whispered, her heart pounding. 'He's there. He's in his room. He must have got away.' She let go of Jonan's hand and reached for the handle. 'Bill? Are you in the there?'

A flash of light blinded her as the door swung away. She almost overbalanced, swaying back, away from the light.

'Well, look who it is!'

A shot of fear burned down Beth's spine, settling in the pit of her stomach. She pushed it back. She would not let this woman control her.

Amelia raised her glass and laughed. 'Come in, little mouse,' she said, gesturing into the room. 'Pour two more glasses of bubbles, Rolo.' A man in a white suit nodded, stood up from Bill's faded old armchair, and walked over to the table of drinks on the other side of the small room. There were already several discarded bottles, and a magnum sat open in the ice bucket.

He was familiar, but Beth couldn't place why. His dark hair was cut short and styled off his face, accentuating the dark, slanted eyebrows that characterised his rounded face. His suit would have been too fitted, if it hadn't been for his well-built but lean physique. As it was, it drew her gaze towards the biceps that almost stretched the fabric of his sleeves. She wondered if she would stand any chance at resisting him if it came to a struggle.

He poured out the drinks, crossed the room and handed them each a glass.

Amelia raised her glass and inclined her head. Her hips swayed in her purple silk jumpsuit as she walked over to the man, hooking one leg between his and leaning against him in a pose designed to be artful rather than comfortable. She angled her foot to show off her delicate ankle and the black stilettos that showed her toe cleavage and ended in two sharp points at the front of her foot. She looked like a fairy-tale enchantress.

'Amelia,' Jonan said, nodding and raising his glass.

'Jonan, how nice to see you. You look as ravishing as ever, darling. Has this little mouse snapped you up yet? Or is she too timid?'

Beth frowned. 'I hadn't had a timid moment in my life until you messed with my head.' She kept her voice calm, but her fingernails dug into her palms as she clenched her fists at her sides.

'Ignore her.' Jonan took one of her hands, and threaded his fingers through hers, forcing her to relax her grip. He turned to Amelia, who had unhooked her leg but was still leaning into the man. Jonan's jaw tensed as he looked at him. 'Where's Bill?'

'Bill? That old fool?' Amelia's high-pitched laugh made Beth wince. 'How the devil would I know?'

'He's disappeared.'

'Well, good riddance.'

Beth forced her face into a smile. 'You don't know where he is?'

Amelia gave an elaborate sigh. 'You seem to think I'm some kind of criminal, Beth. A mafia boss or something. But I'm just a silly celebrity.'

'I know exactly what you are.' Jonan's voice was soft.

Amelia licked her lips.' You always were a pain in my backside, Jonan.' Amelia straightened, and then walked over to Jonan with exaggerated slowness, her hips swaying from side to side as she put one heeled foot directly in front of the other. She stopped in front of Jonan, too close for courtesy.

He stepped back, but his heel hit the skirting board.

Amelia smirked and raised one hand, cupping his cheek.

Beth felt her anger rise a notch as Amelia moved her body in closer, breathing something so quietly into his ear that she couldn't hear it from two paces away.

Jonan's jaw tensed. He glared at Amelia, and then sighed. 'That's ancient history.'

Amelia laughed, tipping her head back, allowing her long, luscious hair to hang behind her. 'And you think she would agree? You think you'd still get your precious destiny if she knew? I haven't forgotten, you know. I still know enough about you to recognise every soft spot. You can't hide from me, Joe.'

Jonan shrugged. 'I'm not going to try. 'Where's Bill?'

'Bill again? What do you care about that old man?'

Beth put her glass down on the top of an upright piano that stood to her right.

'On a coaster please, darling,' Amelia snapped, but didn't move.

Nor did Beth.

The man in the suit stepped forward, slipped a coaster under the glass then moved back to Amelia's side. He sat back in Bill's chair, tipping it onto its hind legs.

A feeling of dread settled into Beth's stomach. 'Is he dead?'

Amelia laughed, but the high-pitched sound was strained. 'Don't be so melodramatic.'

'Well, something's not right.' Beth walked towards Amelia, eyes narrowed. 'If you are so afraid of spirits stealing your soul, why are you living in this creepy place? Why would you settle somewhere so obviously haunted?'

'You're assuming my choices are your business.' Her voice was low, hypnotic. She smiled. 'I don't have to explain myself to you.'

Beth was standing in front of Amelia now. She stood tall, but the other woman still had a few inches on her. 'Maybe not.'

There was silence, broken only by the ticking of a carriage clock on the mantelpiece. Beth looked over at Jonan. He stood in the shadows by the door, hands shoved in the pockets of his jeans. His face was impassive, eyes blank, a very human blue. His high cheekbones, accentuated by the dim light, made his face seemed edgy and unfamiliar.

Roland stepped towards her, standing too close. She smelled garlic on his breath, felt his intrusion. It was suffocating. A smile stretched across his face. It was familiar, but she couldn't place it. His face remained cold, his eyes dark and unreadable.

She took a step backwards.

'Give her space.' Jonan's energy fizzed, creating little sparks of light that flashed so fast she wondered if she'd imagined them. His ears shimmered into little points and his aura stretched, making him appear large and intimidating.

Roland wasn't fazed. Without any kind of show, he matched Jonan's presence at all times. 'Is that all you have to throw at me?'

'Don't take a single step closer to Beth.'

'Or what?' Roland tilted his head and grinned, cat-like, at Jonan. 'What exactly will you do to me... brother?' He stretched out the syllables, emphasising the word so it bounced around the echoing corridor.

'You haven't been my brother in a long time. Don't think you can start now.'

Beth turned to Jonan in surprise. When she looked closely, she saw the similarities between the two men. They both had the angular cheekbones and slanted eyebrows. They had the same lean but strong physique, but Roland was as dark as Jonan was blond, his face rounder, softer.

Amelia rolled her eyes. 'Don't bore me with family reunions. I was over that a long time ago. Rolo, leave Beth alone.'

Roland walked around Beth in a circle, but didn't come any closer.

'Don't push me, Roland.' Jonan's voice was quiet.

Roland laughed. 'What are you going to do? Call Mummy?'

'I might just do that.' Jonan smiled, but there was no warmth in it. His eyes were narrowed, his shoulders tense as he glared at the younger man.

Roland paled. 'She won't listen to you. She has other priorities now.'

'You'd be surprised.' Jonan's voice was soft as he stepped closer. 'She talks about you, often. She isn't the way Amelia paints her.'

Roland leaned against the wall, crossing his arms over his chest. 'She made her choice a long time ago and I wasn't it. You weren't it. I'm surprised you still stand by her.'

'I was cared for.'

'By whom? Doriel?'

'Yes.'

'You're crazy to put your faith, your life, in the care of that Oracle.'

'And yet you put your faith in Amelia.' Jonan shrugged.

'Anyway, you know Doriel's not the Oracle any more. She stepped into the role of Mother when Miranda went into seclusion.'

Roland stepped closer to Jonan. Their noses were almost touching.

'You ruined everything and you have the gall to come here and try to throw your weight around?'

'I ruined everything? On my own?' Jonan's voice cracked. 'You don't hold Amelia accountable at all?'

Roland walked over to the table, poured a large shot of whisky, knocked it back, and slammed the glass back down on the table. 'Oh, I know where you place the blame, brother. My perspective is different. I helped Amelia put herself back together after you left. You may be proud of your teenage self for scoring a beautiful older woman, but I am ashamed of you. I always will be. You were not worthy of her.'

Jonan swallowed. 'You certainly know how to hit a nerve. Amelia has taught you well. But if you stay with her, you will always live in fear.' He looked up at Amelia. She was leaning against the wall, her fingers whitening at the knuckles where she held her wine glass with a death grip.

'Fear I can trust.' Roland walked over to Amelia and slipped an arm around her waist, pulling her in tight against his body. 'Fear delivers what it promises. With fear, you know the worst. And so with fear there are no surprises.'

Jonan sighed. 'You know the worst because you invite it in.'

'And the Oracle, what? Surrounds you with peace and happiness?'

'Doriel gave me space to find my own way and supported me when I couldn't. She doesn't issue orders.'

'Brother.' Roland smirked. 'Amelia treats me like a man, believe me.'

'Nobody's questioning your manhood,' Beth said, her voice cutting through the intimacy like a knife. 'Just your courage. Believe it or not, the two are not the same thing.'

Amelia laughed. 'You're a feisty one, Beth. Come and work at my side. Think how much we could achieve. And what it would do for Jonan to reunite him with his brother.'

Jonan rolled his eyes. Reaching out, he took Beth's hand. 'Ignore her. You don't need to do me any favours.'

Beth stepped round so she was standing in front of Jonan, her back to Amelia. Mirroring the other woman's earlier movements, she cupped Jonan's cheek then leaned in until her mouth was close to his ear. 'I'm going to look for Bill,' she said under her breath. 'Don't follow me. Keep them occupied. I'll come back and find you here.'

Jonan said nothing, but squeezed her hand.

Beth straightened, let go of Jonan's hand and moved to stand in front of the door. 'Tell me where Bill is.'

Amelia rolled her eyes. 'For the final time, I know nothing about the old man's whereabouts.'

Beth turned, grasped the door handle and was through in a moment, pulling the door shut behind her. She took a deep breath as the latch clicked.

She was on her own.

After darting up the stairs, Beth opened the door to the first bedroom but it was empty. So was the next. She tried each room, working her way down the upstairs corridor to the Royal Suite, which was bursting with life. The dressing table was littered with make up in very modern pots. The bed was rumpled and unmade. Clothes and underwear were scattered across the floor. Beth backed out and crossed the hall to the room that had housed the spirit of the girl for so long. Inside, the energy fizzed. She felt fear bubbling up inside her chest. Her breathing became shallow and her heart raced. She forced herself to remain detached, to observe the reactions of her body to the energy in the room.

She heard footsteps downstairs, solid male steps, and the sharp tap of high heels. The murmur of voices came ever closer and the pressure closed her throat, pushing her to the edge of panic.

'Bill?' she whispered.

'*Not here.*' A voice floated into her mind. She recognised the energy signature of the girl.

'You're still here?' she murmured. 'I thought we helped you cross over?'

'I am free now, but I still watch over Bill. He is downstairs.'

Beth shook her head. 'I've been downstairs. He's not there.'

'Further down, below his home.'

Beth took her shoes off so she could move quietly, and then slipped out of the room and down the staircase at the opposite end of the hall to the approaching voices. She ran to the reception desk, padding quietly on her toes and searching for a way down.

'Where the hell is she?' Amelia's voice was high pitched.

'If you don't have anything to hide, why do you care?' Jonan's voice had a hard edge Beth had never heard before.

'I'm not besotted like you are. I don't know this woman and don't want her poking around my private things. I'm sure the police would find that reasonable.'

Beth went back into the small living room. There were two doors, one she had come in through, the other at the opposite end of the room was shut tight. She knocked, and then waited. There was nothing. She grasped the brass handle, turning it slowly, flinching as it creaked. She pushed the door and it swung easily over the threadbare carpet. There was a single bed in the corner of the room. A bedside table with one book and a half-filled glass of water stood next to it. An armchair in the opposite corner was the home of a pair of brown corduroy trousers and a knitted grey cardigan. A dark wood wardrobe and set of drawers sat next to the chair. There was nothing on top of the drawers: no pictures, no ornaments, no hairbrush, can of deodorant, or other sign of life. Apart from this basic furniture, the room was empty.

She went back out to reception. The way they had come in was dark, filled with shadows. The crack of metal on wood caught her attention. She turned. A door she hadn't noticed before swung open on its hinges. She froze, waited, but there was nobody there. A stone staircase descended into inky blackness. The rickety wooden banister was fastened to the wall on the left, offering support on the uneven steps. Beth looked around. Footsteps and voices were coming closer, but right now there was no one to watch where she went.

She felt around on the walls for a light switch. There was nothing. Taking hold of the banister, she gave it a tug to see how secure it was. She wouldn't have wanted to put her whole weight on it, but it was enough to steady her on the dark steps. She stepped down and closed the door behind her, plunging herself into blindness. The next step was lower than she expected and she lurched forwards. The banister rocked under the pressure and she reached out with her other hand, steadying herself on the damp stone wall. The stench of mould filled her nostrils and her throat, but she forced herself to breathe through the thickness. The dread began as a seed below her ribcage and spread, branching out through her chest, her stomach, to the tips of her fingers and toes. The sense of anticipation, of something wrong in this dank and freezing place, was overwhelming.

The floor evened out and the walls dropped away from under her fingertips. She walked slowly, feeling her way with each step. The pattering of feet made her lurch to the left. Her toe caught something large and solid. She staggered, trying to get her balance, but there was no flat surface and she fell forwards, the heels of her hands jarring against the cold stone floor. She scrambled away from the solid mound, hardly daring to breathe. It was cold, immovable. She dug her phone from her bag and opened it, breathing into the comfort of the yellow glow. Turning the light towards the lump on the ground, she ran her hands over it, and finding a layer of plastic wrapping, peeled it back to find a soft, tartan shirt. Underneath was a pair of corduroy trousers like the ones on the chair in Bill's room, but more worn. The clothes looked like Bill's, but that was all that was there. She took a deep, steadying breath. Bill had lived in this place for years. Of course he stored things here. She needed to quit this hysterical drama queen stuff and focus.

A groan cut through the silence. Beth stilled, listened, trying to ignore the pattering a few dark steps ahead of her. There was another groan, fainter this time. The pattering had stilled. She pointed the torch on her phone, expecting to see the gleam of eyes, but there was nothing there. There must have been some kind of hole or gap, an escape route for whatever rodent shared this room with her. She moved closer, scanning the walls and exits. A tail disappeared through a gap in the brickwork. Beth lurched back, and then froze. She walked back towards the corner, running her hand along the cold stone wall.

There was a gap at the end. Sliding her hand in, she felt along the wall. Although the gap started very narrow, it widened and she couldn't feel any barrier at the other side.

The groan was louder this time, and clearly came through the space in front of her. 'Bill? Is that you?' She waited. There were voices in the hall upstairs and the sound of footsteps. Amelia's high-pitched laughter grated on her, and she wondered if the woman's pull over Jonan still held any power. Slowly, she slid into the gap. It was tight and she breathed in, making herself as small as possible. As the space widened, she wondered what waited for her on the other side. The groaning was louder now, but so was the scent of fresh air.

Beth took a deep breath as she stepped out of the gap, filling her lungs and expelling the feel of mould. She shone her torch around the room. It was larger than the one she had left and an external door swung open in one corner allowing cold air in. She shivered. Another groan drew her attention to the corner opposite the door. 'Bill?' she pointed the light in the direction of the sound, but the beam only bounced as far as her next few steps. She followed the light, leaning forwards to get a better view. The groan was louder this time. She lurched towards the sound and her phone slipped through her fingers. The light went out.

'No!' She dropped to her knees, feeling around with her hands as she searched. Broken glass pierced her fingertips, and then she felt something smooth and cold. She pressed the on button. She felt across the screen, her skin catching on the fragments of broken glass. A faint glow came from it, but it was fading fast.

'Bill?' she said again, moving slowly now in the near dark.

'Beth?' The voice was thin, reedy, but she recognised it at once.

'Bill!' She closed the gap in a couple of steps. Close up, she could just about make out the slump of Bill's body. He was sitting, but bent forwards, unable to hold himself upright. She crouched down and put one hand under his cheek, raising his face into the faint light. His chin was covered in stubble that would have been grey without the ingrained dirt. His lined skin was pasty and there was a deep graze on his right cheek. Dried blood mixed with dirt in the wound. He was icy cold and his breath rattled as he fought to draw the damp air in and out of his lungs.

'How did you end up in here?'

'I don't remember.' He coughed and his thin frame shuddered over and over with the force.

'Were you drugged?'

Bill coughed again. 'Maybe. My head feels as though it's about to crack and my eyes just want to close.' He raised his hand and touched the side of his head gingerly.

'We need to get you out of here.'

'I'm stuck.'

'Let me look.' Beth shone the torch over Bill and found a thick rope tied to his ankle at one end, and to a thick, iron ring at the other. 'It's okay, I've got this. Hold the phone and point the light at the knot.'

Bill took the phone.

The light went out.

'Here, I'll do it,' Beth said, reaching for the device. She pressed the button.

Nothing happened.

She tried again. Nothing.

She tried the on switch. Still nothing.

She took a deep breath and put the phone back in her pocket. 'Never mind. It's run out of battery.'

'That's bad isn't it?'

'Not at all. I can handle these knots. Do you know where that door leads to? I want to get you out of here.'

Beth fumbled with the knots. She didn't want Bill to worry. She wanted to reassure him she was in control, but she knew that wasn't the truth.

Was Amelia still looking for her? The woman had told her to look around, but the footsteps and voices in the halls told her Amelia was not as relaxed about Beth exploring as she wanted to appear.

The knots would have been difficult to untie in full daylight. In the pitch black they were near impossible. She kept picking away, ignoring the pain in her fingernails as the tough rope bent them backwards. Time and fear were playing tricks on her mind. She felt Amelia's influence snaking through the dank cellar and tried to hold distance. She wasn't sure whether it was conscious or just the remnants of the woman's energy, but the intrusion thrummed through her veins as though she had been drugged.

Bill was still just about sitting, but was becoming more slumped by the minute. His weight was now pushing on her left shoulder, forcing her sideways and sending pins and needles down her arm. Her back ached, but she adjusted her weight, angling into him to give her more stability against the cold stone floor.

'Bill,' she whispered as the final knot released. 'Bill, wake up. It's time to go.'

He snorted and sank more weight onto her.

'Bill!' She shook him.

He lurched away from her as he woke with a start.

'It's Beth. Let's go.'

He tried to stand up, but his legs were weak from long days in a hospital bed and they crumpled under his weight. 'I'm sorry.'

'It's okay, but I really need you to try your best.'

She helped Bill up, and then took his weight as they shuffled over to the open door in the corner of the room. 'Oh no,' she said, feeling every pound of weight pulling at her back. The uneven steps up to the garden were wet and slippery. 'I'm really going to need you to use your strength up here.'

'Of course,' Bill mumbled, but he took little of the strain as she dragged and cajoled him up towards the path and the garden.

She was breathing heavily by the time they reached the road, and untangled herself from him, leaning him against the wall to claim a moment to recover. 'Can you manage this hill?'

'Of course,' Bill said, but he slumped to the pavement before they had moved ten paces.

The walk should have taken a few minutes, but it was half an hour before Beth stood outside the Third Eye with Bill leaning heavily on her shoulder. She rang the bell.

The silence was deafening. It hadn't occurred to Beth that Doriel might not be in. It was nearly one in the morning and she had assumed the woman would be tucked up in bed. 'Please, Doriel, come to the door,' she whispered. She was just about to turn away when Doriel peered through the glass door. She had a red dressing gown gathered tightly around her, with Chinese dragons snaking up the front. Her long hair was loose for once, and cascaded over her shoulders in a tousled mess. She was dishevelled, but her eyes were sharp with no sign of sleep.

'Doriel, you're here, thank goodness.'

'What's going on? And what happened to the shop?'

'This is Bill. Amelia had him tied up in a cellar. I need to get back to Jonan. He's still at the inn with Amelia. I'll explain about the shop later. You've done a great job of clearing up.'

Doriel nodded. 'Help me get Bill upstairs, and then you get back to Jonan.'

One on each side of Bill, they helped him up the narrow staircase and onto the sofa. Doriel lit the fire and within moments it was roaring, pouring heat into the tiny room.

Bill was shivering and pale. His face was gaunt, his eyes flat, expressionless.

Doriel clasped Beth's hands. 'Don't worry about him, I've got this. Go and find Jonan.'

'Thank you. Can I borrow your phone? Mine broke.'

Doriel grinned. 'Mine's broken too, remember?'

'Of course, I'm sorry about that.' Beth grimaced.

'Oh don't worry. Just take care of Jonan. He has too much history with Amelia already. I hate to think of him getting drawn in again.'

Beth nodded, and then ran down the stairs.

On her own, it took moments to get back to the inn. She slipped through the gate, down the steps into Bill's cell and then up into the corridor. She hoped Jonan was still there, or she would be walking into Amelia's stronghold alone.

CHAPTER SIXTEEN

Jonan

JONAN FORCED HIMSELF not to move. It took all his focus not to walk out of the room with Beth, but then Amelia would have followed them both. As long as he was here keeping Amelia busy, Beth had a chance to explore without interference.

Amelia's face softened as Beth left the room. 'Let her look for the old man, Rolo.' She sat in Bill's old armchair by the fire, leaning her head against the back of the chair and gazing up at Jonan. In that moment, the celebrity was gone. He saw only the woman he had fallen in love with all those years ago.

He swallowed, stepping back to put some distance between them. He visualised white light streaming around him, connecting into his heart and forming a barrier between him and Amelia.

Amelia gave a throaty chuckle. 'I'm not doing anything, Jonan, whatever you're feeling is all you.'

Jonan gritted his teeth and forced his face into a strained smile. Amelia was watching him far too closely. He was used to playing the role of normal, but this was the toughest audience he could possibly face.

Roland held out a bottle of beer.

Jonan shook his head.

Roland rolled his eyes. 'You're far too serious, bro, always were. If you loosened up a bit, you might be able to get things moving with that girl of yours.' He sat on the side of Amelia's chair, draping one arm over her shoulders.

She turned to look up into his face and he dropped a kiss on her mouth that lasted a moment too long.

Jonan rolled his eyes. 'I hate to interfere with your public displays of affection, but why the hell are you staying here? What happened to the London penthouse?

Amelia chuckled. 'We're not living here, as such, but I have a soft spot for this place. I want to keep an eye on how things progress.'

'And this has nothing to do with Doriel and I living so close by?'

'And what if it does? Would it be so terrible for me to want to move closer to my family?'

'Family? You didn't call me that when you were sleeping with me.'

Amelia laughed. 'No, well, you and that mother of yours put paid to that and I moved on. Were you expecting me to hold a torch for you forever?'

'I'm pretty sure you've never held a torch for me in your life.' Jonan leaned against the wall. He had been over and over this part of his history in his mind. He thought he had come to terms with it but talking to Amelia brought up all the old anger.

'That's not true. I didn't leave you, Jonan; I was ejected from the group. Don't let Doriel persuade you into some kind of revisionist history.'

'I know what happened.' Jonan's voice cracked.

Amelia blinked. She looked ashen in the dim light. 'I

know that's not the way you see it, but believe me, it's how I felt. You despise who I have become, but you and yours gave me very little choice.'

Jonan took a deep breath. The faint creases around his eyes deepened. 'My mother put herself into spiritual seclusion when Roland and I were young enough to need her. Roland is right. Neither you nor I are innocent of that.'

Amelia's face hardened. 'Where is that bloody girl?' She stood up, pulled on her discarded heels and strode from the room.

'Wait,' Jonan said, running to catch up. 'You were going to let her look around.'

'I figured she'd have a quick look, not root through my drawers. How long does it take to open doors and see a room is empty?'

'To be fair, there are a lot of doors here,' Jonan said, keeping pace with her now.

'Quite the little knight in shining armour, aren't you, Jonan,' Roland said, just a step behind his brother. 'Trying to live up to your tarot card, are you? Keeping everyone tightly controlled?'

Jonan glared at him but said nothing.

They spent a full twenty minutes trawling around the hotel's many rooms before Amelia gave up and went back to Bill's lounge. She waited for Jonan and Roland to follow her through the door, and then kicked it shut with a force that jarred Jonan to the bone.

'Have you spoken to Miranda?' she said, her voice hoarse. 'How is she?'

'She's... different. There's not much that would have persuaded her to leave her children, but you managed it. You excelled yourself, Amelia.'

Amelia swallowed. 'I didn't do it alone. You were as aware of the risks as I was.'

'I was seventeen, Amelia. Just because I believed I understood the risks doesn't mean I did. You were my mother's best friend. You should have been looking out for me.'

'Stop it, Jonan.' Roland's voice was sharp. 'You walked away, not Amelia. You broke her heart and left me to clear up the mess.'

Jonan narrowed his eyes, watching their auras against the background of the starkly empty wall. Roland's was a strong, shimmering green and pink, flecked through with red. He really did love Amelia. Hers was muddied, contracted smaller than he'd ever seen it. Jonan blinked. Could it be? Amelia was actually scared. What had her so worried? And how could he keep her talking long enough to give Beth a chance to find out?

'When exactly did things begin between you two?' Jonan poured himself a glass of whisky from the crystal decanter on the tray, and then leaned against the bureau. He nodded at Amelia. 'Did you at least wait until my side of the bed was cold?'

Jonan grunted as Roland barged into him. He lurched to the ground, tipping whisky all over himself before dropping the glass onto the rug, where it rolled to a stop against the bureau.

Roland crouched over Jonan, raising his fist above his head.

'Stop!' Amelia shouted. 'For heaven's sake, you're acting like jealous teenage boys.'

Roland turned, face flushing. 'You're going to let him speak to us like that?'

'If I have a chance to win back Jonan's good opinion, I'm not going to waste it.'

Roland was still for a moment, and then he jumped up, rolling his shoulders as he walked over to an upright chair on the opposite side of the room and sat down.

Jonan took a deep breath and got up. His glass lay unbroken in the corner. He retrieved it and poured another drink.

Roland shook his head. 'Honestly, Jonan, it wasn't like that.'

'Well what was it like then?'

'I always adored Amelia in a way you never did. But you wouldn't understand that. It's always about you, Jonan, it's still about you and it drives me bloody crazy.'

Jonan looked at Amelia.

She flushed. 'I would never hurt you, Jonan. Please believe that.'

Jonan stepped towards her, whisky in hand. His heavy boots made a satisfying thump on the threadbare carpet as he approached. 'Every time you target Beth, you hurt me. You know that. It's why you sought her out to work on your little project, and you've been badgering her ever since.'

'You still assume it's all about you?' Amelia laughed and shook her head. 'Do you really think you're the sum total her of her destiny? That she has no more potential than to be your soul mate?'

Jonan frowned. 'No, of course not.'

Amelia kept looking over to the door.

Jonan turned as he heard a creak behind him.

Beth

THE DOOR TO Bill's old living quarters was closed, but Beth heard voices. She put her hand on the doorknob as quietly as possible and turned it, slowly, hoping nobody would notice. The click was quiet but there. Light streamed through the crack and the voices were louder now. She saw Jonan, as well as Amelia and Roland.

'What are you saying?' Jonan's voice was sharp, hard in a way she had never heard it before.

Beth felt Amelia's attention on her. Then everyone was staring.

'What happened to you?' Amelia asked, eyeing Beth's dusty face and cobwebbed hair.

'I tripped, that's all, down in the cellar. The ground is so uneven. I think I've bruised my back.'

'No sign of Bill?' Jonan's voice was casual, but his eyes burned violet as he watched her, his face tilted so Amelia and Roland couldn't see.

She shook her head. 'Shall we get going? I could do with a hot bath.'

'Not so fast.' Amelia strode over, pulling out a chair. 'If you've hurt yourself sit down, have some whisky.' She nodded at Roland and he poured an amber shot into a crystal cut glass and held it out to her.

Beth sighed and took the glass. She sipped at it. The neat spirit made her throat burn and her eyes water, but it warmed her from the inside, and she was surprised to find herself starting to feel better.

'What were you doing in my cellar?'

Beth stared at Amelia. She wasn't showing any signs of panic. If Beth had been guessing she would have said

Amelia had no idea Bill had been down there, but surely that wasn't possible? She had assumed the order to take Bill had come direct from the top, but now she wondered. She didn't trust Roland either. Might he have arranged this without telling Amelia? Was there any way she could be innocent? Beth blurred her eyes, trying to get a read on one of them, or both of them. It was hopeless.

'Stop prying, darling. I know what you're doing and you have no hope of getting past my defences.' Amelia stepped closer, her eyes narrowed. 'Tell me what you were up to. What could possibly have kept you for so long.'

Beth raised her eyebrows. Amelia seemed to be telling the truth. If she hadn't put Bill there, who had? And did that make Amelia an ally?

They were all watching her and the silence was stretching out between them, ever larger and increasingly hungry.

'Bill was down there,' she said, watching Amelia closely for a reaction. 'He was tied up in a hidden room, hungry, thirsty and weak.'

'A hidden room?' Amelia asked, her voice incredulous. She turned to look at Roland. 'Did you know about that?'

Roland shrugged.

'You said he *was* there.' Amelia turned back to Beth. 'Where is he now?'

'Never mind that. I want to know why you had him.' Beth tilted her chin up, hoping to look defiant.

'You silly girl.' Amelia rolled her eyes. 'Why would I *have* him? What do you think I am?'

'Do you really want me to answer that?' Beth asked.

'Right, well, you'd better show us this secret room.' Amelia stepped out of her spiky black stilettos, and slid on some flip flops that were shoved beneath one of the chairs.

'Did he say who took him?' Jonan whispered as they followed Amelia out of the room and down the stairs that led them below ground.

'I didn't ask. I assumed it was Amelia.'

'Tying him up in a basement is far too cartoon villain for her. But it does implicate her, so who would want to do that?'

'It would have to be someone with access to the property,' Beth said, stepping off the bottom step.

'That counts out most people,' Amelia said, pulling a small torch out of her pocket and clicking it on. She peered around. 'Where is this hidden room?'

Beth led them to the gap and they shuffled through one by one.

Amelia crouched down and lifted the iron ring in the floor. 'What's this?'

'It was tied to Bill's ankle.'

'And you, what, just untied it, just like that?'

'Well, yes.'

'And were Bill's hands tied?'

Beth shook her head. 'Why?'

'Well, if you managed to untie it, and his hands were free, presumably he could have untied it himself.'

Beth frowned. 'What are you suggesting?'

'I'm suggesting that Bill hadn't been there as long as you assumed, that he probably tied himself up and fully intended to leave before his next bathroom break.'

'Why would he do that?' Beth shook her head, but a sense of foreboding had started to thread through her.

Amelia laughed. 'You're so sure your precious old man is a harmless victim, aren't you? How long have you known him exactly?'

An image of Bill slumped on Doriel's sofa popped into Beth's mind. 'What are you suggesting?'

Amelia sighed. 'Well, darling, it seems we know a bit more about Bill than you do.'

'How?'

'Did he tell you I'd just bought this place, or did you make that assumption too? I've owned it for years. Always meant to come and do it up, turn it into something spectacular, but there was always a reason I couldn't. The whole process was fraught with problems and every time I visited, the ghosts became agitated and the whole thing ground to a halt.' She stood up. 'Bill is an oddity. I find him interesting. I've spent years watching him, but I would never, ever trust him.'

'You think he was stopping you from doing up the inn?'

Amelia laughed. 'For those who know how, there are many ways to slow down a project. Bill is... unpredictable. And I know he's a more accomplished energy worker than he lets on. It seems he isn't quite so accomplished at framing me. Honestly, a cellar? Could he have been any more obvious?'

'I'm guessing you don't like him because he doesn't fall for your tricks?' Jonan gave an uneasy laugh.

'He doesn't. He never has, but he has come close to rivalling my tricks on any number of occasions, and I don't admit that easily. He has a way of drawing people in, making sure they trust him, and then...'

'Then what?' Beth's voice was barely more than a whisper. 'What does he do next?'

'Oh, don't listen to me, darling. What do I know? I'm just an empty-headed celebrity.'

'You've never been that,' Jonan said.

Amelia walked over to the open door that led to the garden. She peered outside then turned back to Jonan, eyes narrowed.

'Amelia,' Beth said. 'What then?'

Amelia shut the door, deepening the darkness in the room. The light from the torch cast strange shadows over her face so the angles stood out in sharp relief. 'I don't know. I'm guessing he's gunning for me. He wants me out. I have no idea where you fit in to this.' She pointed to the door. 'Beth, was this open when you arrived?'

'Yes,' Beth said.

'Then he could have got up and walked out.' Roland said, raising his eyebrows and peering down at Beth.

'He was far too weak for that,' she said through gritted teeth. 'I had to virtually carry him out of the room.'

'Or so he had you believe.' Amelia laughed. 'He's a clever man.'

'We need to go,' Beth said to Jonan. Dread settled in the pit of her stomach. She had left Bill alone with Doriel.

Jonan looked at her, and then nodded.

'Run away, little boy,' Amelia said.

Jonan stopped. He began to turn, but Beth took his hand and pulled him up the steps into the garden.

'Forget her,' she said. 'I left Bill with Doriel.'

'What?' Jonan said. 'When?'

'Earlier,' Beth said, opening the garden gate and ushering Jonan through. She pulled her coat tight around her against the sharp breeze as she began to run up the steep hill towards the centre of town. Jonan kept pace with her, the thud of his feet on the pavement somehow comforting. 'Would you have known if there was something wrong with him?' Beth said, pulling in air as she pushed her aching legs up the hill. 'Would you have picked it up in his energy?' An image of Doriel screaming flashed through her mind and she pushed faster.

'Everyone has blind spots,' Jonan said, before lapsing into silence. 'Of course, Amelia might be lying.'

A pub door opened and the sound of the TV blared through the open space before the door slammed shut. Amelia's voice seemed to come from every corner. Her voice carried on the wind, sending shivers down Beth's spine.

Jonan pulled out his keys as they reached the wide, cobbled walkway outside The Third Eye. He pushed the door open, leaving it swinging on its hinges behind him as he took the stairs two at a time.

Beth shut the door and secured the shop using the key Jonan had left in the door. Then she followed him upstairs.

The living room was full of chaos and utterly silent. Chairs had been turned over and there were clothes and ornaments everywhere. Even the firewood had been tipped out of the basket.

Jonan stood in the middle of the room, his arms spread, eyes closed. He appeared serene, but stress showed in the creases around his eyes and on his forehead. He seemed to have aged in the few moments since she had seen him last. For the first time, she realised he had to be older than her twenty-six years.

'Jonan,' she whispered, stepping over to him and taking one of his hands. 'Jonan, what happened. Are you alright?'

'They're gone,' he said, his voice tight. 'He took her.'

'You don't know that. Maybe they've just popped out?'

'It's after one in the morning.'

'Maybe she took him back to hospital?'

'No, there's a lot of fear here, but I can't see details. Not many people would be able to block me like this. Thank goodness Doriel has left markers for me.'

Beth sank onto the sofa and dropped her head into her hands. 'So Amelia was right? And it's all my fault. He seemed so nice.'

'That's the way it works sometimes.' Jonan sighed.

'So he did put himself in the cellar?'

'I don't know. The energy of it isn't in here.'

Beth took a deep breath. 'Jonan, I think we need to call the police.'

Jonan squeezed his eyes tight. 'Would you mind? I need to see if I can reach Doriel telepathically.'

Beth picked up the phone and dialled 999.

'Police, fire or ambulance?' The voice sounded tired.

'Police, please.'

Moments later Beth heard sirens, but they drifted away on the wind, leaving her in silence. Jonan sat on the sofa in the lounge, amongst the chaos, his eyes closed, jaw tight. She felt reproach in the deafening lack of sound, felt the rolling of her stomach increase with each passing moment.

She put the kettle on and went into the lounge. Jonan hadn't moved. She went over to the window, pushing open the old, wooden frame and breathing in the fresh air with relief. Heading back to the kitchen, she made tea and put one cup on the table in front of Jonan. He sat so still she almost wanted to check his pulse, but he had asked her to leave him alone, and she was determined not to disturb whatever he was doing.

When the bell rang, she let out her breath in relief and took the stairs two at a time.

A policeman in uniform stood outside. His black hair

was slicked back and his face was all sharp features, cheek bones standing out either side of a narrow, pointed nose.

'Hello,' he said without a smile. 'I'm DC Ainsworth.'

'Beth,' she said, slightly breathless from her sprint down the stairs. She reached out to shake his hand, but he peered at her outstretched palm, sniffed and walked right past her to scan the room. Walking around the shop, he peered into the glass cabinets, buckets of crystals and open bookshelves. He glared at her for a moment, and then pulled a black leather notebook out of his pocket and began a fast scrawl with a silver ballpoint pen.

'The damage is upstairs,' Beth said.

He nodded. 'Lead the way.'

He was far too close as he followed her up the stairs, almost clipping her heels with his shiny shoes. She hoped he couldn't hear the hammering of her heart. This was not a man she wanted to show weakness to.

She knocked on the door at the top. Jonan was striding towards them when she opened it, but stood back to allow them into the flat.

'What happened here tonight?'

Jonan spread out his arms. 'We came home and found it this way.'

'There's no forced entry?'

'No,' Beth said, 'but Jonan's aunt is missing, along with a friend of ours.'

'Their names?' DC Ainsworth raised his eyebrows.

'Doriel McLaney and Bill ... do you know his surname, Beth?' Jonan turned to her.

Beth blanched. 'No. I can't remember. I'm sorry.'

'Is Bill a close friend of Doriel's?'

'No. They had just met. I brought him here tonight to

recover from a hospital stay. Doriel offered to look after him.'

DC Ainsworth's jaw worked. He wrote in his notebook. 'How well do *you* know this Bill?'

Jonan sighed. 'I've met him once. Beth met him a couple of times.'

'He was injured,' Beth blurted out. 'And he's old and frail.'

DC Ainsworth strode over to the chair next to the smouldering fire and sat down on the edge, back straight.

'Sit down, please,' he said, gesturing to the sofa. 'I won't take more of your time than necessary. I need descriptions of Doriel and Bill, photographs too.' The man raised his eyes, holding his pen poised. His right leg jiggled, his heel not touching the floor.

Jonan picked up a picture frame and handed it to him. 'This is Doriel. She's medium height with long, red hair.'

'How was she dressed when you last saw her?'

'She was wearing a dressing gown,' Beth said with a sinking feeling. 'It was red with dragons, like a kimono.'

DC Ainsworth carried on writing, his lips compressed into a thin line. 'And Bill?'

Beth frowned. 'He was wearing dark-brown trousers and a rumpled checked shirt.'

DC Ainsworth nodded. 'Do you have a picture?'

Beth shook her head. 'Wait, where's the polaroid, Jonan?'

He frowned. 'I think it's in my coat pocket.'

Beth picked up his jacket from the back of one of the chairs and slid her hand into one pocket and then the other. They were both empty. She shook her head again.

'Look, is there anything you can tell me about Bill and Doriel that might help me find them?'

'Bill has just come out of hospital,' Beth said, holding the detective's gaze. 'He needed somewhere to recover. He's just lost his home and has no family.' He listened intently as she talked, watching every movement. He was reading them, Beth knew, much as she might read the energy of a person she was trying to figure out.

'And?' DC Ainsworth raised his eyebrows.

'I can tell you about Doriel,' Jonan said, his voice flat. 'You can see where we work. She has been getting abuse from the local community. A brick was thrown through the window recently while she was working. We reported it and were told no action would be taken.'

DC Ainsworth looked at Jonan and sighed. Taking his phone out of his back pocket, he dialled and moved over to the window, looking out onto the dark street as he murmured into it. He was just loud enough to be obvious, but too quiet for Beth to hear what he was saying.

Beth sat on the sofa next to Jonan. She wanted to put her arm around him, to pull him close and comfort him. But even though DC Ainsworth's back was turned, she had a weird sense he was watching them.

'Jonan?' she whispered.

'Would you mind getting DC Ainsworth some coffee?' he asked, turning towards her. His eyes were bloodshot, but dry. 'I need to focus.'

'Coffee, black, three sugars,' DC Ainsworth said, not turning around.

Beth stood up and walked through to the kitchen without a word. The urge to clear up was almost irresistible. She longed to have something to do, something that would make her feel useful. She was so tired she felt dizzy, but anxiety made her stomach squirm and kept her eyes wide.

She searched through the cupboards, trying to disturb as little as possible. There were lots of cups with pictures on the side, goddesses, symbols and fairies. Beth took out one with a mermaid, and then stopped herself. How would DC Ainsworth view them if she handed him this? She rummaged around in the cupboard and found two plain mugs right at the back.

She scooped four heaped teaspoons of coffee into a cafetière and poured on the water. She wasn't ready to go back into the living room. The policeman's energy was spreading through the chaos of the living room. It felt familiar, but she couldn't place why. Stalling, she took her time, heating the milk in the microwave and trying, in vain, to whip it up into a froth using a fork. The smell of the coffee turned her stomach as she poured, so she grabbed a glass from the cupboard and filled it with water, gulping down one glass and then filling it up again, hoping it might somehow make her feel more normal.

The doorbell made her jump.

'I'll go,' DC Ainsworth's voice rang out.

She put his coffee on the table, and then handed one to Jonan. 'There's something not right with him.'

'I know.' Jonan sighed and leaned back against the sofa. 'Amelia has contacts in the police force. We need to be careful.'

Beth went to the door to the staircase and opened it slightly, putting an ear to the crack.

'No, no help needed.' DC Ainsworth's voice was low, but clearly audible. 'I'll close this out than come back to the station. There's nothing important here.'

Beth pushed the door to, careful not to let it click shut. She went over to the sofa and sat down next to Jonan. 'I think you're right. He said there's nothing important here. We're being side-lined.'

Jonan sighed. 'The same thing happened when we reported the brick through the window. We won't get any help. I suggest we tell him as little as we can and get him out of here.

Beth plastered a smile onto her face as DC Ainsworth came back into the room. She hoped it looked more convincing than it felt.

'Well,' he said, sliding his pen into the top pocket of his jacket. 'I think that's everything.'

'What happens now?' Beth asked.

The detective shrugged. 'Get a couple of hours sleep. It's nearly dawn and you don't look as though you've been to bed yet. Is there somewhere else you can go? It's hugely unlikely anyone would come back, but it's probably safer to be elsewhere tonight.'

'We can go back to mine.' Beth stifled a yawn.

'I'll take your contact details in case we need to get in touch, but try not to worry. The most likely scenario is that your friends left the house voluntarily. See if you can think of any places Doriel might have gone, or might have taken Bill. If you think of anything, let me know.' He handed Beth a business card. 'No need to see me out.'

The door swung shut behind him. Beth heard his footsteps on the stairs, and then there was silence. 'Did you hear the front door?'

Jonan shook his head, opening the door to the stairs with an audible click.

The front door slammed, the bells jingling to announce the constable's departure.

Jonan frowned, his eyes darkening.

'Come on, let's get out of here,' Beth said. 'It's not far to my flat.'

Jonan smiled, but his mouth was tight, the edges of his lips whitening slightly. His eyes flashed a deep purple and his ears ran into clearly defined points. 'Thank you, it's very kind, but you don't have to put me up. I'll be fine here. I'm confident there's no risk.'

Beth's heart hammered in her chest. He seemed so remote. 'Don't you want to come to my flat?'

His forehead creased. 'I don't want you to feel pressured just because a crooked policeman shot his mouth off about my home.'

'I don't feel pressured.' She swallowed. 'I'd like you to come.'

Jonan stilled, the rise and fall of his chest his only movement.

'Will Laura mind me coming back?'

'No, she'll love it. She'll quiz me about you for weeks.'

Jonan laughed. 'What will you tell her?'

'That I've nabbed the neighbourhood psychic with pointed elf ears, otherwise known as the Charioteer?'

Jonan nodded. 'Sounds fair. Just give me a minute.' He disappeared into his bedroom and she heard drawers opening and shutting. Then he came back out and grabbed his keys from the table. 'Shall we?'

Beth grinned, and then opened the door and went down the stairs. The shop was dark but after a moment her eyes began to adjust. What had the policeman been doing down here? She walked slowly around the room, peering at the buckets of tumble stones and glass cases of crystals. Nothing looked out of place.

The bell on the door jingled.

She turned.

Jonan held the door open. 'Don't worry, he won't have been able to take anything valuable. I'll have a look in the morning.'

She ducked through the doorway, and Jonan locked up behind her.

She did up her coat, gritting her teeth as a blast of wind caught her in the chest.

Jonan pulled her into his side, putting his arm around her waist. She relaxed into the warmth and felt the ache in her chest start to subside.

'Can you believe how late it is, or how early?' She said with a yawn as they walked through the early-morning town.

A van pulled up in front of them and two men jumped out to unload poles and awnings. They started setting up the market stalls with surprising speed.

'I can't decide whether to go to bed or buy coffee.'

'Let's get some rest,' Jonan said, pulling her closer. 'It's been a long day. We've got a lot to figure out tomorrow.'

They walked in silence for a few minutes. The air was damp and it was still dark, despite the efforts of the market traders to usher in the day. Beth got a strong whiff of bacon sandwich. Her stomach growled. She laughed, embarrassed by the speaking of her body, but Jonan just smiled and nudged her closer to him.

'Jonan,' she said, her voice small. She coughed, and then forced herself to speak louder. 'We should talk about you and Amelia, about what she said. I know I told her I knew it all, and, to some extent, I do. But it was different, hearing her speak like that. I can see she still means something to you.'

Jonan sighed. 'Of course she does. I've known Amelia for my whole life. We have a long and complicated relationship, but I'm not attracted to her any more. She was never who I thought she was.'

Beth swallowed. 'Before we went to The Monk's Inn, it felt as though something was happening between us. If it is, if it means anything at all to you, you really need to tell me what's going on, and what Amelia really means to you.' She took a deep breath, looking pointedly forwards, giving him time to decide what to say.

Jonan sighed and let go of her hand. He rubbed his hands together, cupped them over his mouth and blew on them to warm them. He rubbed one hand over his forehead, not noticing that his long blond hair was coming loose from the ponytail at the nape of his neck. 'We were involved a long time ago. I was so young and Amelia was different then. She was best friends with my mother and Doriel. The three of them were virtually inseparable, so Amelia and I had to keep everything quiet. That's why Mother went into seclusion. She found out what had happened between Amelia and I, and she was so angry that she left us. I was seventeen; Roland was fifteen. I felt so guilty. I had pulled my family apart and had no way to fix it. I couldn't bear to look at Amelia afterwards. I blamed her for everything. That's why I left with Doriel. I tried to persuade Roland to come, but he wouldn't. He'd always adored Amelia and I suspect he was pleased to get me out the way and have her for himself.'

'I can see that,' Beth said. 'But, wow. Your mother left him at fifteen? I can see why he's so angry with her.'

Jonan nodded. 'And with me. He feels I abandoned him too, and he's right. I would do things differently now, but I wasn't much older than him myself and I wasn't thinking straight.' They turned off the main road and crossed the grass outside Beth's flat. Jonan stopped and leaned against the tree. Beth stopped too and stood facing him. Ever since her birthday party, she had thought of this as Jonan's tree. She reached out and took his hand. It was freezing cold.

'Doriel and I kept an eye on Amelia from a distance.' Jonan seemed to be staring through Beth now, watching a place she had never seen. 'Amelia had always been powerful, but she'd begun behaving strangely. We watched as she became more and more entangled with heavier energies. Then she started shielding herself and we couldn't see any more. But with her being in the public eye, we can read the impact she's having on others and it fits with the signature she was building before she started to shield. She works with the fear frequency, pulling people to her by making them feel threatened. She likes to be a saviour, to make others feel as though she's their only option. She takes pride in hijacking people's independence, and influences their decisions, their lifestyles, their choices. Her power was always there, but now it's using her, rather than the other way around.'

'But, Jonan.' Beth clasped his hand between both of hers. 'She's your ex. You're angry with her. Don't you see how that clouds your judgment?'

'It did, I'll admit that. I was angry with her, and hurt that she didn't fight for me when I walked away. But Doriel still loves her. She hates what Amelia is doing, but every day she looks for an indication she can win her friend back. Doriel is an Oracle. She sees the possibility of a future where Amelia can change, but that option is dwindling the more she uses her power to create fear. I know it sounds innocuous but by being in the public eye she has millions of people acting from a place of fear and defensiveness.'

'I know.' Beth took a deep breath. 'I feel the dread whenever she's in the room and I see what other people become when she's around. But when we were together at the inn, I felt the intimacy between the two of you. I'm not stupid, Jonan. I know there was more there than ancient history.'

'There is. You've seen my ears. You know I'm different. Well, Amelia is too. We don't just share ancient history, we share heritage. We share differences in a world where everyone else fits. There is common ground there, because we understand the complexities and contradictions the other lives with every day. That's partly why we happened. I was surrounded by people who had no idea, but Amelia understood and knew how to make life better. I wanted that.'

'Didn't you grow up with people like you?'

'I grew up in London. I know we look different, but we were born into these bodies, on this Earth, through our mothers just like everybody else. The difference is that we remember things most people have forgotten. That gives us access to abilities most people don't know about. Anyone can do this stuff, but most people forget the path when they incarnate. We remember. We were born to bring new energy to Earth and have been working at that our whole lives.'

'But Amelia's bringing fear. That's hardly new.'

'Amelia got distracted. Because she remembers so much, she knows how to work with energy at a high level and she is subverting it. That's why she is dangerous. She has the ability to create panic and when people are afraid they make bad decisions.'

'And you're trying to stop her?'

'We're trying to win her over. So far, we're not doing well and, right now, I'd settle for stopping her.'

A gust of wind made Beth shiver. 'Come on, let's go upstairs. It's freezing out here.'

Jonan followed her in silence as she went into the hall and up the concrete stairs. Her hands were pink with cold as she fumbled the lock, but she managed to get the door open without drawing Laura from her bedroom. Putting her finger to her lips to signal Jonan to be quiet, she got two glasses of water from the kitchen, and then led him to her room. 'There's not much space in here, I'm sorry,' she whispered, darting a glance at Laura's bedroom door.

Jonan paused in the doorway.

'Come on in,' Beth said. 'We'll wake Laura if we talk out there, and I could do without her nosing about right now.'

He came in, looking around, and stood in the middle of room.

Beth sat on the bed and patted the space beside her. 'How does Doriel feel about all of this?'

Jonan sat down. 'Doriel grieves for Amelia every day, but she also feels responsible. She feels that if she'd realised what was happening between Amelia and I, if she'd stopped it, none of this would have happened.'

'So this, Amelia's new direction, this is a direct result of your relationship?'

'It's a direct result of her losing the people she loved. She lost me, she lost my mother and she lost Doriel. Only Roland remained with her, and he was fifteen. She seems to have made the best of that though.' He rolled his eyes.

'How do you know all of this?'

'We were in contact for a long time. She tried to convince me to take her back. She tried to persuade my mother to come out of seclusion. She tried to persuade Doriel to go with her.'

'But nobody would?'

'She was already spreading her fear. We refused to be a

part of that. Doriel would have taken her in if she'd stopped, but Mother vowed never to come out of seclusion.'

'And about that.' Beth shook her head. 'Your mother deserted you and your brother. How could she justify that?'

'She was hurt so she went on an inward journey. She never has tried to justify her decision, but what she's become is pretty incredible. Her energy is purer than you can imagine. She has become more than an Oracle. She is so much in her energy body that she is hardly bound by the physical anymore.

'And Amelia…?'

'Is nothing to me now.'

Beth took a deep breath. She swayed as tiredness overtook her, but her skin was electric with the energy of their connection. She shifted on the bed, just wanting to be closer to him.

'You're tired,' Jonan said, softly. 'I'll sleep on the sofa in the lounge, give you some space.'

Beth sighed. 'Do you honestly want to sleep in the lounge, or do you still think I'm Amelia's little mouse?' she said, her heart pounding in her ears. 'Because, if you don't want me, that's fine. But you can't feed me all this stuff about joint destiny and past lives and then refuse to see me as I am, right now, here in front of you. You're almost impossible to read, Jonan McLaney. I have no idea whether to be blunt about how I feel or to respect *my* need for distance.'

'You pushed me away before Amelia got involved,' he whispered, his voice cracking. His body was so still he was barely breathing.

'No. You pushed *me* away, so I gave you the space you asked for. Don't rewrite history.'

Jonan swallowed then leaned closer, brushing a strand of hair away from her face. 'There is nothing I want less from you than space,' he said, his voice hoarse. He took her hand and placed it over his heart. She could feel it beating as fast as her own, could feel the rough weave of his shirt and the warmth of his body. She felt her own pulse increase. All her attention was focused on the man in front of her, the man whose eyes were burning deep violet, ears elongated into points. In that moment, every ounce of his differentness was on display, but it felt so natural, so real and so obvious. Without knowing why, she was sure she looked the same. She reached up, felt her own ears. They felt normal.

He took her hand, brought her fingers up to touch the silky skin on the curved top of his ear. It felt the same as hers. She felt the rounded edge even as she admired the points. She brought her fingers down to the upward line of his angular cheekbones. He was so perfect, so different, but so completely familiar that he felt like home.

Jonan stood still, allowing her to explore his face. His breathing hitched as she stroked his bottom lip, feeling the softness, the intimacy of the caress.

He bent his head, touching his lips gently to hers, and then pulled back an inch and looked at her. His breathing was ragged as he reached out and took her hand.

'How many lifetimes have we waited, Jonan? How many memories of us do you have?'

'Oh, so many, more than I can count, but they're not all lonely. I have done this before,' he said, bending down to kiss her lightly on the lips. 'I have spent many years with you over many lifetimes, but there's always something that gets in the way. There's always something that breaks us.'

'And that scares you.'

'Not being with you scares me more.' He kissed her again, pulling her into his energy until there was no separation. She could feel their past, present and future surrounding them as she let down her barriers, allowing herself to be swept away in a torrent of feelings and memories. Images flashed through her mind, some strange, some familiar: that other Jonan, the room with the pillars, his face leaning over her, his fury as he rescued her from the theatre, horror as his other-self watched another Beth burn. Grief warred with longing as they clung together, trying to find a point of stability amongst the chaos.

Beth blinked, pushing back the memories and anchoring herself in the present. Jonan's eyes were huge as he watched her, deep pools of questions. It felt so obvious to her what she wanted but, in that moment, she realised how long he had waited, how unattainable she had seemed. She tugged at his hand, grinned as his face lit up in a smile. She wished she had a better room to take him to. She wished she had a double bed. But all that really mattered was that they were together, they had found each other at last. As she pulled him down onto the bed, she knew she was crossing a line, and that she would never, ever go back.

CHAPTER SEVENTEEN

Beth

'BETH!' LAURA'S VOICE was harsh between the pounding thumps on the door. 'Beth, for goodness sake, wake up.'

'Why?' Beth forced her eyes open and shifted Jonan's arm, which was draped over her waist. She sat up, shoving herself off the bed. She grabbed some clean clothes from the wardrobe and pulled them on. Opening the door, she leaned against the wall, taking in Laura's thin-lipped frown.

'What's the emergency?'

'There's a policeman in the living room. He wants to talk to you. What the hell is going on? Why is he here? And who is in bed with you?'

'Jonan. He came to your party.'

Laura wrapped her oversized cardigan around her body, covering her pyjamas. She shrugged. 'He's a hanger-on at the studio, right?'

Beth sighed. 'He's my friend. And this isn't your flat, it's ours. Stop with the melodrama. Just let me go and talk to the policeman.'

Laura didn't move. There was only one way out of the small room and she was standing directly in front of it. Beth raised her eyebrows, staring Laura down until she moved just enough to allow Beth to duck through the opening.

Beth shut the door behind her, giving Jonan privacy to get dressed. A moment later he came out, covering a yawn with his hand as he nodded at Laura. Laura blanched and stepped right back now, edging away from Jonan. Beth frowned. Normally everyone loved Jonan. Why was Laura acting so strangely? Was she picking up on his differentness, or was she even more under Amelia's influence than Beth had thought?'

Beth and Jonan made their way through to the living room. Laura trailed behind them, hugging her oversized cardigan tightly around her middle.

DC Ainsworth sat on the edge of the sofa, one leg jiggling. 'Ah,' he said, leaning forwards, his arms propped on his thighs as he propelled himself up with a bounce. 'Thank you, Miss…'

'Balantyne,' Laura said. 'Ms Balantyne.'

'Well, Miss Balantyne, thank you for your help,' he said. He was dressed in a sharp black suit with a grey tie. His shirt was so white it almost shone and he looked unreasonably bright given his lack of sleep. 'I'm sure your friends can take it from here.' He raised his eyebrows and waited while Laura hovered at the door.

'He wants you to leave, Laura,' Beth snapped. She knew Laura hated to miss out, but she had no patience with her friend right now. She wanted to rub her eyes and her throat felt as though she'd been shouting. She'd had hardly any sleep and was in desperate need of coffee. Instead she had to deal with a bucket-load of questions and Laura's ridiculous attitude.

Laura pressed her lips together, but she left the room and shut the door behind her.

DC Ainsworth watched her go, and then frowned. He walked over to the door and opened it.

Laura was standing outside with her ear pressed up to where the wooden door had been.

'Perhaps you don't understand, Miss Balantyne,' he said, his tone clipped. 'There are penalties for wasting police time.'

Laura blushed. 'I have to get to work anyway.' She glared at Beth.

Beth knew what that meant: You will tell me everything later. Another thing she had no energy for.

DC Ainsworth watched as Laura disappeared into her bedroom.

'Thank you for seeing me so early,' he said, closing the door and turning back into the room. 'I was hoping you could run me through everything again. I want to make sure I have *all* the information.' He sat bolt upright on the soft sofa, glaring at them with raised eyebrows.

They told the story again. And again. The repetition on top of exhaustion ate at the edges of Beth's focus, making her feel dizzy. 'Would you like coffee?' she asked, interrupting Jonan. She had no idea what he'd been saying.

'Is there a problem, Miss Meyer?' DC Ainsworth raised his eyebrows. 'You seem… agitated.'

'I'm just exhausted. I think caffeine might help.'

'Black, two sugars,' he said with a nod and turned back to Jonan.

Beth shut the door to the kitchen, grateful for the moment of quiet. Her phone lay on the work surface, and she powered it up as the kettle boiled. The noise of the coffee grinder hid the incessant beeping of a barrage of messages as they fired their annoyance at her, making her head ache.

She held her thumb on the scanner and raised her eyebrows as the notifications came up.

They were all from Charlie.

She dialled his number. 'No, I haven't read and listened to them all,' she said, hearing the annoyance in her voice. 'Amelia fired me, remember? What possible reason could you have to call me that many times? The headline please?'

'Amelia has brought the event forward. It's tonight.'

Beth's throat tightened. A chill ran down her spine. 'Tonight?' She swallowed. 'Why tonight? We're not ready.'

'Of course we're not bloody ready!' Charlie shouted down the phone. 'That's why I need you here. Now. We need to figure out how we are going to make this thing work.'

Beth sighed. 'I can't. The police are here. A friend of mine was abducted last night and I was one of the last people to see her.'

Charlie was silent.

Beth could hear him shifting on the other end of the phone, but he said nothing.

'Charlie, what is it?'

'That must be what she wants to talk about. Your friend who was taken. Was it the spirits?'

'My friend was taken by a person. A solid person made of flesh and blood. I know, because I saw him too.'

'He may have been flesh and blood, but that doesn't mean he wasn't influenced by the spirits. Look, I know you think I'm crazy, but Amelia has a point. There has been weird stuff going on. People are acting strangely.'

Beth slammed her hand down on the work surface. 'People are acting this way because Amelia has whipped them up into a panic.'

'Is that so, Miss Meyer?'

Beth spun around.

DC Ainsworth stood in front of her, Jonan behind him. He was watching her, eyes dark, brow furrowed, as he waited for her reaction.

'I'm sorry,' she said. 'I've got to go, Charlie.' His protests were cut off as she hung up. 'That was my boss.' She poured three cups of coffee from the cafetière, spooned sugar into one and handed it to DC Ainsworth.

He nodded as he took it. 'I assume you're talking about Ms Amelia Faustus?'

Beth poured milk exceptionally slowly into the other two mugs, trying to buy time to think. 'Yes, yes, she's wonderful trying to save the world and all that.'

He frowned. 'You don't sound convinced. Do you have a problem with Ms Faustus?'

Beth pressed her lips together to stop herself from saying something she would regret later. She handed Jonan his drink and picked up her own. 'Shall we?' she said, gesturing back to the living room.

DC Ainsworth nodded, his jaw tightening.

'Do I annoy you, Detective?' Beth said as she sat on the sofa in the lounge. 'I'm sorry if I seem irritable, but I've had very little sleep and I'm worried about my friends... Both of them.'

'Why *did* you leave them last night? That's been puzzling me. You took an old man, injured and just out of hospital, and left him with a woman he had never met, in the middle of the night. Why would you move him at that time? And if you did, why would you drop him off with a stranger and leave? Furthermore, why would you leave Doriel alone at night, in her dressing gown, with a man you barely know? I'm sure you can see my many problems with this story.'

Beth clenched her jaw. She felt heat flush her cheeks but refused to look away.

'I went to get Jonan,' she said, her voice steady and firm.

'Okay, where was he, and why did you need him?'

'He was at The Monk's Inn, in Fishpool Street.'

The DC jotted the name down in his notebook, and then looked at Jonan. 'Why would you stay in a hotel round the corner from your house? Or were you just visiting the bar?'

'I was meeting an acquaintance,' Jonan said, tilting his head to one side, leaning back in his chair and crossing his legs. He looked so relaxed, so unconcerned, but Beth could feel the tension pouring from him, and the effort it took to portray composure.

'Who was this acquaintance? We'll need to contact them, to check your alibi.'

Jonan flushed. His hands curled into fists, but otherwise he didn't move. 'I was with Amelia Faustus.'

The detective's eyebrows shot up. 'Were you now?' He shot a look at Beth, the edges of his mouth turning up. 'And you needed collecting from this meeting why?'

'We had a prior arrangement,' Beth said.

'Of course you did.' DC Ainsworth smirked. 'And you couldn't call him up? let him know your plans had changed? Or did you not trust him to leave Ms Faustus's company?'

'My phone was broken and out of battery.' Beth said from between gritted teeth. She fished the device from her handbag and held it up.

'And we don't have a landline at the house.' Jonan's voice was hard now, his pretence at cool gone. 'Doriel's phone was at the shop being fixed. I took it in myself.' He fished in his pocket, pulled out his wallet and handed over a slip of pink card.

'Can I take this? I need to verify it.'

'And then you'll return it?' Jonan raised his eyebrows and held the DC's gaze. 'Doriel won't be happy if she doesn't get it back.'

'I suggest we focus on getting her back first,' DC Ainsworth said, standing up. 'If appropriate, once the phone has been properly examined, it will be returned to her, or to you.' There was a faint smile at the edges of his lips now. Beth had the odd sensation that he counted that as a win.

'I will check your alibi, of course, but it would be best if you both stayed away from Ms Faustus for now.'

'I can't.' Beth sighed. 'I'm helping her with an event tonight.'

'Tonight?' Jonan asked. His eyes flashed purple, and then turned back to their normal blue.

Beth nodded. 'She's changed the date.'

'You're going to the charity gala?' DC Ainsworth frowned.

'I organised the charity gala. I work for an events company,' Beth said, not even trying to keep the exhaustion from her voice. 'Have we finished here, Detective? I need to get ready for work.'

'We've finished for now, but please don't leave the area, and keep an eye on your phone. I will have more questions. It goes without saying that if you hear from Doriel or Bill I would like to hear about it right away.'

'Right away.' Jonan nodded. 'Let me show you out.'

He nodded and followed Jonan out into the hall.

Beth slumped onto the sofa, dropping her head into her hands. It was pounding. Her eyelids were so heavy, but when she allowed them to close the world started spinning. Beth forced herself off of the sofa and opened the window, breathing in the cold, crisp air.

'He's gone.'

She turned around. Jonan was standing in the doorway, face pale, hands shoved in his pockets. His protections were down now, his ears pointed and eyes a deep purple. 'Any idea why she's pushed the event forwards?'

'I don't know, but apparently all the guests are able to come, even at this short notice. How unlikely is that? Oh, and Laura's still here.'

'Did I hear my name?' Laura's voice called from the other room. 'Has the policeman gone yet?'

'He has, and I'm going too,' Beth said, grabbing her coat from the back of a dining chair and heading for the door. 'See you later.'

'But, Beth…' Laura stood in her doorway, one shoe on, the other in her hand. 'We need to talk.'

'Not now. I have to get to work.' Beth held the door open for Jonan, ducked through after him, and then closed it before Laura could say any more.

Jonan led the way down the stairs, and then held the door open for Beth. 'We always planned to deal with the monks before we got to this point. We've missed our chance now, but I think that together we could do something to mitigate Amelia's manipulation of the energy. Is there anything you could hire me to do so I have an excuse to be there?'

'You could work behind the bar, but what about looking for Doriel?'

'Whoever is behind Doriel's disappearance, I'm convinced the key to finding them lies in Amelia's plans.'

Beth's phone rang again. 'Charlie.' She sighed. 'Yes, okay. I'm coming in.'

THE OFFICE WAS sinking under piles of paper. There were lists, forms and contracts everywhere. Charlie was speaking on the phone, his voice thrumming out a staccato rhythm that set Beth's nerves jangling.

She waited for him to put the phone down.

'Thank god you're here,' he said, collapsing into his chair.

'How far have you got?' Beth sat at her desk and opened the ring binder in front of her.

'I told you I didn't know what I was doing.' Charlie closed his eyes. 'Now she's changed the date and we're completely unprepared. What do we do now?'

'I'm going to need more coffee.' Beth handed Charlie her purse. 'Get me the biggest, strongest one you can find.'

'I don't have time for—'

'Do you want my help or not? Get out of my hair for a few minutes at least. Let me figure out what kind of mess you've left us in, and then I'll tell you what to do.'

Charlie flushed, but he took the purse and strode away, letting the door bang behind him.

It took Beth an hour to find all the relevant paperwork, and another to get Charlie up to speed. By the time she was ready to start contacting suppliers, her nerves were frayed to breaking point.

When her mobile phone rang, she didn't look at the number. 'Yes?' she said, reading through a list of props.

'Beth, it's me. Please don't react.' Doriel's voice was almost a whisper.

'Are you okay?' Beth let the file drop.

Doriel ignored her question. 'Don't believe anything she says about Bill.'

'Is he with you? Where are you?'

'I've borrowed a phone and it's about to run out. You must warn Jonan. His mother is in danger.'

'His mother? I thought she was in seclusion?'

knee wedged between his. Her feet were bare and a pair of white stilettos lay on their side in the middle of the room. She stepped back, her shoulders stiffly straight. When she turned around, an odd smile twisted her face.

'Look who it is.' She sniffed the air. 'And isn't that an interesting perfume.' She looked over at Jonan, her lips pressed together. He met her gaze, not flinching.

She straightened, smoothing out her fitted, white dress. 'It seems no matter what I do to sink your involvement with my event, you keep rising to the surface.'

Beth walked towards Amelia, holding eye contact. In her heels, she was taller than Amelia, and her lips tilted up as she saw the older woman shift, her gaze darting to the shoes on the floor. 'I do know what you were to each other. Jonan has told me everything. I guess you thought you still had secrets together.' Beth gave a tight-lipped smile.

Amelia laughed. 'He told you everything, did he? In that case, I assume he mentioned that he was ready to dedicate himself to me for life? That he was in love with me?'

'Is that the best you've got?' Beth raised her eyebrows. 'Do you really think you can come between us that easily?'

Beth felt the energy building. She was in her body, but somehow watching it at the same time. She felt overwhelming love for the woman standing in her shoes, and knew her body was just the tip of the iceberg. A bigger part of her knew exactly what she was doing. In that moment she knew with absolute conviction that she could simply allow that part of herself to lead.

She advanced on Amelia, her energy expanding with each step.

Amelia gave a shaky laugh. 'Are you threatening me, little girl?'

Beth shrugged. 'I don't see the point in threats. I'm simply being clear. I see through you, Amelia. If you mess with Jonan or I again, I will destroy you.'

'Don't be ridiculous. You can't touch me.'

Beth tilted her head to one side. 'You think? There's more than one way to get a job done. As I remember, Katherine Haversham wasn't impressed by your simpering. Did I mention I'm friends with Laura from *Deep and Dark*? I'm sure she'd love to do a show on my story. It's perfect for them, don't you think? It has the celebrity angle, the spookiness, the weird, erratic behaviour, and I have so much more information for them now. I think they'd particularly love the bit about the theatre.'

Amelia paled. 'Why, Beth? Is this all because of Jonan?'

'I can see why you might think so, but no. Most people can't see the way you're playing them. I can and I won't stand by and watch you do it.'

Amelia laughed. 'Quite the little superwoman, aren't you? I can see why Jonan is so attached. He's always had a saviour complex too. That's why you fell for me, isn't it, darling, I was a conquest to convert.'

'I fell for you,' Jonan said, 'because at the time you were someone worth being with. This cruelty and manipulation is new.'

'Ah, I'm a fallen angel now, am I? How glamourous.'

'What are you planning for tonight, Amelia?' Jonan held her gaze. He was standing straight now, shoulders back, but he was still pale.

Amelia laughed, a low throaty sound that made Beth shiver.

'Wouldn't you like to know, lover boy?'

'Don't call me that,' Jonan said from between gritted

teeth. He crossed the room in three strides and took Beth's hand.

Amelia bent down and picked up her stilettos, slipping on one, and then the other. Taller now, she stalked closer, crowding Jonan. She was breathless as her gaze travelled over him. She raised her hand, but didn't touch. 'Does she know you've pinned all your hopes on her? Does she know you moon over her, that you've watched her for years, hanging around in the shadows outside her flat? Does she know you've pulled tarot cards to see into her future, that you've been looking at her for as long as you can remember?'

Jonan froze. Then he turned and met Beth's gaze, his breathing ragged. He swayed.

'Yes,' Beth said, stepping in front of Jonan, forcing Amelia back. 'Yes, he has told me. Is that all you've got?'

CHAPTER EIGHTEEN

Jonan

THE ROOM SPUN. Jonan closed his eyes, willing Amelia to shut up, to stop her barrage of incessant talking. The woman had poured his heart out to Beth without his say so. In his confusion, he couldn't remember what he had told her. Had Amelia ruined everything, or just confirmed what he had confided. He knew he was letting the woman get to him. He had experienced The Fear before and vowed never to let her do that to him again, but his mind was careening through so many shades of pain and his legs had turned to water. She had found a trigger and was pressing it as hard as she could. He felt sick. He reached out, feeling the cold solidity of the wall beneath the shaking of his hand.

His path rested on Beth's ability to see past Amelia's manipulation. More than that, his heart rested on her ability to open herself to the depth of love he had to offer. His memories felt like a curse. She had always been his. He had always been hers. There was nothing else for him in this world or any other.

'Jonan.' Her voice was soft and he opened his eyes. His heart beat faster. She moved closer. He felt the prickle of her energy on his skin as her space began to merge with his. His gaze darted to Amelia. She was watching him, her eyes narrowed. He pushed her energy back, snapping the cord that bound them and instead filled his energy with Beth, allowing her into his space as never before.

'Jonan, look at me,' Beth said, her voice hoarse. 'Take my hands.'

She stood so close he could feel the warmth of her breath on his skin. Her glossy dark hair fell in waves around her shoulders. Her flawless, dewy make up and closely fitted midnight-blue suit should have made her seem distant, but the look in her eyes cracked open the last of his resistance. They shone, glinting pools of emotion he could only begin to decipher. That look pulled at him, opening out his insides, leaving him raw and exposed. He could feel the pulse of her heart beating in sync with his own. He felt the connection so strongly he could hardly breathe. His body thrummed with the impact of their closeness. She was in his blood, pulsing through him, filling his mind, filling the space around him with blazing golden light.

For once her energy was unfettered and she dazzled him. She glowed, and in the light, he could see the echoes of all the people she had been, of all the times he had loved her.

'Don't you dare,' Amelia's voice cracked. He turned in surprise. It was rare for her to show emotion. Her usually immaculate face was drawn, more tired than it had been a moment ago. He had once thought Amelia and Beth looked similar, but they had never been less alike than at this moment. She narrowed her eyes and stepped towards Beth. 'This is my space, my energy. I have done this and you will not ruin my moment.'

Beth turned to Amelia, but Jonan could have sworn she

didn't see her. She seemed to look through the woman, to see what lay beyond the glossy exterior.

She turned back to Jonan. He took a deep breath as she stepped closer, his heart pounding in his chest. Adrenaline raced through his system and every nerve ending felt more and more alight the closer she came.

'Beth,' he said, his voice rough.

'You're messing with my event and you're not supposed to be here.' Amelia stepped between them, shoving Jonan back with one hand on his chest. She leaned in to Beth's space. 'I fired you. Do you remember that?'

Beth didn't flinch. 'Charlie has no idea how to run an event. Apparently he is as liberal with the truth as you. All the suppliers report to me. I have the running order, the contracts, the names and numbers. If I walk now, you lose everything except your shiny brass band and table favours.'

Amelia swallowed. She stepped back. 'You're lying. He's your boss. He's higher up the pecking order than you'll ever be.'

Beth shrugged. 'Maybe, but his journey up the pecking order did not venture into event organising country. I'm here as a favour. If you don't want me, I would be delighted to go back to the evening I had planned. And if you still think I'm lying, read me.'

Amelia flushed. She glared at Beth, but her gaze unfocused.

The haunted look that had persisted around Beth's eyes had gone. Jonan had no idea how she had done it, but somehow, here, in this dingy room, surrounded by Amelia's poisonous energy, Beth had looked her fears in the face and stepped past them.

Beth reached for his hand and squeezed it.

Only then did he realise he had been holding his breath. Her skin was warm, and sent tingles up his arm as he allowed himself to pull her closer, to increase the connection. He had spent so much of his life waiting for this moment. He had been so wary of letting her in, of scaring her off and destroying his chances of success and of happiness. Now the time had come to pull down the barriers.

His life changed now.

'Don't you have an event to host?' Beth said, turning to Amelia.

Amelia slammed her hand down on the table next to her. The glass top cracked and splintered, a web of lines reaching out towards the edge of the table. She reached down and grabbed a tumbler with a shot of amber liquid. She knocked it back, and then strode from the room, slamming the door behind her.

Jonan swallowed. He was becoming more and more light-headed. He was the Earth Guide in this relationship. He was the one who had to lead Beth towards her path, to awaken her slowly, but in a moment, she had stepped past him. He was flying and he couldn't find firm ground to land on.

She stepped closer and smiled. She reached up, her fingers trailing his jaw. He breathed heavily, sinking into the moment, allowing the energy to submerge him. Time dropped away. This was forever, past and future. Their bodies were everything and nothing as they shifted closer together, closing the physical gap that separated them.

The touch of her lips jolted him and he pulled her closer, feeling the warmth of her body through his clothes. He wished they were anywhere but here, anywhere but Amelia's space, her hotel, her energy, her event.

Beth sighed. 'I have something to tell you.

Jonan's heart ached as she pulled away, but he nodded and leaned back against the wall.

'Doriel phoned me.'

Jonan stared at her, and then forced himself to let out the breath he was holding. 'Is she okay? What did she say?'

'She told me not to believe anything Amelia says about Bill. She also said your mother is in danger. Does that make any sense to you? Why would Miranda be involved?'

Jonan sighed and sat down on Bill's chair, dropping his head into his hands. 'Amelia is still angry with her, but she is in seclusion and Amelia is focused here, for tonight at least. Did Doriel say anything about herself?'

Beth shook her head. No, her phone ran out of battery and she was cut off before she could say any more. And you're right. We can worry about your mother in the morning. It's time to do this.'

Jonan nodded, breathing deeply and focusing on slowing the adrenaline that still coursed through his blood. 'Remember, she's banking on controlling people through their energy. We can get in the way of that as long as we stay focused, grounded and connected. What we have matters and she knows it. That's why she's trying so hard to get between us.'

'What do you mean?'

'Our energy combined holds a special kind of magic that is powerful enough to unseat her influence. Separately, we are not strong enough to combat her in this place. Together, we can face up to Amelia and the monks. Who knows, maybe we can even bring her back to her path. But whatever you do, don't let her get into your head. She wants to separate us.'

Beth squeezed his hand. 'And your head, Jonan. Don't let her get into your head either.'

Jonan swallowed.

'We didn't have a chance to deal with the monks,' Beth said, her forehead creasing into a frown. 'You said we'd need Doriel's help with that. It's just us now.'

'I know. That is going to make it harder, but I believe we can do it.'

Beth nodded. 'I hope you're right. People make bad decisions when they're scared. It's going to be us against a whole roomful of people under her influence, and she's gathered a very powerful guest list, including the press. If she manages to control them, who knows what she could do?'

Jonan nodded. 'Did you get me a place on the staff?'

'I did, but she'll spot you the moment you walk into the room.'

Jonan gave a tight smile. 'Don't worry. Amelia's ego is her weakness. She won't see me as a problem.'

Beth turned as the hum of noise from outside grew louder. 'I'd better get out there, and you're supposed to be behind the bar. Have you done that before?'

Jonan nodded. 'I've got this.'

Beth straightened her suit and Jonan felt the distance expand between them. She was back in that composed shell, a woman who didn't need anybody. For once, he was grateful she was so good at it.

He held open the door and she strode through, shoulders back. The sheen of her midnight-blue suit caught the light as she walked through the crowds, weaving in and out through the guests without effort.

Jonan forced himself to breathe through the bubbling anxiety that was all that was left of The Fear. She had this. He had to trust her to do her part, just as she had to trust him with his.

CHAPTER NINETEEN

Beth

A HUSH FELL over the room. Glasses clinked as they were set awkwardly on the white linen tablecloths. Chairs scraped across the newly polished wooden floor. The food and drink had done their job.

The atmosphere in the room would have been relaxed, but there was an edginess that had been building all evening.

Beth had been doing everything she could to counteract it. She knew Jonan had been doing the same. She could feel the brightness shining from his side of the room, but it quickly slammed against a heavy sludge that was putting everyone on edge.

Everyone apart from Amelia.

Amelia was growing more animated by the moment. Back in her heels, she seemed six feet tall as she laughed and flirted her way around the room. Men stared down her cleavage and eyed the expanse of leg that that slid through the high split in her slinky dress. Women watched her, measuring their own charisma by her impossible standards. She was irresistible and terrifying by turns.

Beth sighed. She was exhausted and was starting to feel

dizzy. She could feel the energy of the monks pushing at her awareness, drawing in towards the packed room. That could only mean one thing. The Fear was rising.

Amelia was flushed. Her cheeks were pink, her eyes sparkling. She ran up the steps to the stage, not faltering despite her high heels and tight dress. 'Welcome,' Amelia purred into the microphone. Her voice was sultry, seductive and every face turned towards her. 'Welcome to my party, and thank you so much for coming at such late notice. The Children's Refuge is an amazing cause and one very dear to my heart, particularly at this troubling time.'

Beth looked around. People were sitting forward in their seats, leaning towards the stage, angling their bodies towards Amelia. The cameras were wheeling forwards. They were the real target. Amelia's reach would be in the millions.

'I promised I would tell you more about the spirits as soon as I could and I'm here to fulfil that vow. These spirits aren't just permeating our society, they are actively on the hunt for susceptible people, and when they find them, everything is at stake.'

The room broke out in muttering. People fidgeted in their seats, murmuring to each other and checking their watches.

Amelia tapped twice on the microphone. The room fell silent.

'I beg you to hear me out, because something awful has happened.'

The lights dimmed. Only a spotlight on Amelia and the glare of a screen lit the room, filling it with shadows. A picture of Bill filled the huge surface behind Amelia.

Beth frowned. There was something off about the picture. Bill had been unkempt when she saw him, but here he seemed hollowed out. His cheeks were sunken, dark smudges rimmed his eyes and his front tooth was newly missing. Overall he had an odd kind of pallor that she couldn't place. What had happened to him since she saw him last?'

Amelia sat on a high stool that had appeared in the middle of the spotlight. 'Bill spent his adult life caring for *this* hotel. He was a loner, but in all the years he worked for me, he seemed to be a good man. That was until last night when he abducted one of my oldest friends.'

Bill's picture disappeared. The room went dark and Doriel appeared on the screen.

Shock hit Beth as a kick in the ribs. Her chest clenched and her breathing became ragged as the air was squeezed from her lungs. She wasn't sure whether she heard Jonan gasp, or felt it.

'Doriel was like a sister to me.' Amelia put a hand over her heart, allowed her voice to crack. 'Doriel welcomed Bill into her house. She thought he was hurt, but he was strong enough to do this to her home.' A picture of the destroyed flat flickered onto the screen, and then settled. There was a collective gasp.

'You have no right to show that photograph.' Jonan strode towards the stage. 'That is my home.'

'It is. I'm so sorry for what happened to your aunt. I will not let the man, or those who control him, get away with it.' Amelia had her best 'sympathy' face on. Her forehead furrowed in concern, her head tilted. Her eyes lingered on Jonan's face. The cameras zoomed in on them both as she held out a hand to him.

He did not take it.

Amusement flickered across Amelia's face, and then was gone.

Amelia turned back to the room. 'This is deeply personal.' Her breath caught in her throat. She brushed a single tear from her cheek. 'Doriel is one of my oldest friends. I don't want you to have to go through what I am suffering right now. These spirits, they aren't just hovering around us in the atmosphere. They're not benign. They're here with intention. They want to take control, to get into your psyche and take over your will. They want to steal your soul.'

Amelia allowed the muttering to build into a roar. She stood, arms wide, head tilted slightly backwards.

Beth could see shadows shifting in her peripheral vision. They moved around the room, targeting those within reach. A shiver ran down her spine and spread out to the tips of her fingers. It was cold. Far colder than it should have been in a packed room. She called down the light, allowing it to flood her body, warming her where she stood. She looked at Jonan. He was doing the same. His hands moving in a fluid dance that strengthened the light around him and sent it throughout the room. Beth visualised her own light stretching out, pushing back the darkness of the monks. For a moment she felt silly, she felt the coldness start to regain hold, but she strengthened her resolve and the shadows receded.

Amelia looked at her, and then at Jonan. A tightness whitened the edges of her mouth. When she spoke her voice was soft, but it cut through the noise like a knife and the room fell silent. 'I need every single one of you to know the danger so you can protect yourselves and those you love. I need you to be vigilant so no more innocent people are taken. Only this morning a little girl was targeted. Another photograph flashed up on the screen. The girl was pale, with large white-blond curls that sat on her shoulders. She looked about six years old.

Amelia took the microphone from the stand, kicked off her heels and stepped off the stage. Her pale, narrow feet and painted toenails brought an oddly intimate feel to the room.

'This girl disappeared yesterday. She was on a school trip, taking part in a local parade. She vanished into the crowds and nobody could find her for a whole hour. Finally, she was discovered on the flat roof of one of the shops in town. There is no reasonable way she could have got up there unless someone helped her. She said nothing as she ran across the roof, and then jumped as though launching herself into a swimming pool.'

There was a gasp. A woman cried out.

'Was she okay?' a voice called from the back.

'Fortunately for everyone, an off-duty fire-fighter was in the crowd. He acted fast and threw himself forwards, catching the girl and taking all the impact on his own back when he fell. She thought it was a wonderful game. The fire-fighter is bruised, but recovering. But the class's teaching assistant has gone missing. Nobody has seen her since the incident. You have no idea which of the people around you are infected. All you can do, I repeat, all you can do is protect your family from everyone. Stay safe. Avoid anything and anyone that feels different.'

There was a crash from the other side of the room as a woman in a pale blue jumpsuit lurched against the chairs along the aisle. A man shouted as her bag hit him in the face, but she didn't stop.

'Wait.' Amelia's voice was sharp. The woman stopped, her body trembling as she turned slowly.

Beth could see shadowy shapes moving around the edges of the room. The woman in blue was surrounded.

The colour drained from her face as the pressure increased.

'I have help at hand.' Amelia stood up and began pacing the stage. 'I have set up an organisation to help protect you. It is called Amelia's Haven. There is a small fee to join, but in return, you have a protection force ready to step forward for you at any time. You have a vetted database of providers I will personally vouch for, who will only employ approved members of staff. Imagine knowing your children were in safe hands, knowing their nursery or school would not hire anyone infected.'

There was another murmur around the room, but it quietened. People shuffled forwards, chairs scraping against the polished wooden floor, straining to get closer to Amelia.

Several waiters in black and white entered the room with piles of leaflets. They spread around the ballroom, distributing pieces of paper while Amelia talked.

'Join my Haven. Protect your children. Protect yourselves and take care. Stay away from anyone who is different and report anyone who acts strangely. This is everyone's responsibility. We can only be safe if we call out every danger. Join the only group of people who can keep you safe. Join the only group who can keep the Soul Snatchers at bay.'

Silence.

Beth looked at Jonan. His face was dark, furious.

Amelia was at the back of the ballroom now. She walked up the aisle slowly, reaching out and taking people's outstretched hands as she went.

'It breaks my heart to say it, but the ringleader of the Soul Snatchers is in this room.'

One by one, people stood up, turning around, eyes narrowed. Nobody stepped forward, nobody seemed guilty.

Amelia brought the microphone close to her mouth and

breathed into it, her voice husky. 'Jonan McLaney is more than a kidnapper. He'll turn your children against you so they go to him willingly. It's all about free will with Jonan, but he will twist it until they no longer know what they're choosing.'

'For pity's sake, who is he?' a man yelled.

'Jonan, step forward please.'

Jonan stepped out from behind the bar, wiped his hands on a towel, and then put it down on the oak surface. He walked slowly up the aisle through the seats, his presence growing with every step.

'I am not the enemy,' he said, addressing the people who drew back as he walked near them. 'There are no Soul Snatchers. Amelia is whipping up fear in order to control you. She would create a threat, and then provide you with a solution you have to pay for dearly. It looks as though she intends for me to pay dearly too. She has you by the throat. She has you under so much threat you can't think. Try to clear your minds. Try to find a way back to your normal thought processes. Does she really sound plausible?'

'Well you would say that. You're protecting yourself.' The woman in blue edged away from Jonan. 'Keep back.'

DC Ainsworth stepped forwards, smoothing down his already slicked-back hair. His lips were pinched, but a glint in his eye told Beth he was enjoying himself.

'Jonan McLaney?'

A shiver ran down Beth's spine.

'How can I help you, DC Ainsworth?' Jonan said without flinching.

The policeman's mouth widened into a sneer. 'Jonan McLaney, you are under arrest. You do not have to say anything, but it may harm your defence if you do not mention when questioned something which you later rely on in court. Anything you do say may be given in evidence.'

Beth swallowed. She stepped forwards, head held high. 'Why? What are you charging him with?'

There was a low chuckle from the stage. Amelia flicked her hair over her shoulder. 'He is under suspicion of being the ringleader of the Soul Snatchers.'

'That's not even a thing.' Beth's voice hardened. 'It doesn't exist. It's not a crime. You're making this up.'

'And you are obstructing an investigation.' DC Ainsworth stepped closer to Beth. He was half a head taller than her, and tilted his head back to peer down his nose at her with narrowed eyes. His breath stank of red wine and cigarettes. She stepped back.

DC Ainsworth smirked. 'You should know that the police are fully supporting Amelia's Haven. *All* intelligence will be taken seriously.'

Beth frowned. She looked from DC Ainsworth to Amelia, who was almost holding her poker face. Only a twitch at the side of her mouth showed any chink in her composure. 'So Amelia can say whatever she wants, about anyone, and you will arrest them without hesitation?'

The man nodded. 'All intelligence will be taken seriously.'

'Why are you doing this, Amelia?' Jonan's voice was rough. He swallowed. 'You know I'm innocent. I used to mean something to you.'

'Yes, Amelia, what is your plan?' The voice from the door was hushed like the wind. It filled the packed ballroom with a deep in-breath and an exhale that released some of the tension at last.

'Miranda,' Amelia breathed. She was pale now. She grasped the back of the stool, her hands shaking.

'Mother.' Jonan took another step forward.

DC Ainsworth shoved him backwards.

'Let him go to her,' Amelia said, her voice choked. 'Just for a moment.' She lifted her gaze, and then clapped her hands once as though breaking a spell.

'Go my children, go. Protect your families. Lock your doors. Make sure you know who surrounds you and stay away from anyone who might put you and yours at risk.'

'But the man, the ringleader, what about him?' a woman's voice called from the audience.

'He will be dealt with.' Amelia clasped her hands in front of her, nodding her head. 'You can put your trust in me. Sign up to the Haven and I will keep you and your loved ones safe. If you have your forms ready now, please give them to my staff in reception, otherwise, post them to the address on the form. Do your bit and I will do mine.' She raised her arms and tilted her head back. 'Now you are armed. You are empowered to go to your children, to your parents and your friends. Go to them and keep them safe. Now, go!'

Amelia's voice rose in volume as she spoke. With a detached part of her mind, Beth knew someone must have been turning up the PA, because she didn't sound as though she was shouting. As she uttered the final 'go', people gathered their things and there was a rush for the door. A wave of sound swept the room, engulfing Beth in chaos. She swayed on her feet. Fear pounded through her system with a pulse of its own, grabbing her by the chest and weakening her knees. She reached out, steadying herself on a nearby table and forcing herself to remain upright.

People were trying to push their way through the bottleneck at the doors. A man towards the back punched his neighbour in the face. Someone yelled across the room. Beth's head was pounding. She couldn't tell what anyone was saying.

The room felt like poison. Fear dripped from the walls and infected everything. Only Amelia was unfazed.

Jonan and Miranda stood at the far side of the stage. She clasped him so tight her hands went white. Her body shook as he held her head cradled to his chest. His eyes were closed, his breathing ragged. They seemed oblivious to the chaos, but the air around them glimmered.

As the last person rushed through the door, Amelia allowed her arms to drop. Her jaw was tight as she turned to the woman standing next to Jonan. She stepped off the stage and walked towards them, back straight, fists clenched. 'What are you doing here, sister?'

The other woman let go of Jonan and wiped a tear from her eye. She turned and took a step towards Amelia. Closer now, Beth could see that her pale skin was almost translucent. Her hair was spun with grey glints, and there were deep lines around her eyes and mouth. 'We once made a promise to one another. Do you remember?'

Amelia gave a harsh bark of laughter. 'Remember? I have heard those words every day of my life, as a mockery of the love I felt for my sisters, and my own failure in believing that you felt something for me.'

'I do love you, Amelia, and so does Doriel. If you were missing she would stop at nothing to find you, in spite of everything that has happened. Are you doing the same for her? We love you so much that we will not let you destroy these people. We will not let you stray this far from the path you chose when you were still thinking clearly.'

'What do you know?' Amelia stepped back. 'Everything

has changed. None of our promises or plans mean anything any more.'

'They mean everything,' Miranda said. We came here for a reason, to change things for the better, not to make them worse. We came with greater power than the people here were used to, and we intended to use that to raise them up, to help them fulfil their potential. We came here to shine a light, not to block it out. When did you start relying on fear, Amelia? You used to be such a beacon, and now you feed off fear like a drug. When did you ever need to draw on extra power? You have more of it than most people would ever dream of.'

'Don't judge me.' Amelia gritted her teeth. 'You left me alone in a strange world. I had to find a way to adapt. My light blinked out and there was nobody there to help me reignite it. I had to learn to work with the darkness; that was all I had.'

'How can you say that?' Miranda stepped forwards, spreading her hands. 'I lost everything, but I held my peace.'

'Held your peace? Are you kidding me?' Amelia's voice was high pitched. She stepped closer to the two women. 'You didn't lose everything; you threw your kids away because you didn't like Jonan's choices. You didn't like me. You ran away and hid. That's not holding your peace, or your light. It's cowardice, it's selfishness. Those boys were desperate for you and you turned your back all because your pride was hurt. You will never persuade me that you have any moral high ground. You gave away your integrity at the moment you let down Jonan and Roland.'

'Both of whom you have now bedded, I understand?'

Jonan winced.

Amelia laughed and shook her head. 'That's still all that

matters to you, isn't it? A quick hug for Jonan and you're using him already. You haven't said a word to Roland. He was fifteen when you went into seclusion. Fifteen! If you want to talk about fear, talk to Roland. He was terrified. If I hadn't taken him in, he would have been lost.'

Miranda's eyes widened. 'Roland is here?' She looked at Jonan, eyebrows raised.

There was a cough from the doorway. Roland leaned against the doorpost, his white suit brilliant against his dark hair. His forehead was furrowed; his lips pressed tightly together.

Miranda's feet were silent as she walked towards him, her hands held out, palms facing upwards. 'My son.'

'It's a bit late for that, isn't it?' He raised his eyebrows.

She stopped, allowed her arms to drop.

'I've moved on, Mother. Just like you did.'

Beth couldn't see Miranda's face, but she didn't miss the shudder of her shoulders, or Roland's wince. He shook his head and strode over to Amelia, taking her hand.

'I'm sorry you feel I failed you.' Miranda turned. A single tear drifted down her cheek. 'I'm sorry you feel you had to turn to Amelia because I wasn't there. I hope there may be something left for us to salvage.'

'Huh. You think you can just walk back into my life?' Roland's voice was soft, controlled, but it held the keen edge of a lifetime's anger. 'You saw me as unimportant, less glamourous and exciting than Jonan and just too far from your heart. But people listen to me now, Mother. And they are looking for people to blame.'

'I understand, Roland, but know that I am not frightened by your threats. I will be here if you are ever ready for me.'

'You'll be waiting a long time.' He turned and walked over to Amelia, putting his arm around her waist.

'You always paint me as the bad one, sister,' Amelia spat the word, her nose wrinkling. 'I was there for Roland. Doriel was there for Jonan. Only you walked away, abandoned your people.'

'And yet, I am here now.' All trace of sadness was gone from Miranda's voice as she walked towards Amelia. 'And I will not let you move forwards with this fear-mongering. I will not let you use these people and sacrifice Doriel to fuel your own hunger for power. The Triad may have broken down, but it is always ready to be renewed, to be channelled in another way.'

'You wouldn't dare,' Amelia said through gritted teeth.

Jonan walked forwards and held out a hand.

Miranda took it and closed her eyes.

'No.' The horror on Amelia's face was bizarre. She seemed so frightened by the simple touch.

Jonan's eyes went wide, and then vacant as though he were watching something elsewhere.

Beth tuned into her psychic sight. Jonan and Miranda were surrounded by a bright white bubble, and the light was moving towards Amelia, bending outwards on either side of her to encompass the shadowy monks that gathered all around.

It held Amelia's energy in, a sludgy fog that bumped up against the edges of the barrier, trying to get out and spread through the room.

DC Ainsworth swayed. Beth took him by the arm and led him to a chair. He slumped down, hunching over his knees, his body shuddering as he drew in deep breaths. Then he went still. When he looked up, something had changed.

His eyes narrowed at Amelia. 'What did you do to me?'

'Me?' Amelia's voice was shrill and tense. 'Why do you think I did anything?'

'I would never have agreed to any of this in my right mind. You're trying to charge this man with a crime that doesn't even exist.'

Amelia compressed her lips, but said nothing.

DC Ainsworth shook his head. 'I'm out of here. I need to find these people who have gone missing.' He pulled off his jacket and slung it over his shoulder as he strode out through the door. He didn't look back.

'I will never forgive you for this,' Amelia hissed, pushing her energy outwards, thinning the light barrier that surrounded her.

'You can add it to the tally.' Jonan's voice was expressionless, but Beth could see the focus it was taking him to keep Amelia's energy from spreading.

Miranda started to sing, a deep chant that resonated in Beth's breastbone. She felt an expansion in her chest and stepped closer. Both Jonan and Miranda held their free arms out, as though waiting for someone to take their hands. She looked up at Roland. His gaze moved compulsively backwards and forwards between Miranda and Amelia. His skin was sallow, and he rubbed his hand across his forehead.

Beth's palms prickled. She felt a rush of energy as she had in the back room when she had stood up to Amelia. This was her place. She was born to hold her ground against this woman.

Her feet moved forwards of their own volition. Her palms were warm. Energy flickered over her skin like lightning as she reached out and took Jonan's hand. She jolted as a current shot through her. The scent of lavender flared and a rightness settled deep in her chest. She reached out, finding Miranda's hand easily without looking.

At the moment she closed the circle, she felt herself swept up into a whirlpool of light. It carried her upwards, higher and higher. Part of her awareness remained in her body, where she held hands with Jonan and Miranda, but the greater part of her being flew free. She could feel the others beside her. Her energy swirled in the upwards spiral, reaching further and further outwards.

Then the spiral stopped.

She was in a throne room.

Huge white pillars loomed above her. The crystal throne sat empty on the dais. A woman stood in front of her, long, glossy ringlets falling over her shoulders and the draped white fabric of her robes.

'My daughter,' she whispered, taking Beth's hands. 'You have the strength for this. Do not doubt yourself. Do not hesitate. You know what to do.'

Beth felt Jonan's familiar energy next to her, and the still, calm pool that was Miranda. She shuddered as a flare of something else consumed her. It swept into the room, wrapping around her, opening her heart, and breaking all her defences into pieces. In a moment she felt raw and exposed, but more powerful than she had ever known.

'*Brother.*' She felt the word vibrate through her being.

'Sister,' have you felt me with you?'

'I don't know. I was alone for so long.'

The energy materialised next to her as a dazzling light being. He had blond hair that reached his waist, his eyes were a clear violet, and his ears rose into delicate points. 'You are never alone, sister, and never will be.' The scent of lavender filled Beth's senses. 'Jonan has done well to bring you to this point. Do you know who he is, dear one?'

'He is my soul mate.'

Her brother nodded. 'You have work to do together. Are you ready to do this now? The choice will always be yours, but your world needs you.'

Beth inclined her head. 'What do I need to do?'

'Embrace who you really are. Hold on to your connection here. You will be able to hear us if you try. Listen to Jonan. He has spent an Earth lifetime preparing for this moment, but he is wavering right now. He fears for Doriel and he is weary. He wants you more than he wants to complete his destiny.'

'Can't he have both?'

'He can, of course, if you are willing to travel the road alongside him.'

'I am willing. I choose it. I choose my destiny, my awakening. I choose Jonan.'

The light flared. The world turned white. Beth felt a touch on her shoulder that sent energy fizzing through her body.

Then she was back in the ballroom.

Jonan met her gaze.

She nodded.

There was knowing in his eyes. 'I am ready now,' she said, taking a deep breath and feeling her chest expand, allowing the light into her body.

Amelia laughed, and then broke into a fit of coughing. 'You think you're some kind of superhero, don't you? But you're just one girl, a girl who has some talent with event organising and an ability to see ghosts. That doesn't make you anything special. If you stand against me, I will annihilate you with public derision. And you.' She looked Miranda up and down, a sneer on her face. 'You I will paint as the enemy, a Soul Snatcher of the most dangerous kind. You'd be amazed what these people will believe if you tell them in the right way. I will turn you into a target your precious seclusion has left you ill-prepared for.'

Miranda didn't flinch. 'Do what you must. I am willing. I choose it.'

Beth took her hand and turned to look Amelia in the eye. 'Do what you must. I am willing. I choose it.' She opened her heart to the energy. It flared up around them, filling the room with light.

'Do what you must.' Jonan's voice was resonant, filling the room with a vibration that sent the monks reeling. 'I am willing. I choose it.'

'No!' Amelia shouted.

One by one, the monks that surrounded Amelia faded into nothing. As the energy rose even higher, Beth felt the presence of those other beings, her mother and brother from that other place, and wondered how they had crossed. The energy in the room fizzed.

Amelia stood alone now, the space around her muddy in spite of the light that surrounded her. She walked backwards, slowly, towards the door.

Roland still leaned against the door post. His lips parted as she approached, but he shook his head and stepped backwards.

'Come on, Rolo.' Amelia's voice was low. 'Don't let them manipulate you. They can't destroy us. They're not that strong.'

'We do not seek to destroy you,' Miranda said. She released Beth's hand and then Jonan's, breaking the circle, but the light that surrounded them remained. Miranda blazed, her own brightness filling the space now the draining pull of the monks was gone. She walked towards the door, but her eyes were on the man in the white suit.

'Roland, I love you. You are my son, and no matter what Amelia may have told you, I will always be yours. I hope that one day you might see that.'

He took a deep breath, his chest expanding as though he was breathing clean air for the first time.

'Rolo,' Amelia snapped.

He blinked. His eyes dulled. Stepping over to her, he laced his arm around Amelia's waist. 'Let's get out of here.'

'You know that once I'm out of this room, there's nothing you can do to stop me?'

'You're right, of course,' Miranda said with a smile. 'But we will do this again and again. We will find Doriel, we will keep foiling you, and we will tell the truth until enough people listen.'

Amelia swayed.

The energy in the room was so strong now that Beth had no sense of where her body ended and the light began.

Pulling Roland with her, Amelia reached the door. She fumbled at the handle, threw it open and dashed through, slamming it behind her.

There was silence.

The energy fizzed and settled.

Beth slumped onto one of the chairs in the audience. She leaned back, her eyes wide and unseeing. That other place was still there at the edges of her consciousness, and part of her longed to go back.

'You'll never lose it, not now you've been there consciously. Once you've woken up to it, it's always there for you.' Miranda smiled at Beth. 'As am I. You are part of our family, Beth.'

Beth swallowed. 'Thank you. I don't know what to say.'

'No need.' She smiled again, and then turned and walked out the door.

'Does she know where she's going?' Beth frowned.

Jonan rolled his eyes. 'Oh, she'll figure it out. Mother has been in seclusion so long she has got out of the habit of social niceties.' He sat down next to her and took her hand in both of his.

Reality flooded over Beth in a wave of grief. 'Oh, Jonan, how are we going to find Doriel?'

Jonan's face shifted, the faint lines in his forehead deepening. His skin paled and the shift in his energy made her head pound. 'Doriel, where are you?' he whispered. His eyes were unfocused and Beth knew he was looking for his aunt.

She squeezed his hands. 'We will find her. We have to.' She wished she felt as sure as she sounded.

When his eyes came back into focus, they were deep purple and haunted. 'She is completely cut off. I can't find her at all. This has never happened before.'

'Maybe Miranda will be able to locate her?'

'Perhaps.' Jonan turned and gazed out of the window, his expression bleak.

'Jonan,' Beth whispered, 'where did *I* go?'

'You went home.'

She felt an expansion in her chest. 'And where is home?'

'Have you ever thought about life on other planets?'

'I guess I've always assumed it was possible, but I haven't thought too much about it.'

'That's probably a good thing.' Jonan put his arm around her and pulled her close. He felt so familiar, so right, as though their bodies and energy fitted together like a puzzle. 'When people overthink these things, they get tied up in complex and worrying knots. Life exists in so many places and so many realities, but it generally doesn't manifest how people expect. In that other life, we were light beings. We could assume a shape at will when we chose.'

'I felt my brother before I saw him.'

'Yes, Salu has become unused to form. He has been with you here for so long.'

Beth sat up and turned to face Jonan. 'I've felt that, but I still find it hard to believe.'

The scent of lavender flared.

'If you need reminding, tell him. He is always ready to let you know he's here.'

'Lavender,' Beth whispered.

Lavender. The word sounded in her mind.

Jonan smiled.

'You heard that?' Beth raised her eyebrows.

'Does that make it easier to believe?'

'It does, thank you.' Beth sighed. 'I didn't know you heard him too.'

'He's often with me. He's been prodding me over and over to find you.'

'Did you need prodding?' she asked, quietly.

'Never. I have been waiting for you forever, but much as we'd like to, we can't rush the cosmic ordering. Things happen in their right time. Sometimes our path is to wait.'

'And Salu didn't know that?'

'Oh, he knew it.' Jonan laughed. 'But he was determined to make sure I didn't get distracted while I waited. You have a powerful advocate and protector in your brother.'

'I've always wanted a brother. I look after myself, but it

would be nice to have someone else looking out for me.'

'You have me too.' Jonan reached out and stroked her cheek. 'If you would like me.'

Beth tilted her face up to him. She could feel Jonan's energy pulsing through her own, could see how intertwined they were, how their auras melded perfectly to create a whole. This was exactly where she was supposed to be.

The kiss was feathery light and it made Beth's head swim.

'This is a long journey, Beth, but we can do it together.'

She shifted closer to him, feeling the warmth of his body relaxing her own tense muscles.

'Together,' she whispered. 'Can that be real?'

'It's not just real, it's our path. It's what we came here for. Are you ready?'

'I'm ready. Amelia thinks she knows what we've got, but I can't help feeling there's so much more.'

Jonan grinned.

Beth looked up as someone knocked on the open door. Miranda stood there, a tray in her hands with a teapot and three cups with saucers.

'You're not going to have a tantrum about this girl too, are you, Mum?' Jonan smiled as Miranda glided over to them so smoothly she didn't seem to be walking.

She raised one eyebrow as she sat down next to Jonan. 'She's the one I wanted you to wait for.'

Jonan laughed, a deep belly laugh. For a moment his tension eased, then the haunted look returned.

'I've checked outside,' Miranda said. 'Amelia and Roland have both gone. How can we get him back, Jonan?'

'I don't know.' Jonan frowned. 'He always had a thing for Amelia, but he's in so deep now.'

'Don't worry,' Beth said. 'We'll get him out, find Doriel and Bill, and expose her for what she is. I have no idea how, but we'll do it one way or another.'

Miranda smiled. 'Between us, we're more than a match for Amelia. If you agree to join us, our circle is complete. She is alone.'

'You sound so hard.' Jonan frowned.

'Amelia is lost because I allowed her to feel abandoned. I am here to put that right. I want to bring her back into the family, to remind her of who she used to be, and who she could become again, but until then we are working in opposite directions. Only she can change that.'

Jonan sighed. 'It sounds like we need a plan. We need to figure out where Doriel and Bill are fast, and we need to find a way to counteract all this fear. Can you pick up any sign of Doriel, Mother?'

Miranda's brow drew in as she poured the tea. 'No, I've never lost my connection to her before.'

Beth swallowed. 'Do you think she has died?'

The silence was so heavy Beth could barely breathe.

Miranda held her gaze, then shook her head. 'I would be able to find her if she had passed. Either she is hiding herself, or she has been hidden.'

'There must be a way to break through those shields.' Jonan started pacing. 'Amelia feels beaten right now, but she won't stay quiet for long. The threat of the Soul Snatchers and the promise of safety from Amelia's Haven are a huge win for her. She'll be well aware of how much social momentum she has. There's no way she'll let that slide.'

'What about your momentum, Jonan?' Beth looked up at him and smiled at his confusion. 'She accused you publicly, in front of all those TV cameras, and then DC Ainsworth declared you innocent. Isn't that libel?'

Jonan raised his eyebrows. 'Well, that's a new approach.'

'New? Really?' Beth looked from one to the other of them. 'That's what normal people do.'

'So that's it,' Miranda whispered. 'That's why you had to go your own way and find us later.'

'She brings in the normal,' Jonan said, rubbing a hand across his forehead.

Beth snorted. 'I'm the least normal person you could have chosen.'

'And yet,' Miranda smiled. 'This is a long journey. We don't yet know what we'll need or what will turn our lives around and point us in a new direction. All we know is that we are on this path together, supporting each other and helping each other learn. We came here as one, a unified group of souls, but then we split. That has caused a tension that will have repercussions we don't yet know about. But it has also brought the learning it was planned for—'

'But—' Beth cut in.

Jonan shook his head, put his hand on her arm. 'She's an Oracle, Beth. When she speaks in that funny voice, listen to her.'

Miranda paused then carried on speaking, her voice low and hypnotic. 'Amelia is already regrouping. There are many souls who easily fall prey to the fear vibration and they are flocking around her like drones to their queen. We will counteract that flow in every way we can.

'We have spent decades preparing for this moment. Now is the time to act, to fly, and to unite fully with the energies we sought to bring to Earth.'

They sat in silence as the words sank into their minds, through their bodies.

Jonan held Beth's hand and it anchored her, giving her a steadiness in this strange new world that she had never felt in normal life.

She squeezed his hand. 'This is it. This is where it all begins.'

A LETTER FROM THE AUTHOR

DEAR READER,

Thank you so much for opening my book and taking up my call to adventure. If you're wondering what happened to Doriel and Bill, I promise the next instalment of the Starfolk Trilogy is coming soon, as well as a standalone novel.

If you enjoyed *The Starfolk Arcana*, please do consider leaving a review on Amazon. Even a few words help make the book more visible to new readers. Reviews are one of the best ways to support authors, and help them write lots of lovely new stories for you to enjoy.

If you would like to hear about my new releases, you can subscribe to my newsletter to receive news and cover reveals first.

You can also find me on Facebook or Twitter. Please do drop in and chat to me there.

I hope you will join me again soon because I have lots more adventures up my sleeve and I would love to travel with you.

Lots of love, and happy reading,

Martha

ACKNOWLEDGEMENTS

THE ROAD TO publishing *The Starfolk Arcana*, my first book, has been a long one and a series of kick-arse women helped me push my skills and bring this book to where it is now.

Thank you Kathryn Cottam who helped me mould my story, mentored and encouraged me, and gave me the confidence to take the next step. Thank you to Eleanor Leese who copy-edited my work, and helped me with the minutia of blurb writing.

Ravven, I dreamed of your beautiful cover, and your magic made my dream feel real. Your images helped motivate me to take many of those scary final steps towards publication.

Thank you to Heidi Boxer for always being there to brainstorm ideas with me and give me pep talks when I was flagging. Thank you to my wonderful aunt, Janet Hamer, for dusting off her English Teacher skills and proofing my manuscript for me, and to Maria Hayden for pointing out when a character inadvertently left home with no clothes on.

Before these fabulous women, Jane Holland scooped up an aspiring writer and went above and beyond to open her eyes to what needed to be done. Jane, I will always be grateful that you were prepared to give me the tough messages, not the easy ones. Thank you, Barbara Henderson, (Bea Davenport) who instructed and encouraged me by turns, and Anna Katmore who wouldn't let me off the hook for a moment.

Thank you to my family and my friends for being excited about reading my work, and supporting me every step of the way. You know who you are.

But most of all, thank you to Murray, my husband, who believed in me from the very first time I told him I wanted to write a book. Without him, there would be no Starfolk Arcana. I would never have had the courage to get this far, let alone tell anyone about it.

Now, on to the next one!

ABOUT THE AUTHOR

MARTHA IS A dreamer and lover of stories who likes nothing better than spending her days exploring the paranormal and intuitive senses, and getting to know the characters in her head.

She is a tarot card reader and Reiki Master, and loves to chat reading, writing and all things mystical on social media, as well as posting pictures of her fellow pack-member, Bertie the Cavalier King Charles Spaniel.

Martha is a fiddle player who fell in love with all kinds of traditional music, but particularly Irish, and is also teaching herself to play the Irish Bouzouki. She played her way through her English degree at York and remembers that time as much for the music as the books.

Martha started her working life in PR because she wanted to write and in the end she left PR because she wanted to write more. But along the way she had the opportunity to work with journalists, hone her writing and editing skills and adapt to the many voices she was asked to use.

Picture by Gene Genie Photography: genegenie.photography.

You can keep up with all Martha's news in the following places:

Website: www.marthadunlop.com
Twitter: @MarthaDunlop
Facebook: The Story Cave, @MarthaDunlopStories
Facebook: The Curious Mystic, @DunlopMartha
Instagram: @MarthaDunlop